'This ... confirms him as a master of the genre. Ranging from the Soviet Union under Stalin to the Cotswolds via Southern Spain, the stories blend convincingly real characters into surreal situations, mixing acute observations with an anarchic, even violent – certainly violently funny – sense of humour.'
DAILY MAIL

'An impressively original and darkly amusing set of yarns, Sayle's absorbing – and subtly comic – style ensures that the bizarrely believable *The Only Man Stalin Was Afraid Of* and the remarkable *Barcelona Chairs* – with its ruthless manhandling of pruning architect rupert (with a small "r") – will leave you merrily ensconced till the new-born dawn.'
FHM

'Inventive and fascinating ... there is always the faint threat of possibility, the suggestion that any of these stories might actually have happened. And that is probably Sayle's greatest success.'
SUNDAY TRIBUNE

'By turns contemptuously misanthropic (the brainless actress who bashes out voice-overs for murderous regimes without even noticing, the obsessive minimalist driven to suicide by clutter), tenderly observational (the neuroses of middle-aged transvestites or out-of-fashion poets) and blithely shocking (as in the casual cruelty of the title story) ... By the end of this collection you'll be convinced that Sayle is a very good writer. And that you are a very bad person.'
BIG ISSUE

'Sometimes eloquent ... always risqué and funny.'
MIRROR

'This is more than just cultural satire, there are moments of poignancy and beauty in these stories too, proof that Alexei Sayle is definitely barking up the right tree.'
THE LIST, GLASGOW

'Packed with fiery dialogue and sharp social observations, these stories are savagely funny.'
OBSERVER

'Every piece in Sayle's marvellous second collection combines strangeness and familiarity to moving and hilarious effect.'
INDEPENDENT

By the same author:

BARCELONA PLATES

'This book is a complete revelation to me ... It's punchy and real and you feel the real weight of a personality behind it. It's terribly funny, full of characters who come out of reality rather than out of other fiction, and I completely agree with those who say that the final story, *The Last Woman Killed in the War* is a masterpiece. The end of it is one of the most extraordinary pieces of writing I can remember. Brilliant tragedy and brilliant comedy delivered in one stunning sentence. It reminded me of the awesome ending to Evelyn Waugh's *A Handful of Dust*. More importantly, though, it reminded me most of nothing I'd read before.'
DOUGLAS ADAMS

'An excellent collection of dark, funny and bizarre short stories ... brutally, cynically and honestly written.'
LOADED

'A cracking read ... dense with smart ideas, sour observations and loony rants.'
INDEPENDENT ON SUNDAY

'His style is comic – black, attritional, exasperated – but he loves his characters as much as he makes them suffer. Most of all though, his work is full of ideas. This is his strength ... he packs his pages with twists and turns, pay-offs and surprises.'
DAILY EXPRESS

'Sayle is a funny man, and these tales of pensioners-turned hitmen, mysterious white Fiat Unos, and inveterate hypochondriacs defy you not to smile at the incremental absurdity of ordinary life.'
THE SUNDAY TIMES

'A startlingly good collection of short stories ... Sayle has an impressive sense of pace ... and a great sense of timing ... This is an excellent fictional debut, fizzing with anger and glee. Nor has he forgotten that old showbiz trick of leaving the audience wanting more.'
EVENING STANDARD

THE DOG CATCHER

Alexei Sayle

SCEPTRE

First published in Great Britain in 2001 by Sceptre
A division of Hodder Headline

A Sceptre paperback

1 3 5 7 9 10 8 6 4 2

A CIP catalogue record for this title is available
from the British Library

ISBN 0 340 81944 8

Typeset in Fournier by Palimpsest Book Production Limited,
Polmont, Stirlingshire
Printed and bound in Great Britain by
Clays Ltd, St Ives plc

Hodder and Stoughton
A division of Hodder Headline
338 Euston Road
London NW1 3BH

Grateful thanks to Roberta Green, Suzannah Buxton
and Caroline Stafford

CONTENTS

THE DOG CATCHER

The woman came into the valley, whose Arabic name meant 'happiness', at the very start of the summer. She had hitchhiked up from the coast, along the highway that climbed twisting through the gorge into the foothills of the Sierra Nevadas. In the wide delta there had been fields of sugar cane, banana palms, custard apple orchards and waving clumps of bamboo, later on as they climbed into the campo there were steep terraces of olive trees, oranges and lemons, then on the rocky mesas almond trees, their leaves a beautiful spring green and the fruit hanging half formed. Nowhere were there the gigantic sheets of plastic, covering chemical-drunk, sweating vegetables, that disfigured the growing lands further up the coast towards Almeria. There had been decent spring rains that year and the acequias, the irrigation channels that the Romans had built, ran fresh with icy water.

The Dog Catcher

She wasn't running away exactly but there were a number of men all along the Costa Tropical and Costa del Sol, one Latvian guy in particular, who it was better that she didn't see for a while, for his sake really, all that shouting and threatening every time he saw her couldn't be doing him any good. Some people just seemed to get so twisted around her, that was her opinion. She knew the reason for it, it was because she was too trusting, too giving, and individuals, guys especially, saw that as a green light to try and suck her dry. Aquarians were always taken advantage of, it was a scientific fact.

The woman's name was Sue, she was from the North of England, that part of the North West where all the towns ran into each other along motorways and bombed-out high streets. She had come to Spain on a whim not knowing really where Spain was, with a bloke of course – Aquarians had a great need to give and receive love, repeated studies had proved it. A nice posh lad with money who she met in a club in Liverpool. They'd been going round together for a couple of weeks when he said he was going out to DJ on the costa, he paid for her plane ticket and he paid for the rented flat in a smart urbanisation. After a bit she asked him why he didn't have any records or any turntables. He told her that he'd thought she understood that he was a conceptual DJ who played the music that he heard all the time in his head, straight into the heads of other people and the heads of cats and dogs too. Then he said he was also working on a machine to slow down time and reverse the flow of entropy. Then the Civil Guards came and took him away. Sometimes she tried to hear his music but she didn't think she could.

The idea of going back to England was a non-starter, her husband and kids had made such a fuss and her own mother had gone on the TV show *Kilroy* to denounce her. They all had to understand that she wasn't Thirty yet and let's face it she was fantastic-looking so she had the absolute right to have a good time before it was too late. That's what feminism had taught her.

So it was bar jobs in the town and other blokes after that and some of the blokes getting twisted. Then the Latvian trying to run her over and ploughing his Mercedes into the stack of butane canisters outside the supermercado. Once his burns healed she sensed he would come after her again so it was time to move on.

With her bag over her shoulder she walked to a big bar on the road out where the camionistas parked their trucks for one last brandy before slinging the rigs up the sinuous mountain roads. She asked around, looking for the perfect destination as if she were in a travel agent's. The old man in the wheezing lorry loaded down with watermelons, whose name was Antonio, said he was going back to his home, one of the villages in the foothills of the mountains. One with a stout wall around it built by the Moors, with a single gate in and out; where the road ended, he said, and where you could see a car coming from five kilometres away. To her it sounded like it might be a safe place; he said he would take her up there for a blow job which she bartered down to a hand job and a feel of her tits, payment to be made at journey's end.

They didn't go on the highway but took the old road, first through the tourist towns, going so slowly that even car drivers towing caravans kept giving them the finger. Then Antonio swerved onto a narrow serpentine camino that bent up into the mountains, and the straining old truck seemed to be pushed up the slopes by the jets of thick black smoke that roared from its tailpipe. All the time Antonio spoke about his little town, its fine walls, its beautiful church, its lovely white-painted jumble of houses. And as if he had talked it into existence, suddenly, there it was above them, rising out of the orange groves, the red-tiled roofs of the houses poking above the thick stone walls.

She paid for her ride in the parking lot of the orange cooperative, a large modern shed built on a rock plateau just outside the single gateway that led into the shaded web of alleys and lanes that was the little town. He was a fit old boy, she had to give him that; the tit fondling would have gone on all night if she hadn't called time after half an hour, still he seemed very grateful. Afterwards he dropped her at one of the two bars in the village, the one where he said all the English drank.

The place was called Bar Noche Azul. You could tell it was a foreigners' bar because there were chairs on its vine-covered terrace though it was only May with the thermometer reading twenty-nine centigrade. The Spanish did not begin sitting outside until later on in the summer when the temperature started pushing into the high thirties.

She stepped inside the bar and dumped her bag on the littered floor. There was the usual battle of the giant noises going on. Two TVs, one behind the bar and another monster, wide-screen one in the corner, both were turned on and both were tuned to different channels. Over that there was a stereo playing Spanish pop and a fruit machine clonging away to itself. The bar was of course tiled, traditional patterns rendered in acid, factory colours on floors, walls and ceiling so the racket bounced and ballooned back on itself. The place was also quite full of people and everybody had to shout to make themselves heard. Sue went to the bar and ordered the smallest beer, a canya, and took it to a vacant table. After a while the barman came over and chucked a big piece of chorizo on a hunk of bread onto the table. In the traditional Andalucian way tapas were given free up here if you bought wine or beer. If you bought a much more expensive drink like twelve-year-old brandy or imported Malibu you didn't get anything.

Though none paid the slightest attention to her she knew she had been noticed, first because she always got noticed, she was that kind of girl, but in a place as small as this a new arrival, no matter how self-effacing, would be clocked by the inhabitants. She studied the ones she knew were the British. There were several clumps of them, mostly older than her, in their forties and fifties. These British didn't seem anything like the ones on the coast. On the coast you got your tweed-coated Nazis, or your gold-dripping cockney villains or your pulling-their-trousers-down fat lumps, being sick in the streets and calling the Spanish 'Pakis'. This lot in Noche Azul spoke English amongst themselves, like on the coast in a variety of accents you'd never hear conversing to each other back home: High Church Knightsbridge talking to Thick Birmingham talking to California talking to Camp Old-fashioned Queen but the difference was that when they ordered drinks from the bar staff or threw some comment to the younger locals who also seemed to hang in this bar they did it incredibly, unbelievably in Spanish! Good Spanish, too. She couldn't remember a British person on the coast ever speaking Spanish, they didn't need to, they lived in a bubble of Britishness, radio stations, newspapers, bars; up here it was obviously different, they had to fit in.

One of the English, an old queen who'd been at the centre of a shrieking group, came over and sat down at the table opposite Sue. 'And whose little girl are you?'

Sue smiled up at him. 'I'm just passing through.'

'To where, darling? There's no through, to pass through to.'

He held out his hand. 'Laurence Leahy . . .'

'Sue,' she said and shook hands.

'Another drink?'

'Yeah, why not?'

He shouted over to the barman who quickly brought more drinks and more food.

'So "Passing Through Sue", where do you plan to stay tonight? There's no hotel in our little town.'

'Somebody usually rents rooms . . .'

'By an incredible coincidence I happen to do that.'

'How much?'

'Umm . . . twenty thousand pesetas a week.'

'Eighteen thousand two hundred and sixty-five.'

The odd number threw him, as it was meant to. When haggling for anything Sue always did this for that reason. 'Yes erm . . . alright, eighteen thousand and whatever it was.'

He indicated the crowd he'd been with. 'Come and meet everyone.'

Laurence led her over to the gaggle of foreigners he had been with and introduced her around, still calling her 'Passing Through Sue'.

They were mostly British with a couple of Belgians and Dutch (who were sort of foreign British people anyway) and a Europhile Singaporean. The whole lot of them stayed in the bar till about 1 a.m. then Laurence led her to his house; he didn't offer to carry Sue's bag. In the dark it was hard to tell from the outside the size of

Laurence's place, only that she entered through a small door set in a huge studded Arabic gate that was the only portal breaking the run of a long white wall.

Stepping through the gate brought her into a secret courtyard, this was the first of an uncountable number of hidden places she would step into over that summer. She stood and stared in amazement, up at the abundant stars that lit the hidden garden, then at the tall palms that shaded the starlight, then at the orange and lemon trees, their fruit hanging as copious as the stars. Laurence waited, enjoying her astonishment. 'Not bad, eh?' he said.

'It's fantastic.'

'Glad you like it because it costs me a bloody fortune, I'm being drained like a pig. This is supposed to be my retirement, I tell you I've never been more distracted . . . Come and see the rest of it. Fucking thing.' He led her through a door into the house and flipped on a light. It was like one of those houses you see in magazines, not the trashy ones in *Hello!* either, not comedians' places in Henley or Formula One drivers' serviced apartments in Monaco but one of the houses in the magazines that are just about houses and show you how you could live, if you had money, taste and about a thousand years.

Laurence whisked her round the place. 'Living room, you can use that; kitchen, you can use that but clean up after you; my office, stay out of there; my bedroom, stay out unless invited; your bedroom, same goes for Laurence . . .'

The next morning she didn't wake up until ten. She could hear Laurence crashing about in the kitchen. The sun was bleaching the stones of the patio and he had laid breakfast out on a long table under a white awning.

'Is there work around here?' she asked him.

'Cleaning some of the houses the tourists rent. Bar work maybe but it's all at Spanish rates . . .'

'Well, I'll hang about to see what opportunities there are.'

Sue had noticed that in the living room there were a lot of framed sketches round the walls of men and women in costumes: Cavaliers, Battle of Britain pilots, milkmaids, Victorian nurses, all signed L.L. She asked him, 'All them pictures on the wall that you did of people from history do you see them in visions or something?'

'Eh?'

'You're a Pisces, in their dreams Pisces travel into the past and bring secret messages back. I thought you might have done the drawings after you came back to the present.'

'Do they really? Umm . . . Well, I suppose that's one explanation but I'm afraid the real one is that I designed all those outfits. Yes, it was what I did before my so-called retirement, I was a costume designer on films and TV.'

'A what?'

'A costume designer. Well, you know in movies and on the telly the clothes that the actors wear are designed by someone. Then they're made specially according to the designs, my designs. Usually there's several copies of course in case of accidents or so the outfits seem fresh or when there's a stunt—'

Sue broke in. 'Are you sure?'

'What?'

'Are you sure about this?'

'Of course I'm sure, I did it for forty years.'

'If you say so,' she said and they left it at that and talked about other things. She wasn't fooled about the drawings though. What a ridiculous idea, she reflected. What was it he called himself again, 'costume designator'? Yeah right. Maybe he was ashamed of seeing visions of the past in his dreams and was trying to cover it up. Yeah that was it, Pisces could be like that if their Venus was rising.

They went down to Noche Azul for their lunch and had the Menu Del Dia. As they walked through the high-walled skein of narrow alleys they had to step over various dogs lying stretched out on the hot ground, and outside the bar lay, scampered or sat panting in the backs of pick-up trucks all the dogs who belonged to those inside. More or less the same crowd as last night were in there, with a few additions and subtractions. These were the people she would spend her summer with. There was 'Nige', a very tall dark-haired woman of about forty years, a sculptor with a studio and living quarters right in the middle of the village; she had two dogs, 'Dexter' and 'Del Boy', two big matching yellow things. Frank, middle-aged cockney wide boy, doing up a house in the next village and exporting antiques, owner of one wolf with a trace of dog in it, name of Colin. Kirsten, Dutch academic working on a doctorate for the next six months, loosely attached to one nameless hound for the duration. Li Tang, big house on the edge of the village, extremely vague about activities, dogless. Janet, retired BBC executive, small village house, small pension, small dog also called Janet (or more usually 'Little Janet'). Baz, local builder to the foreigners, four dogs of mixed size from giant to a tiny creature that seemed to be half-dog half-squirrel, names Canello, Negrita, General Franco and Macki. Miriam from Macclesfield, small cortijo in the woods below the village, early retirement from the planning department on mental health grounds, three-legged black female mongrel called 'Coffee Table' and, fiercely protective of her, a male Doberman answering to the name of 'Azul'. Malcolm, writer, big house in the village, two little dogs, 'Salvador' and 'Pablo'.

When Sue and Laurence joined them the foreigners were having a conversation about how much they the outsiders should get involved in village affairs. Miriam said, 'If they want us to take on some of the jobs for the Junta then they'll ask us. We shouldn't push ourselves forward.'

'This is a timeless culture, we shouldn't distort it by importing extrinsic influences,' added the Dutch woman Kirsten in much better English than anyone else present.

'My taxes to the EC pay to keep it timeless ... why shouldn't I do what I want?' said Frank.

Laurence laughed. 'When was the last time you paid any taxes?'

This from Nige: 'Well, I pay the amount of tax I paid in the UK. I reckon I bought Domingo's shiny new tractor.'

There seemed a bit of needle between Nige and Laurence, and he said with some asperity, 'I'm sure he'd give you a ride on it, dear, if you asked him. Either way you might have paid for it but you don't own it.'

Malcolm said, 'Those of us with money could help in a non pushy way. During the winter this place is often cut off for weeks. We could buy a snow plough and give it to them. I couldn't get into Granada last year to buy fresh memory cards for my Sony Dreamcast.'

Laurence disagreed. 'No, that's one area where we shouldn't mess with the balance. It's part of the ecology of the village that nobody can get in or out from time to time in the cold months, it is a beneficial quarantine, the snows purify the village.' Which seemed to Sue a pretty whacky thing to say, yet maybe everyone felt the same way for discussion moved on to other matters.

Through the rest of that week Sue, via Laurence's

sponsorship, found herself easily worked into the fabric of the little group of foreigners. It wasn't hard, a group of highly intelligent urbanites such as these living amongst peasants would naturally hunger for new stories and Sue had a whole pack of new stories, even accounting for the forty per cent she had to hold back for what might be termed legal reasons.

That weekend, as if to celebrate her arrival, it was the village fiesta. All along the valley every weekend one village or another would have its fiesta. The saints would be taken out of the church and paraded around. The old women would crawl around on their knees as if auditioning to play dwarves in a panto, the men would get drunk, there would be bands and dancing, paella for a thousand given away free at 4 a.m. for those still standing (which was more or less everybody), there would be a theme of some kind and always the most dangerous possible use of fireworks. In Sue's village the men would hold formidable rockets in their hands, then casually light them from the cigarettes that were draped from their bottom lips. As the flame beat on their arms they would hang on to them looking nonchalant with an 'Oh do I have a rocket in my hand?' expression on their faces, then they would release the sticks letting the rockets swoop into the howling air, where they would explode with an immense concussion.

A pair of recovering Welsh bulimics had rented the house next to the plaza, the very seismic epicentre of the fiesta. Used to France they had thought that a village in Spain would be similarly quiet. At 5 a.m. they came out in their nightgowns to ask Paco the Mayor if he could turn the noise down but he couldn't hear them. They left the next day.

On the Monday the few Spanish who were about walked with the shuffling steps of chemotherapy patients, the plaza was still littered with fragments of exploded rocket and other bits of firework.

As Sue was crossing the square a pack of dogs came skittering round the corner in a happy mood. She recognised most of the canine gang, Colin, Little Janet, Azul, Salvador and Pablo, General Franco, Canello plus three of the effete little yappy dogs that the peasants surprisingly favoured, with Coffee Table unsteadily bringing up the rear. However, bounding and leaping at the centre of the group was the most magnificent dog she had ever seen, the size of a small cow it was, with lustrous grey black fur, and a long intelligent head set with jet-black eyes. The Dog appeared to have been much better groomed and fed than any of the local pack of hounds, and Sue thought it might perhaps be some sort of a pedigree.

Later on that evening as Sue was sitting on the terrace of Noche Azul with Laurence, the pack again came lolloping past. She said, 'Laurence, whose is that big dog? I haven't seen it before.' He straightened from his chair to take a look.

'Nobody's, it's abandoned. Been here since the second night of the fiesta,' replied Laurence. 'It probably belonged to some Spaniards who are going down to the coast for the summer and don't want to pay for kennels, or who didn't realise how big it was going to grow, who knows? They often abandon their dogs on the highway or they leave them in this village because they know there are a lot of us British here and they think we'll look after them.'

'Will we?'

'I'm not sure, I think everybody's fully dogged up at the moment, but we'll see.'

Through the week Sue began to look out for The Dog and became quite friendly with it, feeding it her unwanted tapas when the owners of Noche Azul weren't watching and scratching it behind the ear as it lay asleep on the stone steps of the church.

It turned out to be a week for making new friends as her horoscope in the international edition of the *Daily Express* that somebody had left in the bar had told her it was going to be. For on the Friday of that week the Mayor, Don Paco, a man of at least seventy, wearing the strongest spectacles she'd ever seen, consisting of what appeared to be a pair of zoom lenses held in a thick black plastic frame on his head, came to see her in Noche Azul where she was having her morning coffee. He asked her to accompany him to the terrace of the villagers' bar, which as far as she could tell didn't have a name or indeed any furniture, being a big empty tiled room; its only decoration was a big photodisplay provided by the manufacturer of all the various ice creams that the bar didn't stock.

Sue and Don Paco sat outside under a fig tree, on faded orange plastic stacking chairs placed at a wonky old green-baize card table. The local guy who ran the bar brought them coffees and for the Mayor a giant brandy in a fish bowl. She recalled what Laurence said about the cost of booze in these parts: 'At these prices you can't afford not to be drunk!' Except the Spanish never ever seemed to get drunk, not in the fighting, spewing, brawling, boasting British way that she was used to from Saturday nights in Bolton and every night on the costa.

Don Paco obviously had something serious to say. 'Here it comes,' she thought. 'Run out of town on a rail.'

But instead he spoke to her most formally. 'Senorita Sue, I have heard from Antonio the truck driver that you did a little favour for him in return for a ride up here. I was wondering whether it would be possible, if you could perhaps do something similar for me. What it is, if I could put . . . mi pajaro, between your breasts which are coated with soap and you could squeeze them together, until . . . well, you know what follows on from that. Perhaps once a week might be suitable? I would provide my own soap.'

'Hmm . . .' She thought about it. 'Weekly soapy tit wank. That'll cost you, Mr Mayor.'

'So be it, nothing is free in this life, we must pay in

the end for everything. I had some little money set aside to buy an electric corn husker this autumn, but a soapy tit wank sounds like it would be better value.'

A few days later another old farmer called Ramon asked her to sit under the fig tree with him. 'Senorita Sue, I have a little money, it was intended for my wife's operation but you know she will die soon anyway, so . . .'

So that was a bi-weekly, non-penetrative butt fuck that he was after. Then there was an armpit wank for the bank manager, another soapy tit wank for the baker, hand jobs for innumerable old campasinos and ten thousand pesetas from the priest to let him watch her taking a piss in the orange groves.

Pretty soon she had quite a business going. The average age of her clients was seventy-two and all of them were old Spanish men from the village or the surrounding campo. Laurence told her that the younger men in the village either had girlfriends who let them have sex with them (though it was understood that this also meant marriage) or they visited the something like thirty brothels that lined the main roads between the village and the big city of Granada. These brothels were shabby breezeblock, tin-roofed buildings, always seemingly with a single dusty car parked outside, their neon signs hung dead in the daylight spelling out 'Club Paradiso' and 'Club Splendido'. They were staffed, so it was said, by beautiful Argentinian girls.

Sue did not feel any guilt about what she was doing, she was providing a much-needed service at a reasonable price. She was aware that generally peasants did not have a very enlightened attitude to whores, yet when she passed them in the streets and lanes the old men would greet her in a courtly fashion even when they'd had their dick squeezed between her buttocks half an hour before, and even more surprisingly their wives were chatty and friendly when Sue encountered them in the village shop or when they queued at the bread van that came twice a day.

Sitting in Laurence's courtyard with Miriam, Nige, Frank, Kirsten and Baz and the remains of a zarzuela de mariscos, Sue mentioned she was surprised that she hadn't encountered any opprobrium from the Spanish for her activities. Laurence, as always, reckoned he had an explanation and because they were all too dozy and drunk to stop him he was able to launch into one of his lectures. 'What you have to remember is that for nearly a thousand years, from 711, Andalucia was the most tolerant, literate, liberal, progressive place on the planet. Under the rule of the Moors it led the world in science, mathematics, poetry, gardening even. Jews, Christians, any religions were tolerated and encouraged to play a full part in society. Then after that black year, after 1492, after the so-called restoration when the Moors were driven out by Ferdinand and Isabella, it was the most repressive, intolerant, backwards looking and led the world maybe in torture techniques.' Then he started to veer off his original course. 'Typical, of course, that Torquemada was a convert, a Jew who became a persecutor of the Jews. Why does that happen so often, that converts become so much more fanatical than those born to the faith?'

Sue let him go on, she thought what a good thing it was that she was so in tune with other people's feelings that she couldn't find it in herself to show him up by letting all the others know what cock he was talking. She had a hard job holding herself in because it made her angry and sad at the same time, all this babble about kings and queens and caliphs and not one word, not one bloody word had he mentioned about angels! When everybody knew that until 1492 a quarter of the population of ancient Andalucia had been proved to be angels. There were loads of books about it: *The Andalusian Prophecy*, *White Wings Over Spain*, *The Celestial Costa Connection*. It was angels that had built the Alhambra, the signs were everywhere if you knew where to look, and every serious historian knew that the Inquisition had largely been aimed at destroying the power of angels.

The summer was the time for excursions and one Saturday a whole gang of them got in a flotilla of cars and drove away, the dogs saw them off, barking and nipping each other. They were all going to the fiesta in Lanjaron, which was the biggest fiesta in the whole valley. This spa town in the Alpujarras was where all the area's mineral water came from. Massive petrol-tanker type trucks full of fizzy water ground up and down the narrow mountain roads, refusing ever to slow down or give way, forcing other drivers close to, and sometimes over, the crumbling edge in a lo-cal carbonated version of the *Wages of Fear*.

For years the Lanjaron fiesta had been one that glorified the contrasting characteristics of 'Fire and Water' but even by Spanish standards there had been a few too many terrible burnings, so it had been remade as a fiesta that celebrated the different qualities of 'Ham and Water' thus the damage incurred now, though severe, was primarily psychological. From early on the Saturday of the fiesta there was a parade of people dressed in aquatic costumes, scuba gear, sailors, mermaids, while others threw buckets of water down from their balconies and the fire department went around soaking celebrants with their hoses. The locals would walk up to a tourist with a big smile then throw a bowl of water in their face. In no time at all Sue's T-shirt was soaked to transparency; naked but not naked, she felt tremendously sexy and would have gone to the toilets to bring herself off if they hadn't been too busy and crowded.

The real horror though began after 1 p.m. Those in the know crowded into the bars which then locked their doors, leaving those outside trapped and running from doorway to doorway as they were repeatedly doused. At first they found it amusing but after a while the constant assault began to wear them down. The gang Sue was with laughed manically as a couple of Dutch tourists beat on the glass doors of the bar they were in while behind them a fire truck directed its hoses onto their backs, till they sank to the flooded ground and curled into a sodden ball, their tears adding to the pool in which they lay. Surreptitiously Sue rubbed herself against a corner of the bar as the Dutch couple were spun and battered to the ground by the gushing hoses of the firemen. She realised she needed a boyfriend, it was all very well being non-penetratively shagged up the arse by eighty-year-olds but she needed some cock of her own age.

As usual her own personal angel – who a psychic healer in Totnes had told her was a Choctaw Indian by the name of 'Lightning Dog' who'd been killed at the Battle of Bull Run – must have been listening, for on the Tuesday of the next week there was a new car in the village. By now Sue knew everybody's vehicle. Nige's beat-up old locally made Santana Landrover, Baz's Japanese pick-up truck, Laurence's ancient Mini still on British plates, the little white vans with seats in the back that all the local old boys had. The only cars that came and went were the hire cars, bright little hatchbacks rented by the tourists who leased for a couple of weeks the few villas that were available to let for the summer.

This big new silver Opel Omega with Madrid number

plates stood out, just as the big dog had when it had come to the valley. When Sue first saw it, the car was parked outside the house of an old English guy called Max. She had met him once when he had come out for a weekend. He was a retired engineer who seemed to talk about nothing except the kinds of toast he had eaten throughout his long, long life. Laurence said he came for the entire summer once he had got his mother settled in a rest home in Coventry. The door of the house was open and a young man of her own age came out, shading his eyes against the bright sunlight. He took an old leather suitcase out of the car's boot and was hauling it into the house when he saw Sue looking at him.

'Awright?' he said to her.

'Awright,' she replied. He was English and Northern, home-grown cock.

His name was Tony and he was from the flat brown alluvial Lancashire farm country inland from Blackpool Bay. Home-grown, organic, free-range cock.

They started fucking that night.

Sue introduced Tony to the crowd in Noche Azul the next lunchtime. Of course they already knew he was there.

'So,' said Nige, 'you're staying at Max's place – when will he be coming out to join us?'

'Oh he won't be,' said Tony. 'Not this year. He decided to stay at home . . . for the cricket.'

'Oh shame,' said Janet.

'I'm a sort of nephew of his. He gave me the keys to his house; he wanted me to enjoy it even if he couldn't.'

'Will you be staying long?' asked Miriam.

'I'm not sure, Miriam. I'm on the look-out for opportunities, perhaps here or on the coast, so I thought I'd chill for a bit, see what happens.'

'Did he sort of give you his watch as well?' drawled Laurence.

'Eh?'

'Did he give you his watch? A Tag Heuer that his firm gave him after thirty years' indentured slavery, you . . . you're wearing it.'

Tony looked at the watch. 'Yeah, like I said he's me favourite sort of uncle. He likes to give me things.'

'That's nice,' said Laurence.

Sue had been around dangerous men all her life, she knew this about them that they didn't bluster and shout, they didn't issue funny threats like they did on the telly. They didn't say through gritted-together teeth: 'If you do that again I'll cut your bollocks off and nail them to the letter box as a draught excluder!' It was not the way of the violent to indulge in complex verbal linguistic display. If they could indulge in complex verbal linguistic display they probably wouldn't be violent in the first place. And they didn't issue warnings like the weather forecast either; they didn't say, 'I'll only tell you once,' or 'I'm warning you . . .' or 'I'm giving you one more chance but, I swear, if you screw up again I'll . . .' They just did you right there and then with no prior notice and no right of appeal. The only warning you might get is that sometimes the situation they were in, like for instance it being their first day in a new town, led them, occasionally, once in a while, to consider their actions. Sue could see that Tony was thinking of doing Laurence right there and then with no prior notice and she could also see that Laurence knew he was in danger of being done and yet, strangely, Laurence didn't seem frightened and he didn't seem bothered either. The old pouf went up in her estimation. Still, following that, he stopped needling Tony and the danger passed.

Tony never bothered much with the Noche Azul crowd after the first few days; in the early weeks of June he spent a lot of time driving backwards and forwards to the coast, in the big silver car. When she didn't have a client Sue would go with him and sometimes she would bring The Dog as well. It would lie panting on the black leather of the back seat until they arrived in Malaga or Marbella or Nerja. Then while Tony went off to have his meetings Sue and The Dog would go for long walks. At first she felt uneasy being back on the coast but having The Dog with her gave her courage. A couple of times she did see people who might wish to do her harm but they never got close enough to recognise her; also, she realised, her appearance had changed since she had been in the village. Her hair had grown longer, her skin was darker from the time she had spent in the campo and the muscles of her arms were a lot firmer from all the wanking that she was doing.

One lunchtime back in the village towards the start of July an amazing thing happened: the bar went quiet. Sue looked up from her newspaper to see in the doorway an officer of the Guardia Civil. The Guardia, Franco's semi-military rural police were hated up here. During the civil war the village had been an anarchist stronghold and the Guardia had been in charge of reprisals when the republic was lost. They had shot seventeen of the village boys along the cemetery wall and the village had not forgotten. The officer strode up to the bar and started asking Armando something, she couldn't quite hear what but it seemed to be something to do with a car from Madrid. Getting nothing out of the sullen bar owner the policeman soon turned and left, climbing back into his Nissan Patrol and gunning it back down the mountain. A few days after that, Sue was taking a pee in the campo, the padre a few metres away furiously pulling himself off behind an ancient gnarled olive tree, when she heard a sudden 'Whooph!' At first she thought it was the priest coming, some of those old campo boys she had found went off like hand grenades. Then turning the other way she saw in a distant ravine that a car had exploded and was now on fire, it looked like a silver Opel Omega with Madrid plates.

Tony said his car had been stolen while he was in Almunecar, but anyway he only needed one more trip to the coast. He persuaded Sue to borrow Laurence's Mini for this trip south though Laurence lent it grudgingly.

In the end she wasn't able to go with him and Laurence went on and on saying that he'd never get his poxy Mini back. But Tony did return. When he got back, after a few days, he told Sue what his plan was. 'See all the cocaine in dis country comes in through Galicia, they've got great contact with South America for obvious reasons, funny it's the women who control the trade as well, once the Guardia put all their husbands in jail. The dope, the blow, that comes through here, the south of Spain, after all it's only half an hour from Algeciras to Africa by fast launch. Scag though, heroin, they ain't got any of that, cos they ain't got any contacts with Turkey, Afghanistan, any of them places. Except now on the costa there's Russians and they're looking to shift what they know, scag, up here into the valleys and the mountains. Now I have an opportunity to get a load at good prices and I reckon the kids up here would take to heroin real well.'

Sue had a question. 'Have you got the money to do it?'

'I got some, that's why I'm talking to you, though. I need more, as much as I can get.'

'You're not worried about the locals?'

'They're fucking divvies these people,' said Tony. 'They

deserve to get fucking took. We know that they don't like the Guardia, so what the fuck are they going to do about it? Even if they figure it's me that's dealing the gear. So you in or what?'

Sue gave him the money that she had saved up, plus she stole a watch from Laurence. A Rolex with a gold strap that Tony got a thousand dollars for in Almunecar. He wouldn't miss it, a person could only wear one watch at a time after all (apart from her DJ boyfriend who'd worn six) and she'd never seen him wearing this one so he deserved to lose it really when you thought about it.

Pretty soon all over the valley the Spanish kids were doing heroin. With drink they had been brought up to understand its properties and its dangers but with scag there was no bargain that could be made, no truce. Scag would not talk to the hostage negotiator. The boy in the bakery who'd once been chatty and smiling now stood for hours at a time, white-faced and spotty, with his arms buried up to the elbows in a bowl of dough. In the next village the bar owner had to lock the doors to keep out a rampaging gang, and in the orange groves a young boy was found shot dead with his father's hunting rifle.

Tony gave Sue her savings back plus a big bonus after six weeks and then he went into Granada and bought a convertible BMW from the big dealership on the ring road.

One morning in July before the sun had begun to scour

the white-painted alleys, Sue and Nige were walking back from Anna's shop, they each had a carrier bag in both hands. It had taken them an hour and a half to buy their groceries, which was pretty good going given the lethargic pace of things during the hot months. As Nige talked her two dogs came running round the corner, tongues lolling from their mouths, pursued a few seconds later by a cloud of the other hounds with The Dog, at the centre of things, seeming to be directing operations. The whole furry storm shot past and disappeared down Calle Iglesias on their way to the church. 'That's the first time I've seen my dogs in three days,' said Nige. 'That big one seems to have taken over the pack with its big city sophisticated ways.'

'Nobody's taken it in though,' said Sue.

'No, and they won't now, it's too wild and flea-bitten.'

'So what'll happen to it?'

'The usual Spanish thing. They'll let it run round for the summer then one day, after the hot months are over, The Dog Catcher comes . . . and deals with it.'

'Takes it to a dogs' home?'

'Silly girl. Shoots it.'

'No!'

'They reckon they're being kind, letting it have its summer. By their standards they are.' Then, appearing to change the subject. 'Sue, tell me something. How did you travel here, to Spain, in the first place?'

'Plane. Scallyjet from Liverpool airport to Malaga.'

'Ah yeah. Everybody comes by plane now but see, when I left my husband, left Devon, I drove down here in an old post office van. I'll never forget that trip. The mountains and pastures of the Basque country, your senses tell you you're in Switzerland. La Mancha, the flat table lands that seem to go on forever, they were once forest you know, they chopped it all down. South from Madrid, this was before they built the highway, it was just a dead-straight road through a desert. After the foothills of the Sierra Morena you eventually come to the Gateway to Andalucia. It's a pass through the mountains, a defile, a natural cutting. You know what its name is? "Despenaperros", "Desfil de Despenaperros", literally in Spanish, "The Place for Throwing the Dogs off the Cliffs." Some say that the dogs referred to are infidels, foreigners, those who do not belong. I believe the other explanation. That the bandits who certainly infested this pass in the nineteenth century would pelt travellers with dogs that they threw down from the high places.'

'You're having me on,' said Sue.

'Not at all. Whether it's true or not, the name of the pass tells us two things about the Spanish. One, that dogs are as plentiful as stones, as rocks, as dirt in this part of the world; and two, that given a choice between throwing a dog or a rock, then the Spaniard would choose to step to the edge and throw the dog. I don't know. Perhaps it had a practical purpose, I suppose it must have disturbed the travellers mightily to find that the sky was suddenly full of flying dogs but it never does to rule out pointless sadism in your dealings with these here Spanish.'

They were at the door to Nige's place. Another studded gate in a blank white wall.

'You want to come in?' she asked Sue.

'Sure why not.' She had never seen inside Nige's place. Nige opened the gate and they stepped through. Unlike Laurence's house they were not in an open courtyard but instead in a high-ceilinged space that was Nige's workshop. Her sculptures were dotted around all over everywhere. Sue had been expecting something perhaps oldee worldee, nice framed oil paintings, like they sold in the rastros of Granada and Seville. Authentic studies of whitewashed cortijos with peasants sitting outside on straw chairs, still lifes of pewter plates piled high with Serrano ham and Andalucian figs, farmyards full of chickens, the plains of old Castile as seen from Toledo. All the paintings signed 'Chavez' and 'Milagro' and 'Romero' and all of the paintings created by painting factories in Southern China where, on a production line as regulated as the nearby Toyota van plant, Chinese workers ground out studies of a country they had never seen and never would see, each one specialising in a fragment of the painting, this one concentrating on chickens, this one doing skies, this one the best sad donkey eyes painter in all of Ghanzu province.

Nige's sculptures were nothing like that. It was a big room and it was hard to see where the mess on the floor ended and the sculptures began; all over the hidden ground, a foot deep in places, was soil, straw, clay, plaster, paint and rising out of this derangement were figures compounded out of the same stuff. Dogs snarling and snapping at each other, men with the heads of bulls and huge cocks drooping in an arc, pigs, ducks, leaping fish, some white, some grey, some stained with the dust of the mountains, some blood red, some midnight black.

Sue stared for many minutes before speaking. She wove in and out of the figures then she said, 'This is fucked up. This is the most fucked-up thing that I have ever fucking seen. You never, ever, know what is behind these fucking doors.'

Nige laughed, she thought Sue was saying a good thing, which she might have been. The sculptress led Sue into a dark side room, its walls of rough-cast plaster hung with beaten copper plates, the tiled floor piled high with oriental cushions, a dim light spilling from coloured-glass-studded Arab lamps.

'This is almost normal,' said Sue as she dropped straight down into the cushions. Nige landed next to her.

'I bought all this stuff when I was backpacking in Northern Pakistan and Afghanistan. Then I shipped it back. The markets in Peshawar are just unbelievable.'

Nige reached behind her into a carved box and drew

out dope and skins. She began to roll a joint and kept talking.

'You can buy, like, literally anything there, stolen Range Rovers from Britain, any drugs you want, they hand-make copies of any kind of gun in the world, gold-plated Purdey shotguns, Kalashnikovs, M16s, pirated Snoop, Doggy Dog CDs, all this next to the most beautiful, timeless, local handicrafts, rugs, lamps.' Nige lit the joint and took a luxurious pull, languorously exhaled and passed it to Sue.

The younger woman drew in the smoke. Before she could breathe out Nige placed her wide open mouth over the other woman's lips. Sue expelled the smoke and Nige took it down into her own lungs, then they both flopped back against the cushions, laughing.

Sue leant forward and began kissing Nige's long neck, while her hand crept down and unbuttoned the older woman's jeans. She slid her fingers inside and began to stroke between Nige's legs. After a while, with all their clothes off, it was hard to tell where Sue began and Nige ended.

August in the frying pan of Spain, all the villas were rented and it was too hot to go out at night before eleven. It was so hot that Don Paco even took his cardigan off and he didn't need to bring his soap along to the orange groves as the sweat between Sue's breasts was all the lubricant that they needed.

Heroin continued to seep down into the valley like the

water that ran along the acequias from the high Sierra Nevadas. Though entirely without conscience, empathy or kindness, Tony thought himself to be a good man who only did what had to be done to get by. He thought that in other circumstances he might have been a doctor or a fireman, helping people instead of poisoning the youth of a valley with narcotics. Partly to prove his decency to himself he would be good almost at random. He was good to Sue, for example, he gave her a regular cut of his earnings even though he was self-financing by now. And he suggested that she could give up servicing the old boys if she wanted to and she could move into Max's house with him.

Sue declined. She said her work with the old men made her feel that she was providing a vital service to the village. The wives of the old men were as polite to her as they were to any foreign woman so there did not seem to be any anger against her, though she did not delude herself that everybody didn't know what was going on. Plus she was enjoying what she did, giving the old boys a thrill, and she was even picking up a fair bit of farming knowledge from her clients, for example they were all very insistent that things, tasks, had to be carried out on a specific day, or during a specific short period: vines had to be pruned on 25 January and, most important of all, the Matanza, the day of pig-killing, absolutely had to be done between Christmas and New Year. Maybe she'd become a farmer one day, Aquarians were very good at farming.

September came and the hot weather ran away like a coward that owed money. The tourists went and all the crops were gathered in. As Sue walked down to the bar she could hear the sound of Paco swearing as he noisily husked corn by hand-cranked machine.

The village already seemed to be drawing in on itself for the winter, the bus had stopped coming from Granada two days ago, the locals no longer drove or walked as often down into the valley.

One day Laurence asked her if she would go to the shop to get him some stamps. Sue didn't really feel like it but she hadn't paid him any rent for six weeks and she wasn't in the mood for a row so she grumpily pulled her boots on and stomped out of the gate, into the shaded alley.

When Sue got to where Anna's, the village shop, was, for a moment she thought it had gone, that it had somehow taken off into the air like the spaceships disguised as houses that the angels sometimes used, or it had vanished in some other way. Then she realised what the sense of dislocation was: the shop hadn't gone it was just that the door to the shop was closed! Previously Sue never knew that Anna's even possessed a door! Up to that point, in all the time she had been in the village, the entrance had always been covered solely by the coloured strips of a plastic fly screen; now suddenly a peeling but substantial, ancient olive wood door barred the gap. She slammed on the door a few times with the heel of her palm but there was no reply. Vaguely confused she turned away and headed back to Laurence's. There was something missing, a vacancy, an omission she hadn't been able to put her finger on at first, but now it suddenly struck her what it was. There were no dogs! Jackie, Salvador, Pablo, Little Janet, they were nowhere about. Their absence made the village seem strangely empty.

Up ahead of her Tony was standing in the middle of the little plaza at the corner of Calle Solana and Calle Santiago looking bewildered.

'Alright Sue,' he said. A tone of uncertainty she'd never heard before in his voice. 'I don't understand this, Noche Azul's closed. I've never seen it closed in all the time I've been here, it's always been open day and night. Laurence said he wanted to meet me here at eleven to discuss something really important, when fuck me I finds it's fuckin' cerrado and that old pouf nowhere to be found.'

Sue was about to tell him both that Laurence was back at home and that Anna's had also been shut when, very close, perhaps two streets over, they heard a sudden loud crack, the sound amplified twenty times, cannoning off the white stone walls. Tony jumped. 'What the fuck was that?' He yelped.

'Must be a firework or a rocket, you know what they're like,' said Sue.

'I guess,' said Tony.

Just then a little yellow dog that used to run with the pack came racing across the square. Another firework went off, nearer this time and the little yellow dog did a somersault and then flopped onto its back with its legs wide open, the way it did when it wanted to be stroked, except when it wanted to be stroked it wriggled about in the dust in a rather disgusting way and this time it was lying still.

Sue and Tony went slowly over to where the little dog lay, the right half of its head was missing and thick tarry dog blood seeped slowly into the dust.

'The Dog Catcher,' said Sue. 'The Dog Catcher must be here.'

'You what?' said Tony.

'It must be the day for The Dog Catcher. Haven't you heard of him? The Dog Catcher comes at the end of the summer and shoots all the stray dogs. I thought he'd take them away somewhere to do it. That's why everybody's locked their doors! They must be keeping their dogs in, away from The Dog Catcher.'

'Shittin' 'ell, it's a bit much that he shoots them right 'ere in the street. That's fucking dangerous, that is. The 'ealth and Safety wouldn't allow that back in England I can tell you.'

'Well you know what they're like, the Spanish and danger. Macho isn't a Spanish word for nothing. They probably think it's great, bullets flying about. Danger and killing animals, I'm surprised they haven't brought their kids out to watch.'

She looked up and down the deserted lane. 'Come on. Let's get back to Laurence's house.'

So they hustled down the lanes to Casa Laurence but when they got there the little door in the big studded gate was shut and bolted from the inside.

'Oi, Lorenzo mate, lerrus in!' shouted Tony and kicked the door.

Suddenly there was another explosion, even closer this time.

'Christ!' said Sue. 'This is gettin' a bit bleeding silly.'

But Tony wasn't listening to her, he was looking down at a hole that had appeared in his stomach. 'Sue, I think I been . . . I think I been . . .' Another bang and where his lips had been there was a pulpy mass.

Sue took off, running. Turning skidding into Calle Santiago she saw The Dog coming the other way, its ears flat against its head, it tail low in terror between its legs. As she flew past it The Dog turned and followed her. Together they bounded down one lane and up another, cutting across squares, racketing off the high mute walls and finding no sanctuary. The church was shut and barred, the gates in the fortified wall locked and immovable. They cut back into the centre, the woman and the dog.

Suddenly as she fled down a lane a familiar door opened in a wall and a voice called to them, 'Quick, inside.'

They both leapt through. They were in Nige's workshop. Hastily she slammed the door and bolted it.

Sue and The Dog stood trembling amongst the clay figures. She went up to Nige and hugged her.

'Thank you, thank you, thank you. There's somebody out there trying to kill me.' Then, indicating The Dog, 'Kill us.'

'Yeah,' said Nige. 'It's the Day of The Dog Catcher.'

'But he shot Tony. Tony's not a dog.'

'Wasn't he?' said Nige. 'You should pay more attention. I tried to tell you when I spoke about Despenaperros. They don't distinguish between outsiders and dogs. If they're a nuisance they get rid of both of them, when the time is right, on the appointed day. Half the kids in the valley are going to be doing cold turkey when the snows close them in this winter because of Tony. Tony was a mutt. Like I said, they let the dogs and the mutts run around for the summer and then The Dog Catcher comes on the day when The Dog Catcher has always come and deals with them both.'

'What about the Guardia?'

'You've seen the Guardia don't count up here. It's that strange mix of tolerance and cruelty, remember Laurence talked about it? And there's also that thing that if you're a local, a real local or a foreigner local, it doesn't matter. Then you know when The Dog Catcher's coming. You lock yourself and your dog inside and you're safe.'

'Shit Laurence, the bastard! He sent me out this morning. He knew The Dog Catcher was coming! And he sent me out, the old cunt!'

'Well, you're a mutt. If you keep a mutt away from The Dog Catcher then you have to be responsible for it. And you did steal his Rolex watch and you stopped paying rent. That wasn't very nice. He took you in when you were obviously running away from something and you stole from him.'

Sue felt a momentary shame replace her self-righteous anger but it faded. Nige was going on again and getting on Sue's nerves.

'Let's face it, you have done a few things this summer, Sue. If you keep a mutt and it kills sheep or steals or attacks a child or deals drugs, or turns tricks, then you, not the mutt, *you* have to answer for its bad behaviour, and the punishment is . . . well, you don't want to know what the punishment is, they learnt some things from the Inquisition.'

'Holy shit! But you took me in, you've saved me . . . Christ, thanks Nige . . . I won't let you down, I mean not that I've really done anything bad anyway. So I'm alright as long as I'm locked inside when The Dog Catcher comes?'

'Umm . . . Well, yes usually you would be alright, if you were locked inside when The Dog Catcher comes,' said Nige rummaging in an Indian trunk.

'Eh? What d'you mean, usually that I would be alright?' said Sue.

'Umm . . . What I mean is that usually you would be alright, fine, if you were locked inside, except, you see, I'm The Dog Catcher.' Nige turned back from the trunk with a bolt action copy of a British Army Enfield .303 rifle, the kind that you can still buy in the gun markets of Peshawar, the kind that the Peshawaris called a 'Britannia Mk 3', held loosely in her hands. Nimbly she worked a round into the breech and raised the gun to her shoulder.

'This is the first time they've allowed a foreigner to be The Dog Catcher. I don't suppose you ever can understand what a tremendous honour that is because you simply do not comprehend what it is to be part of an ancient culture. I can't afford to screw it up by letting dogs go now, can I? They'd think we weren't serious about being here.' And she shot Sue in the head, the round smashing through her pretty forehead and taking a chunk out of the wall behind. In the enclosed courtyard the concussion from the round was huge, Nige felt displaced air from the passage of the bullet smack her in the chest and rock her back on her heels.

As soon as the gun went off The Dog leapt up, mad with terror and raced round and round the rough stone walls, its ears back, urine streaming from its trembling flanks. Nige worked another cartridge into the breech and tried to draw a bead on the careering canine but it was impossible to get a good sight picture. Nige felt stupid and dizzy trying to aim with a rifle at a dog indoors. She was most likely to shoot one of her own sculptures so she simply lowered her weapon, cradled the rifle in her arms and stood still, waiting for the creature's panic to subside. Eventually after fifteen minutes or so the beast slowed down and flopped, its legs too weak to hold it up, whimpering in a corner, its black eyes fixed pleadingly on Nige.

She stepped up to The Dog and pressed the stubby barrel of the .303 against the side of its long head. The creature's ears flattened as it waited for what it knew was its end. After a few seconds Nige lowered the rifle.

'Fuck it,' she said to herself. 'One more dog won't make that much difference around here.' Then she spoke to The Dog, looking straight into its big fearful eyes, 'Just don't cause any trouble, OK? You know what'll happen if you do, don't you?'

The Dog nodded.

DESCENDING

The rider jumped away from the pack as soon as he passed The Devil. He rose out of his saddle, stood on the pedals and sent his bike powering up the last hundred metres of the Col De Tourmalet. He thought he heard the whisper of a groan from the rest of the peloton as they went out the back. He knew none of them had an answer to his strength today plus, as insurance, his two remaining team members, his domestiques, who had come to the front with him suddenly slowed, disrupting the counter-attack and giving it no time to form before he crested the hill, after which there was only descending. And no one descended like him.

The plan had always been to jump as soon as The Devil was reached. The Devil was really a bike builder from some Eastern German town who positioned himself and his giant bicycle on a trailer towards the end of every stage of the Tour De France, dressed in a full scarlet Satan outfit complete with trident, tail and horns. When the leader appeared he ran alongside him, gibbering and jumping for the TV cameras.

For the last minute on the steep upward slope the rider had been riding through a huge, screaming crowd in a space only just as wide as his bike. Hands reached out and touched him on his head, his back, slapping him and trying to push him along. Then he felt a sudden ice-cold shock, which he always forgot was coming. There were always some of the crowd whose fun was to throw water in the faces of the riders; they pretended they were helping to cool them down but really the rider thought they were taking the rare chance to piss on the face of a sportsman. This was one of the many ways in which cycle racing was the greatest, most difficult sport of all. There was no other sport where you got a chance to do that and for free, no entry fee at all.

Then the crowd were behind the barriers, he was at the top of the hill and they were gone. The very last five metres were almost vertical, suddenly he felt a stab of pain in his chest and a spin of dizziness that put him in a confused fog for a second; when that cleared he was at the very pinnacle of the climb – below him was a twenty kilometre road more or less straight down the mountain to the finish line at the bottom. He sat back briefly and zipped his top up to the neck in readiness for the sandblast of alpine air that was to come. As long as he didn't crash, the stage was his and tonight the yellow jersey would be on his back. All – all! – It was a very big all. All he had to do now was to freewheel down the mountain at speeds of up to ninety kilometres an hour, not touching his brakes, ass in the air, head on the bars, leaning in and out of corners, slender tyres shimmying on the gravel at the bends, looking out to a drop of clear oxygen miles below.

Descenders are the bravest men in a brave sport. Sure the sprinters pushing to the front in the last quarter mile risk slipping down and bringing fifty riders on top of them, sure the climbers push themselves to bursting, pedalling fast up the sides of mountains so steep that spectators standing looking back down the road find that the tarmac is almost touching the back of their head, and sure every rider in the Tour De France has pedalled for nine hours and more with leaking abscesses in their skin and blood trailing from wounds in their knees, and sure they all take the new drugs which leave no trace except that your life is decreased by a month or a year or two and they all know that the average life expectancy of a racing cyclist is fifty-eight, so what the hell. But the descender goes through all that and still it is only the descender who risks sailing out into space at ninety kph, legs milling away, like some aeroplane explosion victim still strapped in their seat, his feet locked into the pedals, unable to break free even when they bounce to the ground.

His speed increases as the drop begins to pull him along the road, past the pine woods that flicker away on either side in a susurrating rush. The rider changes into his top gear, biggest front cog, smallest back, but after a few seconds of grip his legs spin uselessly, the wheels turning faster in their belabouring cones than he can pedal, gravity is doing all the work now but gravity won't be getting a bonus from the team sponsors tonight, gravity won't be standing on the podium in a yellow jersey waving a stuffed lion about and making sure the cameras see the name of the insurance company that is written all over him, gravity won't be the winner of the Tour De France – he will.

He notices the motorbike-borne TV cameras have gone and he is alone, their pilots can't keep up with a descending racing bike, titanium alloy and carbon fibre, wires and chain weighing only seventeen pounds and a rider who weighs not much more. He glances down at the computer on his handlebars, forty kilometres per hour, forty-five kilometres per hour coming up and now there is nothing to do except hang on.

Unusually during a race he has time to think and to look around.

The police keep all the cars and the crowds away from the drop so he is by himself, himself and the onrushing air. For a few seconds the woods stop and the road flattens, on one side there is a meadow coated with alpine flowers, a lovely small, crystalline pond filled with water lilies. At the side of the pond a family is picnicking. A woman, two small children, they wave and call to him in his own language to stop and rest with them, are they crazy? This is the culmination of his life. This day is what he has avoided the entanglement of friendship and family for. He can't stop now.

When he had started racing as a boy the communists had still been in power, at the academy they had told the boys and girls that their deeds brought honour on the people's republic. Well, not their deeds but their wins, their losses counted for nothing. To win, they were told, was simple; all they had to do was to dedicate their entire lives to the idea of winning. To only associate with winners, to eat what winners ate, to think what winners thought. Sometimes there was no medicine in the hospitals but the state's laboratories could always manufacture poison for him to put into his body, or there might only be size two shoes left in the shops but he always had the latest Italian components for his bike. He didn't think about it, a winner didn't.

After the communists went and the democrat playwright briefly took over, and then the democrat playwright went and the gangsters who seemed to be a lot of the old communists took over, he joined a team based in Belgium. His life didn't change that much: the people's republic was replaced by the insurance company, he didn't take much interest in the world outside of cycle racing, he never went to plays or the cinema, never read a book, the only thing he watched on the TV was sport. Somebody had told him that things were bad back home, he couldn't remember who or what.

The trees seem darker now, almost black and very tall, shutting out a lot of the light as he rips past. Then a gap appears and he gets a view of the valley below: a man in strange old-fashioned dress is ploughing and behind him, unnoticed, some kind of hang-glider with wings made out of feathers seems to be about to fall into the sea. Sea? There shouldn't be any sea here, he must have imagined it. He can't check, the trees close around him again, a fast right-hand bend comes up, he sticks his knee out to add a little extra gravity and hurtles round it not touching the brakes, then a plateau, and another gap on the right. There seems to be a huge lake, black and polluted with dead trees around its edge and half-sunken ships poking out of the tarry waters. Then that vision too is gone and it is more rocks and scrub on both sides and steep downhill again, faster and faster, flicking left and right and left again, not slowing for a second.

The road flattens now, almost coming to the end of the drop and a village is approaching. Doesn't look like a French village though, more like the wooden board and picket-fenced houses from back home. Several of the buildings are on fire and others are black burnt shells. In the main square just off the road, an armoured personnel carrier pulls up to the door of an onion-domed church and opens fire with its turret-mounted machine gun, the tracer rounds soon set the building on fire. A woman and two children run out into the road and wave at him but the rider swerves round them – after all, the Tour's own corps of gendarmes on their blue BMWs will be along in a second and they'll be able to deal with whatever the hell is going on. Some kind of farmers' demonstration perhaps.

Around the final bend now, doing a steady thirty-five K, the finish line coming up, but where are the crowds? Must be something to do with what's going on in the village up the road. The only one there is The Devil – how did he get down here so quick?

MY LUCKY PIG

The door when she found it was not what Zoe expected. Usually, in her experience, sound studios these days were in pretty swanky office buildings. This was not a swanky office building, it was the sort of apartment block that she imagined was used as safe flats by the secret services of countries that didn't have a lot of money. She wondered if Salman Rushdie had ever stayed in Mycroft Mansions, and if so did he and his coppers have happy memories of it? Still it wasn't that unusual, she told herself; after all, she had recorded voice-overs for documentaries and radio ads and training films in all kinds of strange buildings all over London. At least the studio was in a part of London where a lot of the best voice-over studios were, north of Oxford Street in the garment district which spreads east from Regent Street for a couple of blocks till it runs up against the straggle of the Middlesex Hospital's many outstations of sickness. Pity though, it was the pukka proper studios that she really liked, where a boy in baggy pants went and got you any kind of coffee you wanted and there were bowls of sticky chocolate stuff for you to clagg up your mouth with.

Radiotracks, where they only had bowls of apples and mini choc bars for you to eat free, was in the next street, she'd done the narration there for a documentary made by the Discovery Channel about blunderbusses. And of course there was Saunders and Gordon back of the Tottenham Court Road with its big squishy sofas and help-yourself bar stacked with pain au chocolat and Danish pastries, loads of different teas and coffee, all the mags and the day's newspapers. Though like any leading actress she didn't actually read the newspapers, it was considered bad form. You were allowed to bring a copy of the *Guardian* to rehearsals or onto the set but only to do the crossword between takes. Other actors were disapproving if you were too clued up on foreign affairs or the stock market, if you ostentatiously read the *Economist* or *Frankfurter Allgemeine* at rehearsals; it implied a lack of interest in the real world, which was the interior world of the actor. When Zoe got a commercials job at Saunders and Gordon she tried not to eat the day before and to turn up as early as possible and get discreetly stuck in. Rory Bremner was usually in there talking about cricket to the pretty receptionists in six or seven of his four hundred different voices but as far as she could see he wasn't getting a free meal, he just didn't seem to have anywhere else to go.

Zoe looked down the brass plate that seemed to have at least a thousand door bells on it. There it was at the bottom: Soda Soundstudio, Basement. She pressed the button, there was a buzz and the iris of a little video camera squirmed open and stared at her. 'Errogh?' said a mutilated voice in the wall.

'Oh hi,' she shouted, 'Zoe Renoir, twelve o'clock, I'm here to do the voice-over for the CD Rom thingy!'

'Baismeng!' said the voice and let her in with an electric rattle of the lock. She entered a long dark hallway with blank doors leading off every couple of feet, suggesting each flat was about thirty inches wide. A voice called her from a stairwell leading down into blackness at the other end of the corridor. 'Sonsoodio, don ear.' Her fingers found one of those timer light switches that you press into the wall. For perhaps one second the hallway was grimly illuminated before the switch sprang back out with an emphatic 'boing!' like it wasn't its job to light up the corridor. So instead she felt her way along the wall till a dim light from an open door at the bottom of the stairwell allowed her to descend the stairs.

The basement flat had a large metal studded door painted a dirty white, the head of a small Oriental-looking man was poking round it. 'Sonsoodio in ear,' he repeated and held the door open. Zoe entered and found herself in another ill-lit passageway. The man led her into what had once been the living room of the basement apartment. It was rather charmingly decorated and would have been a nice room if there hadn't been a huge sound mixing desk of the latest kind, several gigantic speakers and a bank of TV monitors rammed into it. Sitting at the desk in a big leather office chair, like that black boy with the weird sunglasses thingy who drove the *Starship Voyager*, was a tubby young man with long greasy hair; on a low sofa were three other men, one instantly spottable as a London advertising type in the standard issue Paul Smith suit, the other two smartly dressed Orientals in suits not made by anybody called anything like Smith. The sound engineer ignored her while twiddling various knobs on his desk in a random way, the other three on the couch rose as Zoe entered.

The Media bloke held out his hand: 'Zoe, um Tom Mantle from Earwig, the production company, these gentlemen are the clients, Mr Urapo and Mr Sweichian.' Both men bowed and shook Zoe's hand. Tom waved in the direction of the engineer, 'That is Beanie.' An abstracted wave. The man who had shown her in did not get introduced. 'Now I don't believe you've seen the script.'

'No,' said Zoe. 'Which is a pirry, 'cos I usually like to have a good look at the script, get familiar with it, almost learn it,' she lied. Zoe did at least one voice-over a day and she forgot them as soon as she did them, indeed she didn't pay much attention as she was doing them, singing the words up and down while thinking of other things.

'Yomp, sorry about that, still you'll pick it up as you go along. You'll be voicing a CD Rom with pictures which will be distributed to certain key figures in the industry that our clients are wishing to enter as new players, they can play it on der computers. So here's the script.' He handed Zoe five stapled-together sheets of paper with closely typed words on them. 'Might as well get started, you wanna go into the booth?' For the first time she saw in one corner what was formerly a small box room, now converted into a sound-proof booth. She skipped in. Beanie shut the door behind her and locked it with a chromed metal lever. She was in a space four foot square, looking back out into the living room through a small double-glazed window of thick glass. Inside was a table with a TV monitor on it, a table lamp, two pencils, a chair, a set of headphones, a green light on a wire and a big German microphone on a stand with a mesh shield in front of it to catch spit and flying food.

Zoe sat down in the chair. No sound entered the booth. The actress stared out at the quintet moving their mouths like well-dressed men-fish in an aquarium. She felt not quite right. It had been dinned into them at the youth theatre then at drama school that they had to do everything they could to advance their careers, it wasn't nearly enough to be talented, the business of acting had to be the only thing in their lives, they had to make contacts, get along with people – but she didn't know where she was with this lot, there was a funny vibe she'd never encountered before. Her friend Trink from drama school had one of those Psion Organisers, a 7a, the most advanced kind he said. He could talk into it, tell it things and later it would talk to him and tell him things back. What he did was, he would make a note of anybody who could help his career, up and coming directors, casting directors, writers and so on and enter all their details into his Psion, then if he met them at a first night or something he could slip off to the loo and get a briefing, then come back and act like their biggest fan. Many people had been freaked out to hear Trink's voice coming from a lavatory stall at the Old Vic, whispering secrets to himself in RADA-trained tones. Still, she thought a Psion, even the more powerful 7a, was no substitute for a nice pair of tits. Most actresses were good-looking, beautiful even, and being amongst so many pretty ones taught you not to value your looks but it was also implied that you would use them whenever you could. Zoe wasn't stupid though, she knew instinctively not to try anything fresh with anybody in that other room; she might as well have tried to get off with the Procurator of The Free Church of Scotland as to try anything with Tom, Beanie, Mr Urapo or Mr Sweichian.

She turned in the chair and put her Tellytubby backpack

on the floor, looked inside it and realised with a jink of fear that she didn't have her lucky pig with her. Well, that wasn't a good start. She liked to have her lucky pottery pig with her when she did a job or went for an audition or had a cervical smear. She was so frightened so much of the time and she thought her pig kept her safe, protected her like a guard pig, standing square on its stumpy pottery legs, defying the forces of evil to harm her . . . brave pig. There were so many of them, actors, actresses, like you would watch in *The Bill* and apart from the regular cast there were loads of actors in it and in the next episode there was a whole different bunch of actors and you never saw the first bunch again on the telly ever, and those were the successful ones who got on the telly even the once.

The CD Rom had a timecode running along the bottom of it, giving minutes, seconds and tenths of a second. The bits that needed voice-over would be played to her and a green light would tell her when to start talking, the timecode was also printed on her script and that told her when she needed to stop speaking by. Beanie spoke to her over her headphones. 'I need a sound level, tell me what you had for breakfast.'

'A nice piece of grilled lettuce dressed with lemon juice and there's this new live bacteria drink tha—'

'Yeah that's fine. I'll run the picture and give you a light.'

The small TV on the desk in front of her came to life. A big clock appeared on it then the images began, bright blue sea mixing to coral reefs, tropical fish darting in and out, then small tropical islands covered in palm trees. The green light flashed and she began to read. 'The South China Seas, famous for azure blue lagoons, palm-fringed beaches and . . .'

She paused as the script told her to and waited for the light to come on again. As it did the image cut to shaky footage of small boats rammed with armed men smashing through the surf.

'. . . pirates! Rapacious, bloodthirsty, rampaging pirates!'

The pictures stopped and Tom spoke to her over the headphones.

'That was great, Zoe, fablious. Let's try it once more for luck. Have a bit more fun with it.' So they did.

Then the pictures fast forwarded a bit up to the next section they wanted her to voice over.

'Nearly a century after Joseph Conrad wrote of the colourful robbers he called "vagabonds of the sea", the pirates of the South China Seas are highly organised, technically advanced criminals and now they are expanding into Europe.' She thought this sounded like one of those documentaries she'd done but why had they said it was a CD Rom? On screen the speed boats were bucking in the wake of a huge merchant ship. Grappling hooks were thrown and the men in the boats, rifles slung across their backs, climbed like racoons up the ropes and onto the unseen deck of the ship. She read on.

'We are those pirates, the pirates of the South China Seas and we are looking to make alliances in your area. If we are your friend we are loyal and true, if you are our enemy we are implacable.'

On the deck of the freighter the gunmen had the crew lined up in front of them. The pirates began firing with their rifles and the sailors staggered about for a bit and then fell down in a heap.

Zoe suddenly had a horrifying thought. Her agent, who she usually told what she was doing every second of the day, didn't know she was here, in fact she'd lied and said she was going to an auction of unwanted greyhounds. It would be up there on the board in the office in big felt-tip letters: '9/6 Zoe auct, unwnt grhnds.' The CD Rom people had phoned her direct and offered her a buy-out flat fee of five hundred pounds which had seemed like a lot of money for something that wasn't going to be broadcast. So Zoe's agent didn't know about this job, she was cutting her out of her fee, in fact the CD Rom people had expressly told her not to mention it to her agent. What suddenly struck Zoe was, was she getting paid enough for this? What if it wasn't sufficient? What if she was getting shafted? She thought she might try phoning her agent and asking, all casual like, what the right fee for a thing like this might be. Would her agent be annoyed with her? She'd phoned her yesterday when Zoe'd thought she was pregnant to ask if she thought Zoe should get an abortion now or wait till after the *EastEnders* audition. How was she supposed to remember the woman's fucking IVF treatment had failed for the ninth time? She decided to phone, after all her agent was one of her best friends. She took out her mobile but there were no 'steps to heaven', that's what she called the little ascending bars on the display that showed what the signal strength of her phone was; there was no whisper of a signal here. The pictures had frozen on the screen with a grinning pirate brandishing his gun. She spoke into the microphone, 'Erm, hello . . . erm can I make a quick phone call on your landline, I can't get a signal in here on my mobo?'

Beanie's voice came back at her through the cans. 'No the phones aren't working.' She was sure she'd seen one of the Orientals on the phone a few minutes ago, but anyway it would have been difficult to talk about the fee in front of them so she would just have to make the best if it.

Pictures, green light. 'Throughout the reefs and islands in the South China Seas the pirates are feared for their recklessness, cunning and lack of pity. Take the practice of phantom ships, you simply order or buy a vessel for US$350,000 and we seize a ship for you. If you want a crew on board we will keep them for you. If you don't, we will simply throw them overboard. Or let us say you have an enemy, would you like this to happen to them?' The picture on the screen was of a large bare room, in the centre was a Chinese man tied to a chair and naked to the waist. He looked like he was in some kind of abandoned factory. Above his head there were bare pipes hanging from brackets, dangling chains, large industrial metal doors and around him rough unpainted brick walls. But you never knew; for instance, there was a sound studio called Space, off Carnaby Street, that was done out like a spaceship, the doors to the sound booths were like airlocks and all the speakers were housed in swoopy blobby cabinets that looked like they were in the middle of a flashback, and there was this other very weird studio called ADR round the back of Kings Cross where there was a stream running half-way up the walls, all the seating was made out of the boots of cars, Minis converted into couches, and you got upstairs to the recording suites through a door opening out of a large tree in the corner of the reception.

Green light blinking. 'This is the famous Chinese actor Tony Cho, he thought himself a big man, big Kung Fu expert, didn't think he needed his old friends from Macau.'

She recognised the guy, she'd read about him in the *Stage* in an article concerning the dangers of working overseas unprotected by the mighty power of Equity, though it didn't look like Peter Postlethwaite and the general council were going to come swinging through the

windows to rescue Tony Cho. Several other men came
into view, wheeling what Zoe recognised from a week on
Casualty as one of those machines they shock heart-attack
patients back to life with. But of course Tony was alive, at
that moment. One of the pirates put the paddles on Tony
Cho's chest and gave him a jolt of electricity. He twisted
in pain. Zoe watched this intently, she hoped one day to
play in *Death and the Maiden* and you couldn't pay for
research material like this. They waited a bit then gave
the actor another higher shot of electricity. Suddenly he
pissed himself, a fountain of yellow urine.

Zoe wondered if she would be able to piss on demand;
she'd been naked at the Almeida and she'd wanked herself
at the National but a stream of piss once a night and
twice on Saturdays, well that would be a thing to get
a girl noticed. It wasn't that she wondered whether
she could do the pissing from a physical point of
view, more whether she was mentally prepared for it.
She hadn't minded the nakedness at the Almeida that
much really after a while, but she'd hated the wanking
at the National. Thing was though you couldn't demur
at any of that stuff, you couldn't even act like it was
an issue: 'Want me to wank? to fuck? to pee? Sure
no problem, I'll do it right here in this church hall in
Shepherds Bush, I'll do it at a festival in Dundee, I'll
do it in front of my Auntie Janice and go for cannelloni
with her afterwards.' If you didn't jump to it, directors

wouldn't use you, you'd get a reputation. And for once it was actually worse for the boys, you couldn't go more than three visits to the theatre these days without seeing some poor actor's wizened dick. Her friend Mong from drama school said his mum had seen more of his penis in the last few years than she had when he was a baby. It was funny really, in the non-acting world you got a bad reputation from wandering about with your cock out, in the acting world it was the reverse.

The pictures started up again and the nagging green light blinked; the screen was split into four showing various types of criminal activity, drug smuggling, piracy, prostitution and people being gunned down on the streets of some Chinese town.

She was on the last page of script now. 'Whatever you want we can get it for you, drugs, slaves, ships and a speciality of ours is contract killing to a very high standard. In many instances the authorities will not know that a murder has occurred thinking it an accident, or an unexplained disappearance and the target will never be aware that they have been singled out for extermination. But be very certain before you hire us – remember, your own life is at risk if you do not keep up payments.'

They went over some things a few more times and then she was finished.

Beanie came and let her out of the booth with a gift of fresh cold air. Zoe went back into the control room to say goodbye to Tom and the Chinese men. This was always an awkward time for the insecure voice-over artist, an uneasy saying of goodbyes when they want you gone but you'd like to sniff out what they really thought of you, but you find yourself out in the street with thoughts of the engineer hitting the 'delete' button and the producer already on the phone to Caroline Quentin's agent. 'Bye, bye, bye' (she said) to everyone and Zoe was out in the street, surprised that it was still daylight. She felt like she'd been filmed underground for a month.

She must have walked for quite a while though she couldn't really remember. She stopped suddenly in the middle of the pavement, so that a grumpy man walked into the back of her. Looking around Zoe saw she was on a street near Broadcasting House, standing outside a minuscule old-fashioned sandwich bar called the Sandwich Boutique (how Sixties was that?). So tiny was it that for storage they used the space above the ceiling tiles. The sandwich bar man was right then coming down a ladder backwards from a square black hole in the roof. She had a sudden overwhelming impulse to sneak in there while the sandwich bar man was fussing over his Snickers bars and climb the ladder up to the black square. It looked so safe up there in the ceiling, suspended above the diced watery ham egg mayonnaise and minty lamb on ciabatta. But just then she saw her friend Mook from the RSC over the road so she waved to him and ran across the traffic, shrieking. They kissed and stood there for ages chatting and then they went and got a new kind of Brazilian bikini wax together.

BARCELONA CHAIRS

rupert's haircut (whenever people referred to him as 'Rupert' he'd say, 'No, no, it's rupert, no capital, I've got a small r' – to which more than one person thought 'You've got a small something') cost him ninety pounds, which came out at about six pounds fifty a hair. Still it was worth it, there was something Trevor Scorbie did, even with such slim pickings, that was just wonderful, the man really did deserve the term 'genius'. What remained after each strand had been individually trimmed with tiny silver scissors, was pale yellow going on white with a hint of urine. Below were eyebrows of vaporous grey, scallop-coloured eyes, skin the pink of a prawn cocktail. On his thin body a lapel-less suit by Yamamoto, collarless shirt by Paul Smith, slip-on shoes by Patrick Cox. He thought that there was something purposeful about the 'lessness' of his clothes, like he just didn't have the time to fuck about with lapels and collars and laces and buttons and shit like that. (Not that any of these people with their names on these things had actually made them. They had told somebody else who'd told somebody else who'd told somebody else who'd got some hard-up women in lands far away to really run up the clothes.)

rupert looked in the mirror and liked what he saw. But then what he saw possibly wasn't what you saw. rupert was an architect and after modern artists, architects are the next best people in the world at seeing what isn't there. You might see, for example, a building that was a rust-streaked concatenation of concrete forsaken on a traffic island, they would see a subtle evocation of the baroque cathedrals of Europe set on the confluence of mighty rivers. They talk a very good edifice, architects do; pity they aren't quite as good at building the fuckers.

Still smiling into the mirror, rupert dwelt on how his life in the last few years had really turned around, after all he hadn't always been so content. At one point, like one of the modernist buildings he so admired, rupert had been going nowhere. It had dawned on him after seven years of university and fifteen years of private practice that apart from the big bastards of the building world, the Richard Rodgers and the Norman Fosters, the work tended to be of the piddling kind. Mostly in rupert's case it was too rich, too little taste, private clients who spoilt his grand designs by whining about mundane practicalities, demanding shelves to put their horrible knick-knacks on and ruining his spatial flow by insisting on stupid things like walls and doors. At least, he consoled himself, he hadn't fallen so low that he'd been forced to do any work for local authorities. If you worked for them, apart from the more or less continuous meetings, you had to design hideous bloody ramps all over the fucking place, just on the off chance that any passing spastic (or whatever they were called these days) chose to drop in. Though he had made a very good living, rupert had not been satisfied with being piddling, who would be? He wanted to be a player like Norman Foster or, even better, he realised he wanted to be the top half of a player couple like Richard and Ruthie Rodgers. Richard was pretty much the architect of choice for the new Britain and Ruthie of course ran the River Café in Hammersmith, which had been at the forefront of a revolution in British catering by setting new standards for what you could get away with charging for stuff you could have bought in a shop and plonked on a plate. See that's why Norman wasn't as big as Richard because nobody knew what Mrs Foster did or even if there was a Mrs Foster. Equally, if Norman was gay he should start taking the boyfriend to awards dinners and stuff like that and should get him to give an interview to the papers about a friend who'd died of Aids, if he really wanted to get on that is. rupert'd observed that if both you and your wife were famous, then there was an exponential increase in your celebrity. When you stood in front of some bloke, said some words, signed some forms, then right away the media power of the two of you wasn't suddenly just doubled or tripled, instead it was squared or cubed, thus all kinds of incompatible people got strapped together till falling ratings did them part. Fame-research scientists called it 'The Liz and Hugh Effect'.

So at that low point in his life rupert decided to take it all in hand and his first project had to be his own wife who'd been dragging her arse for far too long. Helen, who he'd met at college, had seemed to be satisfied with being at home, raising their two kids, Mies and Corbu, but he was having none of that.

Once he knew what he wanted then rupert generally got what he wanted. As a child he would simply go on and on at his parents or his Scout troop leader or his sister till they did what he wished them to do, moved the family to a lighthouse, made him troop leader or jerked him off. He even gave this process of going on and on a pet name: after trying out 'Persuagement', 'Coercetration' and 'Argueforcement' he finally settled on 'Forcesuasion'. He saw no reason not to continue this behaviour as an adult. So once it had been decided that Helen his wife needed to get out of the house and play her part in his rise he would, day and night, go on at her. He would point out successful women in magazines and say how good they looked, he would point out younger, more successful women at parties and imply he might fuck and then marry them if she didn't pull herself together. She got the message.

Now Helen had her own highly successful, flag cleaning business. Casting around desperately for some way to make herself a big success she had noticed one day how grimy and torn were the flags of all nations flying from the Arding and Hobbs department store in Clapham (just like life, Zaire was in a particularly tattered state). Enquiring of the manager she found that the care of the flags was nobody's responsibility. She pointed out to this woman that not only did the condition of the flags make the store look scruffy but they were risking offending wealthy Zairean shoppers by the state of their flag and they also risked annoying peripatetic Ukrainians, whose beloved national standard, symbol of freedom, icon of the throwing off of a thousand years of Russian imperialism, was flying upside down. She got the contract to clean and maintain the flags and since then had obtained many more. At the moment she was in the midst of pitching to look after the flags of the entire Italian Navy, that'd be a big job if she pulled it off. If it hadn't been for rupert she would be a simple housewife instead of a woman with her own Audi A6, internet capable mobile phone and six hundred thousand unused air miles.

It was reading that had made rupert want to be an architect. From an early age he had read everything he could get his hands on, except fiction. rupert simply had no time for works of fiction; he would happily read a newspaper or a hi-fi magazine or an engineering text book, or of course any sort of web site. You could learn something from them, fiction though? He couldn't see the sense in it. Who could possibly care about the actions and doings of made up, non-existent, fabricated persons? Whether they jumped under trains or solved crimes or got married, who gave a fuck? They didn't exist! They didn't have identities! They didn't have phone numbers or dicks or lawn furniture and they most certainly didn't give dinner parties where rupert could meet powerful people. They were no fucking use at all.

When rupert was growing up in the 1960s all the features in the newspapers seemed to be about the future, the past you couldn't give away for sixpence. Papers and magazines were overflowing with visionary line drawings, Rotring-enscribed prophesies for the rebuilding of the World. Siefert's plot to replace Covent Garden with tower slabs; the long-forgotten 'traffic expert' Colin Buchanan who schemed to lay six-lane motorways where Canterbury Cathedral stood, taking up valuable land, doing nothing and looking old; T. Dan Smith's Newcastle. Abroad, whispering the names of future cities with impossible enchantment: Brazilia, Canberra, Ottowa; and at home, of course, the magic that would become Milton Keynes. All done by young men in architects' offices, thin black lines rendering stark towering workers' housing, shopping precincts, industrial zones, flowers growing where they were told to grow in conical concrete tubs, white families walking hand in hand. There was usually a monorail in there somewhere and the sun always shone. Who wouldn't want to live there, in Skelmersdale New Town? Or even better, how great must it be for 'there' to be your creation. To change the real world, to jumble it up and to spit it out looking different, not for good or ill but simply to change it, to say: 'I put that there, that building. The particular headache that its abiding ugliness gives people, that's my doing.'

But at his low point rupert wasn't changing the world, he was lucky if he got to change a step or a walk-in wardrobe a little bit.

So once he had sorted out his wife and she was a player in the flag cleaning business, rupert started to consider how he could bring power to himself. It came to him in his dissatisfaction that politics, that had to be the game, that was all about reshaping society, wasn't it? Closing down hospitals, letting terrorists out of prison, starting minor wars in little countries, moving people around like the cursor on your computer screen.

'The wastebasket contains fifty thousand miners. Do you want to remove them permanently?'

'Click yes I do.'

'Find/change five hundred cottage hospitals into ten gigantic, super sickness centres.'

'The find/change feature is not undoable. Continue/cancel?'

'Continue, continue, continue, you stupid machine, the future is not undoable. Click!'

So the problem now was how was rupert to get into politics at this late stage? Certainly not standing as an MP or any of that nonsense, who had the time for that? Going around housing estates kissing Pakistani women, then being unelected if you'd unpleased your ungrateful constituents.

It was during the early Nineties when rupert was thinking these thoughts and one day he heard two magic words: 'Think tank'. He knew right away he had to find out more about these cognitive panzers. Like all the best ideas, the idea for 'Think tanks' came from the United States. What they were was groups of brainy individuals who were paid to think up all kinds of new ideas for how society should be organised and then to suggest these new ideas to the government.

Sensing the way the wind was howling, it was a left-wing think tank that rupert joined. It was called 'The Lozenge Institute', and was financed by a group of left-wing individuals who were involved in the businesses of vivisection, nuclear reprocessing and Formula One motor racing.

After the inevitable avalanche election victory rupert then set about moving from where the ideas were thought up, to where the ideas were put into practice. He had to jump out of the think tank, towel himself off and leap into the 'Taskforce'.

Tony's government had created more than four hundred

taskforces so that Tony could stick his snout up every crevice and cranny of your life, which was what he liked. Taskforces were groups of the right people who studied burning issues of the day and could be relied on to fiercely, independently and freely come up with the answers Tony wanted. They had names like 'The Creative Industries Taskforce', 'The Achieving 20% Market Share Sub-group' and 'The Review of the List of Nationally Important Sporting Events Which Must be Made Available to Terrestrial TV Channels'. Taskforces were great for the likes of rupert, real power and no responsibility. There was only one wasp in the lemonade: there was a terrible, shocking shortage of the right kind of tonythinking individuals to stock these taskforces and because there weren't enough reliable right thinking persons to go round, taskforces as often as not reported to other taskforces with exactly the same people on them. Ruthie Rogers often found herself reporting to herself. So the initiatives just went round and round, important initiatives in the field of fire-proofing pet toys went uninitiated.

rupert knew, with the signals he gave off and the work he'd done at the Lozenge Institute, that it would be easy for him to get onto some ordinary, bog-standard taskforce (though perhaps not the 'Cowboy Builders Working Group' or its four sub-groups, since none of the sixty-three people involved in it were architects or surveyors). Instead he wanted to get into a taskforce that was right up close to the juice, to the power, which of course meant Tony, because even when your taskforce came up with some dazzling new ideas in the field of the regulation of artificial meat products nothing happened unless you reported to some big bastard on the way up with real spunk. rupert was determined to get onto a taskforce that reported to Tony, the biggest bastard of all. If rupert wanted to discuss something he just bloody well wanted to get on the phone to Tony or walk over to Number 10 and bloody well talk to Tony.

So rupert waited and wheedled till he could get an invite to a dinner with Tony so he could explain his ideas. Finally it happened at Helena Kennedy QC's (Baroness Kennedy of the Shaws) place. Once Salman's bodyguards and Tony's bodyguards had gone into the other room to eat the pizzas that had been delivered for them by a boy on a scooter, rupert went into his dance.

It came in two parts. The first part. rupert explained that the work of his heroes, the architects Mies van de Rohe and le Corbusier, had been unfairly traduced by the enemies of progress like that reactionary cunt Prince Charles with his organic oatymeal biscuits and his visions of self-effacing stone cottages. In fact it wasn't that they had gone too far but rather that they hadn't gone far enough – what was needed was more organisation, more planning, more control. The second part. People had to be convinced that they wanted this themselves, that's where his childhood creation of Forcesuasion came in. Through Forcesuasion rather than the government doing what the people demanded (which when you thought about it was terribly old-fashioned) you could get the people to demand what you wanted to give them in the first place. If all the powers of the government, all the ministers, all the civil servants, simply went on and on and on and on without deviation or deflection, ignoring all interjection, then in no time at all the populace would be clamouring to be given the chance to live in planned housing, in controlled housing zones, eating nutritious balanced meals in airy spacious communal canteens (Ruthie Rogers was already hard at work designing the menus).

'I've proved it in my own life,' he said to the Prime Minister. 'I've proved it over and over again. It's not undoable, Tony,' he asserted feverishly over the granita of summer fruits. Tony leant forward to hear more.

On the doorstep of Helena's house, as the Jags growled smokily in the night air and the bodyguards' eyes snapped this way and that, Tony said to rupert, 'rupert, I want you to do the undoable.'

'I'll do it, Tony,' he replied and they shook hands, staring into each other's eyes like lovers.

As he was driven home rupert thought about what somebody had told him was the epitaph of the German poet and playwright Bertholt Brecht: 'He had opinions and people listened to them.' He had opinions and soon they would be rammed down the throats of the Strasbourg Goose of the populace. That was rupert now, a man who had everything: an influential position, a powerful good-looking wife, a family and a house.

Or rather, he thought happily, A House. His House deserved the capital letters that he forswore. His house in Belgravia, a mere half a mile from Richard and Ruthie Rogers' place. A dream of a house. When he bought it, it was a dark poky six-bedroom, end-of-terrace London house and now it was transformed into an oasis of light and space. As soon as you entered the plain front door you were met with a vision, a spectacular glass staircase which shot vertiginously up in front of you. The staircase was not, rupert would insist, 'an object', something with which to impress the neighbours, it was simply what it was, a direct link from the new roof lights right down to the basement. A conventional staircase would have destroyed this sense of lightness and space which he was trying to achieve. The treads of the staircase were etched with three rows of opaque dots to make it easier to see the stair edges. rupert had not wanted them and they had not been there originally but one night, finding his son Mies half-way up the clear glass staircase in a puddle of urine, clutching the treads in terror, Helen forced him to have the dots put in. They gave him a twitch of revulsion every time he descended the stairs. The sitting room was sited up these stairs. The only thing to sit on once you got up there were four of the cantilever steel chairs that Mies van de Rohe had designed for the German pavilion at the 1929 Barcelona International Exposition, the famous 'Barcelona chairs'. Apart from that the room was empty.

If you looked closely you could see that one wall was all cupboards which were crammed with the couple's books, music, TV. There was an absolute lack of clutter. rupert and Helen even kept the phone in the cupboard, which meant that occasionally they did miss some important phone calls – such as the one from Corbu's school saying his stitches from the foot wound he'd received from the sharp steel edges of the floor in the kitchen had sprung open again and they'd sent him back to the hospital, so he'd sat alone in casualty for eight hours being molested by blood-encrusted drunks – but it was better than clutter. Because that was the thing about minimalism, it was demanding, it asked a lot of you, everything that was in the minimalist room was balanced on a hair trigger of harmony, every object was precisely where it was supposed to be and the slightest thing out of place threw the whole delicate equilibrium into utter chaos. One pencil out of its box, one picture at the wrong angle and everything was completely ruined, a single toy on the floor and you might as well wallpaper the room in a Laura Ashley print and order matching velour sofas from DFS. And disorder you couldn't see couldn't be allowed either, it still seemed to give off telepathic waves of disharmony, seeping under the door and polluting the pristine atmosphere, which is why he had to insist that the kids kept their sleeping space in the same ordered state as the rest of the house, even though he never visited it. Minimalism is becoming increasingly de rigueur but most are just playing at it. By her own admission not the tidiest of people, Helen now said to friends at dinner parties that 'once you start living here you get into the habit of putting things away'.

This pleased rupert but then he had found out she was renting a small bedsit in Vauxhall, rammed to the ceiling with pottery turtles, leatherette footstools and flowery, appliqué table mats, where she would sneak off as if visiting a lover and would sit for hours, rocking backwards and forwards stroking a ceramic clown amidst a mountain of knick-knacks. He didn't shout at her when he found out but they had a long, long talk about it and of course she saw in the end that it was best to give the place up. Anyway these days she was too busy cleaning flags to have time to stroke a ceramic clown.

The only really showy aspect of the living room was a piece of glass, a metre square, set in the floor just over the front door. Sometimes rupert thought he could see a faint stain of yellow on the crystal-clear glass from another pool of Mies' urine, after the boy had blindly chased a ball onto it, then frozen in fright, seemingly floating in thin space above the front door.

Though Helen went on as usual, he refused to mutilate

this glass, pointing out that Mies would no longer go within ten feet of it without violent spasms accompanied by vomiting. Also he insisted that as the glass was bonded with acrylic even if it cracked it wouldn't go anywhere, surely they could all see that.

So on the night when Tony gave him his task, he sat happily in the back of the Jaguar, dreams of power seemed to seep out of the car's heater and wrap him in a contented fug. The long black limousine turned into his street and the headlights, the powerful new sort that shone like blue stars, lit up the side wall of his beloved house. Lit up the end-of-terrace side wall that had been smoothed, over and over again, to the finish of an egg and then coated five times in a special paint imported from Germany. On that wall which had been beautiful and clean and pristine and white as a sea mist when he left it, on that wall was now written in letters perhaps two foot high a single word: 'PATRICK'.

He got out of the car and stood on the pavement, shaking. rupert couldn't have felt more violated if he'd been forcibly fucked up the arse by some Irish labourers on Hampstead Heath. This couldn't happen to him, he was part of the power. He felt awful and sick with rage. Just the single, stupid, cretinous name 'PATRICK', spray-painted in the shaky tentative hand of an illiterate. He wouldn't have minded so much, he told himself, if it had been some sort of a political slogan, something to do with tortured Kurds, say, or that bloke in Peru who looked like one of the Grateful Dead. It wasn't even as if the name was a proper graffiti artists' tag, which at least had some aspirations to funky street art; he'd read all about it in *MSR* magazine, how generally these tags were the products of teams or crews wending their way home from clubs, late-night, hit-and-run signwriters, enscribing their 'Noms de disco', 'Wot', 'Hemp', 'Waste' as a homeward slug's trail. Never, though, something as bland as an ordinary name: 'PATRICK'. Indeed rupert suddenly remembered that he actually owned a Keith Haring painting, done with a spray can, of his trademark little jumping men, that's how down with graffiti art he was.

This, though, well this was vandalism pure and simple. He briefly thought of asking Jack to get his cops to investigate but quickly dismissed it, part of being part of the power was knowing how far you could go. rupert assumed the work had been done by some idiot, lower-class child of the slums, but how had the child got here? He reckoned it must have taken a taxi from the working-class suburb where it lived. There were no buses or tubes that penetrated this upper-class faubourg and he knew from reading the government reports that no proletarian kid was capable of waddling for more than a few hundred yards without having to sit down for a packet of crisps, a bottle of Sunny Delight and some crack cocaine.

rupert had thought the term 'hopping mad' was simply

an expression, but that's what he did; he hopped, right there on the pavement he stood and he hopped. He had to do something to stop the hopping. Even if he phoned his decorators now to come and paint out the graffiti he knew they wouldn't turn out till the morning if they turned out at all, bloody obdurate British workmen. He wished he could fly them in from Germany like the paint. Fumbling with his keys he jacked the front door open and brushing the au pair aside ran downstairs to the dark-filled basement, and immediately felt utterly confused. When he had designed the house he had insisted that he didn't want handles on any of the doors and that indeed the doors shouldn't be distinguishable from the walls so that you couldn't tell where wall ended and door started, simple flat planes everywhere. He said that if you were down there in the basement then you should know where you were going and if you didn't know you shouldn't be down there. Helen had pointed out that guests might need some guidance as to the whereabouts of the toilet so after hours and hours of discussion late one night he'd conceded a sandblasted square cut into the spare bathroom door; they'd have to locate that or pee in their pants, he would go no further.

Now his house, suddenly unfamiliar to him, seemed to sway and turn. He spun round and round, all around him blank walls. What he wanted was the door that let out into the small open area between the basement and the street. Frantically he pushed and shoved at the walls until one bit gave with a click and he was thrown into a narrow space smelling of soap, grazing his face on the brickwork as he cannoned into it. Out there to the left was another door that gave access to what had been the house's coalhole, now a damp-dripping brick cave under the pavement.

The damp must have made the wooden door swell because he had to tug hard to open it and in so doing a projecting nail tore a huge rip in the three-thousand-pound Ozwald Boateng suit he was wearing. Swearing to himself and wreathed in cobwebs he rootled through the coalhole until he found a quarter-full tin of the paint that had been flown in from Germany and used for the mutilated white wall. He grabbed a big paint brush from a shelf and ran back upstairs to obliterate the offending word. With big broad strokes he painted over the name, getting splashes of paint on his Boateng but not caring. After he had finished he stepped back to admire what he had done. Though his breath was ragged and shallow the unaccustomed physical effort had filled him with a happy feeling of fatigue, in addition to which he felt what every man longs to feel, a sense of having vanquished an enemy.

The feeling didn't last long. Something must have happened to the paint while it was under the stairs in the coalhole because it had come out a much darker shade of white than when it had coated the wall, or perhaps it had reacted with the black spray paint underneath; either way it was now grey, quite dark grey at that, and because rupert had merely followed the contours of the word, the name, there was now written in much bigger letters on his wall: 'PATRICK'.

Ruthie's dinner rose up in his throat and he vomited all over the pavement, soiling the few previously unblemished bits of his Boateng. rupert realised he had made a big mistake, he shouldn't have let passion seize him. That was the thing about the big bastards, the Richards and Tonys and Alastairs, they were as cool as a sorbet, as frosty as a granita, they never got taken over by their emotions; in fact, come to think of it, they didn't seem to have any emotions, the only time they showed emotions was when they were faking them for the TV cameras. He'd foolishly given in. Well, he could learn. There was nothing for it, he had learnt an important lesson: patience, the long view, that was the thing. He would have to get the whole wall re-painted, he knew that now, by professionals, like he should have done in the first place.

Helen got home at 2 a.m. crabby and tired. She'd been attending 'Drycleanex 01' a dry-cleaning convention in Glasgow and couldn't really see why he was so agitated. 'It's only a bit of graffiti for God's sake,' she said. At that point rupert couldn't see why he had married her, she was his partner, she was supposed to understand. He would have gone and slept in the spare room if they'd had one. They didn't. There had been six bedrooms before he'd turned their house into a temple of light and space, now there was only one, the boys slept on a sheet steel landing suspended by wires above the light well, their hands clamped on the edges of their beds. rupert and Helen's bedroom looked out through plate glass doors on to the light well, inconspicuous doors in the wall led to a utility room, cupboards and walk-in wardrobe for all of rupert's identical Boateng suits. They'd had another of their long debates about the tall strip of clear glass in the outside wall of the attached bathroom, which admitted extra light but also allowed the neighbours to see them on the lavatory.

After a restless night he got on the phone to his painters first thing in the morning but they were doing up Lord Winston's place and couldn't get back till the day after tomorrow. He would have to spend two whole days with the desecration on his house.

It was torture, those two days; though he was in the house with the door slammed behind him there was no relief. Notwithstanding that he was inside it made no difference – the wall might as well have been made of his beloved glass for the violation had given him X-ray vision, he could see straight through it to the sacrilege on the other side: 'PATRICK' 'PATRICK' 'PATRICK' 'PATRICK' 'PATRICK' 'PAT-RICK' 'PATRICK' 'PATRICK' 'PATRICK' 'PATRICK' 'PATRICK' 'PATRICK' 'PATRICK'. And as his office was at home he was trapped with 'PATRICK' patrolling up and down outside like an escaped tiger.

After the long wait the painters turned up in their

horrible van at 7 a.m., got out their special builders' portable radio which seemed to be tuned to two stations at the same time and set it blaring, hissing and honking on the pavement. They then went off for a fried breakfast leaving the radio yodelling and scraping to itself. They came back over two and a half hours later, big fried breakfasts being hard to hunt down in Belgravia. Then they set to work.

About ninety minutes later the head painter, a tall laconic black man called Tommy, who always had a copy of the *Sun* in the back pocket of his overalls with the daily xenophobic headline clearly displayed, rang at the door and asked to speak to rupert. 'Mr ... erm ... Mr ... rupert. I fink you should come outside, we ... erm ... dere's a bit of a problem.' He led the trembling rupert round the corner.

What must have happened was that there appeared to have been some chemical reaction that had gone on between the paint underneath and the paint being put on top, so that rather than obliterating the offending name, it was now rather splendidly picked out in bright orange against an immaculate white background. And it seemed to have got bigger: 'PATRICK'. It shouted as if rupert's house was some new kind of bar called 'PATRICK' or something. 'We give it tree coats,' said Tommy. 'But de damn ting keep comin true.'

rupert went back through the front door quite calmly then turned into the kitchen dining area which led off the main entrance. He lay down full length on the nice cool stainless steel floor. A stainless steel kitchen with a stainless steel floor. They used to have a cat but it went to live over the road because it got sick of sliding and skidding all over the place on the slippery floor. rupert was frankly glad it had gone because it had made the place look messy, lying on its back with its legs open in hot weather. The boys must have loved it though because they spent a great amount of their time now over the road with the Saudi Arabian family who had taken it in. From his nice place on the floor rupert looked up at the wire Bertoia chairs he had insisted on for the kitchen. They were originally without cushions, as they should have been, so that dinner guests were left with savage criss-cross lines on their bottoms, as if they had spent the evening with a particularly savage dominatrix. On this one, this one time, Helen put her foot down and went out and bought cushions for the chairs from Liberty and rupert let her and was secretly relieved she'd done it, after all he didn't want people to be getting the wrong idea about Baroness Jay from marks his chairs had given her on her bottom.

'There's sharks in the deep end of my think tank,' he found himself thinking, and then he thought that he no longer understood his own thoughts. He had to get off the floor, he knew that, it was extremely important; Tony wouldn't like him lying on the floor. At that point his mobile phone rang and seeing it was in his pocket, down there on the floor with him, he got it out and answered it.

As if he had sensed his distress it was Tony ringing him in his hour of need.

'Awright, geez?' Tony said in the funny wide-boy voice he used sometimes when he was larking about.

'Yeah sound geez,' replied rupert.

'Listen,' said the Prime Minister reverting to his normal tones. 'We've got the President of Indonesia over here and he's a bit sick of being a dictator. Alastair was telling him about your ideas. Wanna come over and tell him yourself? Marco Pierre White's doing us all Nasi Goreng.'

He still mattered. 'I'll be there in twenty, Tony.'

Then he went back outside where his workmen were perfecting their oafish impersonations. He had a special cockney voice he used with his workmen. 'Listen, yew cunts,' he said, 'I just want you to get rid of this fucking word. Do you understand me? I don't care what you have to do. Get shot of it, chop it out if you have to, but get the fucking job done!'

Then he went to Number 10 Downing Street for Nasi Goreng.

Coming back later in his own car, swinging into the street, rupert turned his headlights to high beam to look more clearly at what his workmen had done.

What they had done was this. With their sharp chisels and their little hammers the workmen had chipped the name out of the brickwork, painfully they had hacked away the plaster leaving the rest of the wall completely untouched, so that now there was carved into the wall in huge letters, perhaps eight foot high, the one word, the one word: 'PATRICK'.

More or less without thought rupert drove his foot almost through the floor of the car as he pressed the accelerator pedal and drove the Audi straight at the word, the wall, the word was the wall, by now so big that he couldn't miss the word wall.

They're known for their safety, big Audis are, so he walked away without a mark on him, the German car's crumple zones having crumpled and all its airbags dangling like big used condoms. Inside the kitchen he hunted under the sink for a bottle of bleach then sat down on the nice cool stainless steel floor to drink it. As it poured down his gullet he felt it scouring him, reducing the untidy tangle of his insides to a minimalist shell.

He would have died if the varnished pine-coloured Finnish au pair hadn't come in looking for some polenta for a late night snack. Being Finnish and with suicide being so common in that country that they teach antidote administration at junior school, she immediately knocked the bottle out of his hand and poured bottle after bottle of Evian down him till the paramedics came.

After he got out of hospital rupert and Helen and the kids went to stay in a whitewashed farmhouse just outside a lovely little walled town in a valley in Southern Spain. All the time he'd been in the Chelsea and Westminster none of the government had come to see rupert, though Gordon Brown had sent some balloons. Now the family was back together. They went walking through the orange groves, swam in the pool, had simple dinners on the Arabic-style terrace. Over the phone Helen sold her flag cleaning business to the Granada Group and they were free of all worries, the money she got allowed them to live in delirious clutter, the kids running in and out all day.

rupert let his hair grow and tied it in a little pony tail at the back. They talked about buying a small farm and raising sheep and goats. But then slowly rupert began to return to the world; he bought a radio that could pick up the BBC World Service and would impatiently sit through reports of government reshuffles in Malawi, falling groundnut prices in the Congo and requests to play Celine Dion records for teenagers in Damascus ('I am most wishing to hear the marvellous Canadian songbird trill her hit song from the film *Titanic* . . .') all so he could catch a fragment of news from back home, a sliver of information of his former pals, Gordon and Jack and Tony.

Helen caught him looking discontentedly at the mess in their farmhouse, studying the shape and the layout, thinking of improvements. One day he shouted at Corbu, 'For God's sake, can't you clear up some of this bloody mess.'

Helen and the two boys stood frozen, it was like a Siberian farmer hearing the howl of the first wolves of winter. They knew He was back.

The Dog Catcher

In the middle of that night as rupert lay sleeping, wrapped in dreams of towering cities, Helen rose and went outside to the white moonlit wall of the farmhouse. With a Pentel pen she wrote in tiny letters on the wall, the one word: 'PATRICK'.

A CURE FOR DEATH

The anti-gravity hover ambulance lifted off in a halo of dust from the special landing pad that he'd had built in the grounds of his home on the tax-free haven of the Isle of Morrisons. Inside he lay on a stretcher plugged up to a rats' nest of wires and tubes. The man was one hundred and sixty-nine years old and barely alive. The pilot/paramedic headed the flying machine east across the Irish Sea, soon they crossed Liverpool Bay and without pause began travelling inland. High above the town of Stoke-on-Tescos, the pilot tilted his control column, causing the rotors to swivel in their housing, and the craft turned south. About an hour after take-off from the billionaire's island they glided in to land at their destination, the giant laboratory complex that he had had constructed on the outskirts of Milton Kwiksave Old Town, Berkshire Sector.

This was where they were working on a cure for death.

The Dog Catcher

The patient's name was Edmund Chive and he had been a happy but poor man until the age of twenty-eight when he had become immensely rich by inventing a new kind of thing: not a completely new thing but an exciting new twist on a thing that had been around for years and everybody had got used to and a bit bored with. If he had invented a completely new thing he probably wouldn't have prospered because the geniuses who do that seldom do; it is the plodders who come after who make the gravy. At first all the money had made his life great: three girls in the bed, four Ferraris in the garage, that sort of thing. Then one day while he was licking crème fraîche off a light-skinned Dominican lesbian, a bad thought descended like an anti-gravity hover ambulance. It was an idea so horrible to him that it froze him in mid-lick with his tongue sticking out and dairy product dripping off it. His life was so great, so brilliant, so fantastic, so wonderful, he thought, and yet one day it would end – because he was at some point in the future going to die just like the lowliest tram driver. That couldn't be right, could it?

From then on his money was spent not on making his life happy but on making it infinite. He sought a cure for death and hired the finest anti-death scientists to bring it to him. The answer lay somewhere in genetics, they were all sure of that.

While he waited for the cure to be discovered he employed the finest health experts to keep him in the best shape for the longest time. His days were entirely taken up with yoga, exercise, positive visualisations; his mealtimes were taken up with munching his way through piles of fibre, nuts and raw vegetables. He kept away from women and wanking because the Bhuddist monk he employed on a part-time basis told him to on no account spill his vital fluids into women or paper tissues. He didn't watch TV because his fourth, ninth and twenty-second personal trainers had told him that bad ideas leaked out of the set from news programmes and made the watcher lethargic. And he didn't mix with people because he might catch something.

So he lived for one hundred and sixty-nine years, though they were not by and large happy years, certainly not the latter ones, for although science could extend life it turned out it could do very little about curing the painful conditions that came with ageing. Just as Alzheimers only came to be known about once people started living long enough to get it, so as humans started passing the hundred and thirty mark in large numbers a huge variety of new conditions appeared, all of them excruciatingly painful and many of them embarrassing and depressing. Apart from the usual faithful companions of old age, Arthritis, Angina, Thrombosis, Prostate Cancer, there now appeared illnesses such as Poliakoff's Syndrome where the sufferer's body fat became so tired and worn out that it caught fire and burned from within like a fire-bombed council house, there was Clutterbuck's Disease in which the excessively old person's bones calcified to such a degree that they more or less turned into a pillar of salt, and the memory loss that occurred in those of seventy, eighty, ninety, was replaced by memory gain in those of one hundred and thirty, forty, fifty. But the memories that re-appeared were entirely faulty so that many aged folk ended their lives thinking they were chickens or trees or Bruce Springsteen (apart from Bruce Springsteen himself who thought he was Dag Hammersholt, a secretary general of the UN in the 1950s).

So Edmund Chive's health gradually deteriorated, despite all the effort of the finest medical minds in the world, and he was in the middle of his eighth bout of pleurisy and on his twenty-seventh pet labrador called Sparky 9 when the call came from his scientists that they had made the breakthrough and they were there. The cure for death was waiting for him in a glass bottle. The hover ambulance kept on permanent standby was started up and the journey was made.

The two scientists in charge of project CFD, Professor Drew Cocker and Professor Lindy Wheen, were waiting for their benefactor as he was wheeled into the central chamber of the complex.

Edmund Chive managed to crowbar open his clag-encrusted eyes and croak at his two hirelings, 'Where is it?'

'We've got it here, Mr Chive,' said Professor Cocker

holding up the bottle. 'As we thought, the answer is essentially a question of genetic mutation, by altering the DNA chromosome of—'

'For God's sake, inject me, there's not much time le—' said Edmund and then he died.

But this was not the end for Edmund as he had feared it would be. After he died Edmund felt himself travelling down a long, gently sloping tunnel. It reminded him of the time in the happy days before he was rich when he'd been to a water park and had dived down a spiral tube, head first. There'd been no time for that in the last one hundred and forty-one years. Following some seconds, or perhaps minutes, it was hard to tell, of gentle floating, a bright white light appeared, small as a pinhole. He drifted towards it as it grew in his vision. The light resolved itself into the end of the tunnel; light as a rice cracker he slipped out of the tube and into a huge vaulted chamber lit by a kind, lambent light. Waiting for him were a group of people all smiling at him. The first person there he recognised was his father, not as he had died, etiolated and grey, but fit and hale as he had been in his late forties, behind him was Edmund's mother as she had been around the time of the war in Korea, a beauty capable of stopping air traffic. Behind them in a spreading phalanx were all his uncles and aunts, his friends, his teachers from primary school, girls he had slept with at university still looking as they had then, and running in and out of their feet all the pets he'd ever had, Sparkies 1 to 8, cats and kittens, lizards and snakes. Edmund's father approached him, his hand outstretched, his smile rueful. 'I bet you feel like a right silly cunt now,' he said as he embraced his son.

'Fucking hell, yes,' exclaimed Edmund. 'What a twat! I didn't think for a second there was a cunting afterlife!'

His mother came up and took him in her arms. 'We were all silly shites,' she said. 'None of us shagging believed there was anything after we fucking died.'

Without looking at himself Edmund knew his body was as it had been when he was thirty-five years old, round about the time when all the exercise he was doing had temporarily given him a physique that was buffed and perfect, glowing with health and happiness. 'So is this bollocking heaven?' he asked.

'Fuck knows,' laughed Abigail Watts, the first girl he had had sex with.

'This might be heaven or it might just be another stage on the shitting journey,' said his Uncle Leon.

'There is still pain here,' said his father, '. . . and death.'

'But it's a different kind of pain and a different kind of death,' explained his primary school teacher Miss Wilson. 'A better kind.'

Suddenly Edmund was embarrassed thinking about what he had caused to be done back in the life before. 'Erm, I think I might have made a bit of a fucking rick back . . . erm . . . there,' he mumbled.

'What's that son?' said his dad.

'Well, I've . . . fucking invented a fucking cure for death. I'm not sure anybody else will be coming here soon.'

Everybody laughed like a drain at this.

'Knackers,' said his mum.

'Fuck 'em,' said Uncle Leon. 'If they don't want to come that's their twatting problem.'

'They can stay where they are, the wankers,' said a man who'd been his best friend over a century ago.

'Well, that's a fucking relief,' said Edmund.

'I'm fucking gagging for a pint,' said Miss Wilson.

'Let's go then,' said Edmund's dad. 'The rest of you tossers coming?'

There was a general murmur of assent and they all went off to get what constituted, in this new place, pissed.

Back in the previous life Drew and Lindy stared at Edmund Chive's cadaver, lying mute and sparkless on its trolley. 'Well, this is unfortunate,' said Drew.

'Bad timing,' said Lindy.

'What do we do now?'

They both knew what they were talking about: the little glass bottle.

'No point in wasting it,' said one.

'No point at all,' said the other.

So they injected themselves with the anti-death serum. Then stood in silence for a few minutes. Finally Drew said, 'Fancy a coffee?'

The Dog Catcher

Lindy looked into an infinite future of coffees, coffee after coffee after coffee for tens of thousands of years.

'I think I'll wait till later,' she said.

WHO DIED AND LEFT YOU IN CHARGE?

Miss Cicely Rodgers strapped her cock and balls into the Miracle Deluxe Vagina, which was made from skin-like flesh-coloured latex and came with fully adjustable straps to ensure a perfect fit and to hide any last sign of maleness. It was complete in every detail including soft vaginal lips and a simulated clitoris. Over this she slipped Femme Form padded hourglass panties to give her womanly curves, and onto her chest she put a lacy padded bra. Next came make-up, beard coverer and on her head the popular page-boy wig, suitable for all face shapes. Finally a sober women's business suit in charcoal grey and on her feet simple court shoes, though huge in a size eleven, with a restrained, ladylike, two-inch heel. Cicely wasn't one of those trannies who dressed like a Chechen prostitute. When she was Clive he wore clothes that were a bit too young for a man of forty-five, trainers like dead pigs' noses in grey and orange with light-reflecting strips on the back, designer combat pants so expensive it would be cheaper to join the army for a year and T-shirts with 'Quack, combust, shithouse squad' or similar gibberish written on them. Cicely considered herself superior to Clive, with a more innate sense of good taste. After all, they both thought, what was the point of being a part-time woman if she was going to be the same sort of woman as you were a bloke?

This transformation from Clive to Cicely was taking shape in a place called Transformations, which is right opposite Euston Station in Eversholt Street, Camden Town. It is in a row of shops, a couple of the type where you can't remember what it is they sell even though you looked in the window five seconds ago and two old-fashioned cafés that serve chicken curry with boiled potatoes, and spaghetti with chips on the side and two slices of margarined bread for the consumption of solitary men wearing hats in all weathers. Euston and Kings Cross used to be surrounded with cafés serving this kind of grub, as if the first thing a fellow fancied after coming down from the North was a weird combination of food? As it turned out, what a lot of fellows seemed to want as soon as they got off the train from the North was to be a woman. Transformations was opposite the station so that nervous businessmen from Tring and Liverpool and Glasgow could slip in there and be transformed into nervous women. The windows of

Transformations are painted red, the writing on them says: 'Wigs, waist cinchers, make-up'. There is also a big before and after photo, on the left a young man in chinos who a market researcher might put in the B2 socio-economic group, self-employed graphic designer or something similar, and on the right the young man is now done up as a woman from a Bradford council estate who has had a hard life on account of her daughter being pregnant and on crack and who sings at the Trades and Labour Club on Fridays to keep her spirits up.

Once or twice a week Clive would visit Transformations to change into a woman, then he would go out for the afternoon with his friend Ashlee (usually Archie). They would walk about then go for tea and a bun or maybe for a little drinkie in a fashionable bar. Being Cicely out for a walk was, Clive imagined, rather like being a slightly forgotten celebrity, Mel Smith perhaps or Kenneth Branagh. Most people paid no attention but one in thirty looked once, looked again, saw something not right, a remark or a thought would come up to the surface by which time Cicely was past, leaving turned heads, pokes in the ribs, sometimes aggressive shouts or sniggers in her trail. Being a trannie also resembled being a minor celebrity in that the glances you got were related in inverse proportion to the coolness and hipness of the area and the inhabitants' resulting indifference to people from off the telly. In Camden Town, where in the local

115

starship trooper Sainsbury's there were more pierced than unpierced shoppers, Mel or Kenneth would go a long time before they got asked for their autograph unless it was on their Switch card. Ashlee and Cicely could walk for hours in that neighbourhood untrammelled by any interference.

Cicely had always really enjoyed their walks, they had been the highpoint of her week until Ashlee pointed out the cyclists, then she never enjoyed them again. Clive and Cicely were alike in that they were prone to having things ruined by pointing out. Years ago Clive had loved to take long drives up the motorway in his car which was called a Gordon Keeble and was an Italian-styled Sixties British-made sportscar. Then one day he'd been going to Leeds and he took his friend Leonard with him. After a bit Leonard asked if he could drive, so they pulled into Leicester Forest East Services and changed seats. Leonard raced straight back onto the motorway and was soon doing eighty-five in the inside lane, ahead of them in the distance a small hatchback was travelling at about seventy in the middle lane. Rather than swing across two lanes to overtake, Leonard got right up behind the Vauxhall Astra and started flashing his headlights. Clive was a very conscientious driver, he believed in keeping a safe, two seconds' distance between vehicles; he achieved this by watching the car in front pass an object – a sign or a bridge – and then saying to himself 'only a fool breaks the two second rule'. If he could complete this sentence before he passed the same object then they were a safe distance apart. He tried this with his Gordon Keeble and the Astra and got as far as 'only a f—'. After a lot of flashing, the other car moved over. Leonard passed it then moved back into the inside lane himself.

'What was that all about?' said Clive.

'The middle lane should be solely for overtaking,' explained Leonard in a pedantic voice. 'Cars should travel in the inside lane at all other times. If they don't it slows everybody up, as that only leaves one lane for overtaking. Driving in the middle lane is selfish and thoughtless.'

'Oh, I didn't know that,' said Clive and he never enjoyed a drive again. From then on the motorways, instead of being a ribbon of pleasure for Clive, unrolling with merry welcome, were concrete channels of anger, full of selfish dawdlers creeping up the middle lane with inflaming insensitivity: each licence-plated rump sneered at him personally. Like Leonard, Clive would now get behind them all (and there were thousands once you noticed), blip his lights and if they didn't move he'd honk his horn, get closer and blip his lights again. Often the cars wouldn't move, either not noticing or refusing to budge. In the month after his drive with Leonard, Clive had four near crashes, he was shot at once and had two knife fights on a slip road. In the end Clive sold the Gordon Keeble for a big loss, the bottom really having dropped out of the classic-car market, and now, if he ever travelled outside London, he took the train.

So it was with the cyclists. Cicely and Ashlee were walking up Camden High Street one day, chummily arm in arm. They were crossing on the Pelican opposite the Acumedical Chinese healing centre when they were forced to jump back and apart by a cyclist riding the wrong way down the road.

'They make me so mad,' said Ashlee.

'Who do?' said Cicely with a dizzy sensation in her head as if she were on the edge of a high diving board; she knew something bad was coming but she couldn't get out of its way.

'Bloody cyclists, especially round here,' replied her friend. 'They're a fucking menace. They ride on the pavement, they ride through red lights, they ride through red lights against the traffic, they ride through red lights against the traffic on the pavement and worst of all there's just something so horribly smug about them, like they're doing you a favour by making the world a worse place to be in.'

Instantly to Cicely Camden High Street was filled with swooping, careening machines and her heart was filled with hate. She had always thought of the bicycle as a rather benign machine but now these people she saw zinging about might as well have been mounted on HIV-infected Rottweilers for all the fear and anger they contaminated her with. They were very various. There were forgetful women on folding shopper bikes, black youths talking into mobile phones while riding no-handed, claimants on wrecks of racing bikes with the drop handlebars turned upside down so as to make sure their brakes didn't work, serious mountain bikers with front suspensions made from impossibly light alloys found only in crashed asteroids, hip twenty-five-year-olds in big baggy pants twiddling away on chromed BMX bikes (she couldn't even begin to figure out what that one was about) and messengers, messengers, messengers. These pedalling freelance postmen wore expressions fixed on their faces that said 'Don't stop me now, bastard. Last year's VAT receipts must get to Chemical Bank ere night falls! The script rewrite must be on the desk of Tim Bevan at Working Title by yesterday morning or there'll be hell to pay! The tickets for the charity ball must get to Mel Smith right now and no old lady on the zebra crossing will stop them', so up in the air she goes, arse over zimmer frame.

In all his wanderings around Camden Town the only cyclist he saw more than once who stopped at the traffic lights and pedalled on the road and behaved in a generally non-malignant way, obeying the law like in the olden days, was the writer Alan Bennett riding around on his dark green lady's bike with the wicker basket out front like something from a film about the Cambridge of F.R. Leavis.

Cicely tried to keep the thing about the cyclists from Clive but he heard about it soon enough and his life was ruined too. If anything, it hit Clive harder than it hit Cicely.

Clive was even more prone than she was to taking things hard; he was barred from several 24-hour mini marts and his local Blockbusters Video for arguing about things and he couldn't go back to Cheltenham any time soon.

They had a good job Clive and Cicely. They were bookbinders. Clive had served his apprenticeship at a venerable firm in Bermondsey. He was amongst the last intake of working-class kids before that craft became a middle-class, Art School shut-out. Now he worked from home, surrounded by glue and card and skin in a council owned live/work apartment in The Brunswick Centre, Holborn, a bold 1960s experiment in concrete eyesores where a Georgian square used to be. He made a good enough living, enabling him to buy Cicely the finest in giant lace panties, by repairing ancient manuscripts, binding lectures and other modern texts for the nearby British Museum and London University and by doing the occasional fine art job, binding a limited edition set of etchings in rat skin, that sort of thing.

On the days when he didn't go to Transformations Clive would work all morning then, like ten thousand other lone craftsmen all around London, painters, sculptors, makers of modern jewellery, writers on internet matters, he would stop at one o'clock to have soup and a grilled cheese brown bread sandwich, listen to a politician being toasted on Radio 4's *The World At One*, then go for a walk, as himself. Every day he took the same route, past the drunks bungling round the DHS emergency payout place in Upper Woburn Place, then the Kosovans washing car windscreens while their women begged at the corner of Upper Woburn Place and the Euston Road, after that Eversholt Street past Transformations then more drunks at the start of Camden High Street. Clive often thought that rather than being paved with gold the streets of Camden Town were paved with alcoholics, seeing as so many of them were sprawled on the ground. A surprising number were foreign, Clive imagined a lot of them were on drunk-exchange schemes from other countries. One thing he noticed about the drunks was that many of them sported the most magnificent heads of hair. 'What a waste,' thought the almost completely bald Clive as he passed yet another comatose figure displaying a splendid mane of luxuriant jet-black tresses. Then one day he heard on Radio 4 while drinking his lunchtime soup that alcohol abuse promoted hair growth and prevented baldness as it led to the suppression of testosterone production in males. Clive reckoned he might have given heavy drinking a go if he'd found out about its tonsorial qualities before most of his hair had gone. He suffered particular hair problems; because of his dressing Clive couldn't even grow a strange little beatnik beard in compensation as many baldies did, seeing as it would pretty much give the game away on Cicely.

Thirty minutes' brisk walking would find him heading

west up Delancey Street then round Regents Park Road to Primrose Hill where he would have a cup of cappuccino sitting outside one of the many patisseries and coffee bars. Just up the road from where he had his coffee was the headquarters of a big, successful record company, so walking up and down on the pavement was a constant parade of men exactly like Clive, thinning-haired forty-somewhats dressed in clobber aimed at eighteen-year-olds. Like US mailmen who 'Neither snow nor rain nor heat nor gloom of night stays these couriers from the swift completion of their appointed rounds', Clive and his fellow coffee drinkers would stoically huddle on the outside seats of the cafés of Primrose Hill no matter what the weather. Inside, the patisseries would be empty even in the middle of a January meteor storm. Twenty years ago you absolutely couldn't get an Englishman to sit outside a gaff. They wouldn't do it. Even in summer temperatures of ninety-five degrees, drinkers would barricade themselves inside pubs behind frosted glass, glazed tiles and mahogany. Now you couldn't keep the bastards indoors no matter what.

But even here in this crescent of chi-chi shops the cyclists were up to their dirty tricks. Even when he saw one doing nothing wrong, Clive would find himself thinking 'Fucking bastard' before he realised he was riding on the correct side of the road through a green light, not doing no harm to no one.

Until the pointing out of the cyclists Clive had managed

to force himself to enjoy, indeed to revel in, the wild drinkers, the dirt, the litter, the terrible record company tosspots, the whole gritty urban shmeer of north London – but the cyclists spoilt it all. Everywhere he went they taunted him with their lawless ways and though he tried there was nothing he could do either to un-notice them or to find a way to cope with their behaviour. Clive tried shouting at them as they hurtled towards him at thirty miles an hour on the sidewalk but one person more or less, shouting in the middle of the street in Camden Town, at either cyclists or lampposts or imaginary six-foot-high dung beetles, was neither here nor there and nobody took any notice, least of all the cyclists.

He tried remonstrating reasonably with them. One time while he was on a zebra crossing, traversing Regents Park Road, a girl zipped across it behind him, clipping him on the ankles as she sped up the pavement. 'This is a pedestrian crossing not a bike crossing,' he said quite mildly. She just looked over her shoulder at him but, unusually, he caught up with her half a minute later as she stopped to look at her *A–Z*. It wasn't often you got one of them stationary so he went up to her and said, 'You shouldn't ride on the pavement and that, you know. It's really intimidating for old people and stuff.'

She just looked up and said, 'Who died and left you in charge?' Then rode off, her behind waggling contemptuously at him. Clive knew then he was going to have to kill one of them.

At nights he couldn't sleep, imagining arguments he'd have with this girl though even in the self-justifying cavern of his brain he came off worst. She always had the snappy rejoinder: 'Who died and left you in charge?'

'You or one of your kind,' was all he could come back with but you could see on her face that she didn't believe him. Well, he might not be able to kill a cyclist but he knew a woman who could.

The first thing he did was to become a member of The London Cycling Campaign: it was important to know his enemy. He soon found out that the major cause of death amongst cyclists was them being crushed under the wheels of trucks. Clive reckoned it would be going too far to buy himself a truck and get an HGV licence and so on. However in another whining article about how great they all were, these pedalling pricks, he read what terrible havoc four-wheel-drive vehicles, Range Rovers, Toyota Amazons, Mitsubishi Shoguns, were carving through the pedestrian and cycling population with their big bumpy bumpers. Their huge flat fronts smacked the unprotected human form with a metal punch of bone-vaporising ferocity.

One dark evening a few days later a second-hand car salesman with an ill-lit car lot sold for cash a Mark One Landrover Discovery on an M plate, to a tall ugly woman.

Clive hid it in the parking garages underneath the

Brunswick Centre. The Discovery leaked black diesel smoke from its rusty anus and the inappropriate pale blue clunky interior designed by Sir Terence Conran was filthy and falling to bits, but Cicely felt it would do the job. The huge pitted chrome bull bars screwed to the front of the Disco would be especially good at mashing up a biker.

Cicely had great fun clothing herself as a middle-class mum on the way to pick up her kids from one of the posh private schools in Hampstead, then she went hunting for a cyclist pedalling the wrong way down one of the many streets of Camden Town.

As she drove, her eyes swivelling back and forth, Cicely daydreamed about her family life, her husband, her kids, the dinner parties she'd cook for his boss at the bank.

Kate Maguire strapped her small son into the child seat of her bicycle. She was late getting to her friend Carmel's place where she was going to drop off Milo then go on to work on the night shift at the Neurological Hospital near Russell Square. She had been forced to go back to work at the Neuro after her husband died and the old pig-pink Raleigh ladies bike was the most economical way for her and Milo to get around town. If she'd had to pay bus fares or, heaven forbid, own a car, she and Milo would be having privet leaves for tea every night. Today, though, she had a problem: if she didn't somehow shave fifteen minutes off her journey she was going to be late for work. That was the thing about bicycles, you always knew to the second how long a journey took. Not like a car, where in central London the same hundred yards could take twenty seconds or two hours to drive depending on what butterfly was flapping its wings in the Brazilian rainforest that day. The simplest way to make up the time would be for her and Milo not to turn left into the long one-way system on leaving her little house in Lyme Street. That was suited to fat-arsed car drivers sitting down but it was an annoying detour when you are pedalling yourself, taking you down Bayham Street along Pratt Street across the High Street and up Delancey Street. It would be much quicker for her to ride the wrong way past the tube station then go against the flow of traffic, up the hill at Parkway, the way she had seen thousands of other cyclists doing. Many times she had sensed other bicycle riders' perplexity as she stopped at the lights and waited while they bumped up onto the pavement or raced through the traffic lights even though the little green man was showing, scattering pedestrians left and right.

Kate buckled up her shiny plastic helmet, gave the straps holding in Milo one last safety check and set off, resolving, for the first time ever, to go head on, into the traffic.

But she didn't, she couldn't force herself to do it; she went through the one-way system as usual and was a bit late for work.

Instead Cicely drove into and killed a bicycle messenger called Darren Barley who was a complete waste of fucking space and deserved to die.

CLIVE HOLE

1

Tatum and Cherry were two television producers who were married to each other and who both worked for the BBC. They were having a proper tea at Cherry's mum's house. They both liked a proper tea with cakes and sandwiches and scones and clotted cream and home-made jams but Tatum refused to pay inflated hotel prices when Cherry's mum would do it for free. Cherry was a very handsome woman, like her mother (Tatum sometimes fantasised about shagging them both). Tatum wasn't handsome, he was the other thing, with prominent buck teeth and a haystack of black hair. What attracted Cherry to him was that he was funny – with an instinctive understanding of comedy, he could make her laugh for hours on end. This was what she loved about him; for her it even excused his remarkable meanness, an unlovely aspect in any man.

Every time Cherry's mum went out of the room they talked about Clive Hole. Cherry's mum, who had been an SOE agent in France during the war, had been captured and tortured by the Gestapo and then, after her husband's suicide, had had to bring up six children alone but who did not work in television and therefore had not had an interesting life, came into the conservatory carrying a spare cake she hadn't thought she'd need and finding her daughter and son-in-law waist-deep in the same conversation they'd been having since last Christmas said, 'Who is this Clive Hole you keep talking about? I've never heard of him.'

Tatum and Cherry thought themselves pretty unshockable (after all they had devised the TV show *Anal Animals*) but they were shocked.

They said in chorus, like in one of the bad sitcoms they produced, 'You've never heard of Clive Hole!!!?'

2

'But I'm Clive Hole,' said the man sitting in the front passenger seat of the black BMW 7 series, with his feet awkwardly propped up on the dash. The man in the car was wearing a baggy unstructured Armani suit and frantically clutched a silver metal briefcase to himself with both arms. He was in his mid-forties, balding, with a grey-flecked beard.

The BBC security guard on the gate of Television Centre was unmoved.

'I know who you are, sir, but it doesn't make any difference, we are at Security State Tangerine, which is a high state and I have to search everybody's bags.'

'But I'm Clive Hole, I'm head of media facilitation.'

'And I've still got to look in your bag.'

Clive thought for a minute, had an idea, then pretended to think for a bit longer. 'Oh ... erm, yes ... I've just remembered I've got a meeting with some people from the circus ...'

He spoke to the large black man who was his driver.

'Clayton, take me to the circus.'

Without a beat, Clayton threw the car into reverse with a cry of, 'Righto, Mr Hole!'

The car shot backwards into Wood Lane did a hand-brake turn like in the movies and sped away, northwards, fishtailing strips of rubber onto the road. The security guard watched it depart with bemusement.

'Loony!' he said to himself in Armenian.

At Clive's instruction Clayton slowed down and turned left so that they were now running round the rear of Television Centre. On a quiet service road they came to a back lot that was being cleared to build more offices. One part of the chainlink perimeter fence of this building site was sagging so that it was only about two metres high. In the distance between the buildings he could see his office window.

Clive shouted, 'Clayton, here, stop here!'

When the car stopped he climbed out and stood looking at the fence. 'Could you give me a boost over?' he asked his driver.

'Certainly, Mr Hole,' replied Clayton. He cupped his hands. Balancing unsteadily on one leg Clive put his foot into those hands and Clayton tossed the other man up into the air and on top of the fence like a little Jewish caber.

Clive straddled the fence like a man clinging to a wild horse that he'd unexpectedly found himself riding, one hand still holding on to his briefcase.

'Shall I pick you up from the reception as usual at four, Mr Hole?' asked the driver.

'Yeah,' mumbled Clive, then: 'No, meet me here instead. At this hole.'

'Righto, Mr Hole.'

Clayton began to get back in the car. Clive hung still semi-impaled on the fence. A thought occurred to him.

'Oh erm . . . Clayton, did you get a chance to look at that series proposal from Tatum and Cherry?'

A thoughtful look crossed Clayton's face.

'You liked it? You didn't like it?' guessed Clive as he swung in the breeze. 'Not enough black people in it?'

Clayton finally delivered his verdict.

'I liked it, Mr Hole . . .'

'Really? Right . . . OK . . . I might speak to them . . . about it then.'

And with that he fell to the ground, then he jumped up again, waved at Clayton and scurried off through the building rubble in the loping crouch of a member of the Special Boat Service. Taking the back roads of the complex where the little electric tugs rattled past, towing trailers of scenery labelled 'Gen Game' and 'Kilroy – not wanted', the top executive eventually arrived at the ground-floor windows of his office suite. He tapped on the glass of the secretary's office. Helen, his assistant, a middle-aged, competent-looking woman glanced up from her work. She did not seem to be fazed to see her boss standing in a flower-bed.

'Helen, can you open my office window please?' he mouthed through the double glazing.

Helen got up, went into Clive's office and opened the window. He clambered gratefully inside.

'Thanks . . . thanks a lot. Now I'd like no calls for half an hour please, Helen.'

'Certainly, Clive,' she said and left.

Clive crossed purposefully to his desk and sat down, placing the briefcase in front of him. From inside it he took a large colourful box marked 'Rainbow Valley Ant Farm', and a jar of honey. Humming happily to himself he crossed over to a corner of the room where there was a large TV and a VCR machine. Kneeling down he took the ant farm out of the box and broke it open. He then poured honey over the fleeing ants. Next, using a pair of tweezers, he began to stuff ants through the loading slot of the VCR, then he poured more honey into the machine. Clive then repeated the process on several VHS tapes that were lying by the machine. He surveyed his handiwork with contentment and then returned to his desk, picked up the phone and dialled an internal number.

'Paul Cliro, please,' he said, 'it's Clive Hole . . .'

He continued to hum to himself while waiting for Paul to come to the phone.

'Paul? Hi, it's Clive . . . about those tapes you sent me of actresses for the supporting role in *Airport Padre* . . . No, I haven't looked at them . . . It's the strangest thing, when I came to try and play the tape it wouldn't work and when I looked inside the machine, well blow me, it was full of ants! . . . Yeah, ants and honey! . . . You couldn't make it up, could you? And then I remembered you said once that one of your kids had an ant farm . . . so I guess somehow the ants got into the tape when it was at your house and then into my VCR . . . and it's not just your tape, there are several other tapes ruined, pilots for shows I'm supposed to decide whether they should go to series. Now I'll have to put the decision off . . . bloody nuisance, eh? . . . No, it's not your fault, mate . . . no . . . What I suggest you do is wait about a month then send me the tape of the actresses again because it'll take that long for Helen to order me another machine . . . you know how useless she is . . . no, don't apologise.' He laughed merrily. 'Just tell your boy to keep his ants to himself . . . speak to you soon, mate . . . yeah, bye.'

He put the phone down and sat looking at it for a minute then picked it up again.

'Helen . . . can you get me Monty Fife's agent? I've decided to give the go-ahead to that thing about otters.'

He was swiftly connected.

'Betty? . . . How are you? It's Clive Hole here . . . fine, fine . . . Listen I've got good news for Monty, I'm finally going to green light *Mudlark Springs*.' His expression changed. 'What . . . dead? When? . . . A year and a half ago? . . . Well, I guess I must have . . . no . . .' He considered for a second. 'What about the otters? . . . Extinct, really? . . . Oh well, bye then.'

He put the phone down and stared as if it was an untrustworthy dog.

3

The next afternoon Clive sat at his big desk made out of logs from New Mexico. He didn't want to be sitting at his big desk, he wanted to be drinking a diet coke from his fridge, the fridge hidden behind an adobe-coloured door that was built in the South Western-style bookcase that was in the opposite corner of the room to where he sat at his big desk, and was stocked with New World wines, juices and other beverages twice a week by the licence payer. A couple of minutes before the automatic part of his brain, the part that usually gets on with stuff and that you hardly listen to, said, 'Right, let's get up, go over to the fridge hidden behind the adobe-coloured door, built into the New Mexico-style bookcase and let's have us a Diet Coke.' He was just about to do that thing when another voice, the voice that had for months been stopping him making any decisions about programmes by endlessly weighing the pros and cons of every tiny detail, chose this moment to expand its operations into other areas of his life. It said, 'Hang on a minute, Clive, are you sure you really want a Diet Coke, how do you really know that is what you want? How do you know you don't want to have a fruit smoothie? Or how do you really really know that you don't want to get up and wee on your Navaho rug? How do you know anything, Clive?' So he had sat there now for twenty minutes, impaled on uncertainty; he was only brought back from this internal inferno of boiling thoughts by the sounds of shouting from the outer office.

Helen looked up from her work as the door was thrown open and Tatum and Cherry bundled in. Before Helen could speak Tatum started talking in a rush.

'Alright, Helen, we're here for our four o'clock meeting

with Clive and don't tell us he's not in because we've been watching his office since he came back from lunch and we know he's still in there.'

Cherry added, 'And he can't say we haven't got an appointment like he's done the last five times because I recorded him saying we've got an appointment on my Psion . . .'

She held up her personal organiser and pressed a key. First there was the sound of some muffled shouting then Clive's voice came out of it sounding agitated.

'Please Cherry, for Christ's sake, I'm trying to donate sperm here for my wife's IVF, I'm . . . oh, oh, oh, Jesus . . . shit . . . too late.' There was a pause, then Clive again: 'Look are you satisfied? That is never going to come out of suede.' Then there was some more mumbling, followed by: 'Alright. OK. This is stupid but alright . . . do I speak into this here? I, Clive Hole, swear on my word of honour as head of media facilitation that I have a meeting with Tatum and Cherry in my office at four on Thursday . . . Are you happy now? Can I have my magazine back if you've finished with it?'

Helen leant forward and spoke into the intercom on her desk. 'Clive? Tatum and Cherry are here for their four o'clock meeting.'

Clive's voice came out of this other machine.

'Sure, just give me a couple of seconds and then send them right in.'

Tatum and Cherry smiled in triumph, hovered and then entered Clive's office. The two producers stared about them in consternation: the office was empty, the summer breeze blowing through the open window stirred the curtains.

4

Tatum was feeling terribly agitated because of Clive Hole. He blamed Clive for the fact that he was having this little relapse. He said to the young man, 'We've written this detective thing called *Bold As Bacon*, it's about this father and son team who go around the markets of Lancashire selling bacon from a stall, they've still got some fabulous Victorian markets . . . Preston, Lancaster . . . but they don't just sell bacon, they solve crimes as well! Plus it's set in the Seventies so you get all that great glam music for the soundtrack. Took us nearly a year and a half to write six one-hour episodes, I gave Clive the scripts nine months ago and since then nothing! I've called, I've e-mailed, I've sent jokey little cards on Valentine's day and he just won't speak to me about it. I bumped into him in the street a few weeks ago and he pretended he was a Portuguese tourist.'

The young man just looked bored so they went to the cemetery. Once they had found a nice mausoleum the young man got down on his knees, undid Tatum's trousers and began to suck his cock. All the time while this was going on the only thing Tatum could think of was Clive Hole, Clive Hole, Clive Hole. On his face was an abstracted and worried expression, his mind miles away and not concentrating on the blow job in hand.

5

The five-a-side pitch was part of the sports centre, the sports centre was part of Arsenal's football ground. In the British style the building had no aesthetic attributes whatsoever. It was a big ugly shed with a lattice of girders holding up the roof and pitiless neon lights shining down on the ten middle-aged men who huffed and limped up and down the pitch chasing the ball. Their shouts and the squeak of their trainers bounced off the shiny brick walls. Several of the men were strapped into corsets or their legs were encased in bright blue supports, velcro and carbon fibre vainly trying to hold up their drooping muscles. One of the men wearing the most body armour was Clive Hole, he was pretending to be a striker dropping off behind the front two and pulling defenders out of position: in reality he was an old man stiffly running about.

On the sidelines in the banked seating Tatum and Cherry sat watching the men. Tatum was dressed in football kit. He pointed at the men playing football, 'Look at them, the heads of every major TV channel and production house in the country . . . what do they think they look like?'

Cherry said, 'They think they look quite . . . well, alright; not great, like when they were young but OK. They think that at least they keep fit. And that'll mean as long as they keep fit and can keep playing football then they won't die. They're not playing each other, they're really playing death.' Tatum hadn't been listening.

'And you think this is a good place to force him to talk to me?'

'He can't get away from you if you're on the pitch with him.'

'How do you know I'll get a game?'

Cherry laughed. 'Look at the state of them. There'll be an injury in the next five minutes, I guarantee it.'

Tatum gave voice to a variant on the only thought he'd had for months.

'It's bloody ridiculous this, why won't he make a decision about anything?'

'Cos as long as he doesn't make a decision he can't be wrong about anything. He can't be accused of making mistakes if he doesn't make anything at all.'

'But he fought so hard to get the job, remember those rumours that went round about Tony Cliff who everybody thought would get the job? Well, it turned out Clive had bought the goat . . . Oh he loves the job, he loves it so much he doesn't want to do anything to lose it . . . like making any programmes. The other neat touch is that he doesn't like the thought of anybody not liking him. He won't tell anybody he's not going to make their show because he doesn't want to upset them.'

'But everybody fucking hates his guts!'

'But he doesn't know that because people are always nice to his face, they still think he might green light their shows . . .'

At that moment one of the fatter, balder players dove wildly for the ball, from inside his groin came a snap that could be heard all over Islington. He squirmed on the green-painted ground yelling in pain until he was taken away by paramedics.

'There you go,' said Cherry. 'Paul Feinberg, head of programming at LWT and winner of the Christopher Reeve award for self-inflicted sports injury.'

Tatum got up and stood by the pitch.

'Er . . . you need another player?' he said to the men. Several of them recognised him as BBC, one of themselves, so they gave their assent before Clive Hole could stop them.

Tatum jogged onto the pitch and took up the same defensive position as the injured man. After a time Clive got the ball and despite the fact that he knew Tatum was waiting for him he headed for goal. The younger man skilfully got in front of Clive and prevented him from moving forward while at the same time not taking the ball off him. At one point Clive even tried to pass to a teammate but Tatum simply kicked the ball back to his feet. 'Clive, I've really got to talk to you about *Bold As Bacon*,' he whispered into his ear.

'Can't we talk about this at the office?' gasped Clive.

'I tried to talk to you at the office and you climbed out of the window . . . And I want you to make a decision, right now, about whether we go ahead or not.'

A look of complete panic came into Clive's eyes. Abandoning the ball he ran full tilt into the wall, knocking himself out cold. Tatum looked on in exasperation as everybody else gathered round Clive's prone form. Back in the seating Cherry rose and took off her coat. Underneath she too was wearing football kit.

'Looks like you need another player, boys?' she said.

6

Tatum and Cherry were going for dinner at the home of their friends Victoria and Miles. Victoria was a make-up artist and Miles was a set designer at the BBC. They were buzzed into the mansion block via the entryphone. It sounded like Victoria was sobbing but those things often made you sound like that.

The couple got up to the flat and knocked on the door. It was flung open and a naked Victoria threw herself into

Tatum's arms, weeping solidly. Tatum tried to comfort her without touching any body parts with his hands, in the end he resorted to stroking her with the inside of his elbows while sticking his behind out so his groin didn't rub up against her triangle of thick black pubic hair.

'Vic, Vic, what is it, babe?' he said but there was no room between the crying for her to speak.

Over her lovely naked shoulder he could see into the entire open-plan apartment. The whole place had been painted black, not just the walls but the furniture, the carpets, vases, the flowers in the vases, pictures, posters, the TV, coats hanging by the door, everything.

'So, you been decorating, Vic?' said Tatum.

This seemed to unlock Victoria's words.

'It was my Miles . . . he did it. See he's spent months working on the set designs for this production. Then Clive Hole . . . Clive said he wanted some changes in the script, like the lead character should be a dog rather than a woman and it should be set in Finland rather than Barnsley . . . stuff like that. So last night he came home and he did this and now he's in a mental institution and . . . Oh hell.'

A big black dog came out of the bathroom barking madly.

Victoria sobbed. 'That was a Dalmatian yesterday . . .'

7

Deep underground in a long corridor at Television Centre, Clive Hole was walking along accompanied by a large group of tourists trotting behind him. Speaking to the group he indicated one of the doors leading off the corridor.

'And this is one of our new digital editing suites, each machine contains a thousand gigabytes of memory and can perform ten million processes a second. Would you like to see inside?'

A Spanish woman said quickly, 'No, no, Mr Hole, you really have given us too much time already. To meet the head of production at the Media-facilitation was thrill enough, at Disneyland you do not expect to be shown around by Walt Disney Junior himself, certainly not for three hours anyway . . .'

'Oh it's no trouble at all, it's important to keep the licence payers informed, after all you pay our wages.'

'Well, we don't actually,' said the Spaniard, 'seeing as we are all foreign tourists.'

'Yes, but . . .'

At that moment an older man in a Savile Row suit with the big flaps at the back that denote an aristocrat came out of one of the offices. He showed surprise at seeing Clive in this technical place, then quickly approached.

'Ah Clive, it's handy bumping into you like this,' he said

in a languid patrician drawl, 'I've been trying to track you down for weeks.'

Clive looked uncomfortable.

'Oh ah, erm . . . Yes. Oh can I introduce you to some of our foreign guests.' He turned to the group. Indicating the older man he said, 'This is Sir Marcus Wilbey, our head of finance.' Then turning back to Sir Marcus, 'This is Senora Aznar from Seville, Mr and Mrs Nomura from Kobe, the Willigers from Boise Idaho, Mr—'

'Yes, yes, if I could just have a quick word I'm sure the ladies and gentlemen will excuse us . . .'

The tourists gave their fervent assent, Marcus took the reluctant Clive's arm and led him a few yards away. The tourists took the opportunity to make a run for it, Clive watched them go as if they were the last hovercraft out of Khe San. Sir Marcus spoke.

'Really a corridor isn't the place to discuss this but seeing as you're so elusive . . . I was at a board of governors' meeting last week and one of the first items on the agenda was your spending . . .'

Clive's heart began to quiver and flutter in his chest like a caged canary.

'Yes, well . . .'

'And everybody agreed what a terrific job you're doing, you seem to have got the spending on programmes right down . . .'

The canary thumped to the floor of its cage, claws up.

Clive didn't know what to say. The bad voice suggested he might like to speak in Spanish for a bit.

'Si, bueno pero mi amigos esta argh umpmm . . . yes, no, yes ergh . . . well, we certainly aren't spending as much as we used to on shows . . . Though there may be a slight shortfall in . . . erm, product . . . actually in actual programmes in a few months but . . .'

Sir Marcus smiled indulgently.

'Oh that doesn't matter, somehow something always gets put on, doesn't it? I mean people have to have their telly, don't they? Whatever awful rubbish is showing. After all if there was no telly they'd have to look at the appalling terrifying random meaningless nature of existence and nobody wants to do that, do they?' Sir Marcus smiled and patted Clive on the arm.

'This expenditure cut though, excellent work, well done, keep it up.'

And with that he turned and walked away humming Tchaikovsky's 1812 overture, making a reasonable fist of the cannons firing and the bells of Moscow ringing out in triumph.

8

Cherry had just got into their flat, hot and sticky from a midnight to 1 a.m. kick boxing class, when the phone rang.

She called out, 'Tatum! Tatum!' But her husband wasn't in so she answered it herself. She listened for a bit, said only a few words then hung up. When Tatum came in half an hour later she was sitting on their big white couch.

'Tatum,' she said, 'there's been a phone call. It's bad news I'm afraid . . .'

'Oh God, what?' he squealed.

'It was your sister on the phone, your dad's had a stroke, he's in the hospital in Ipswich.'

'Oh thank Christ for that . . . I thought it was Clive Hole phoning to say he wasn't going to make our series . . .'

Then realising what he'd said he burst into tears.

'Look what he's done to me, I'm pleased my dad's had a stroke. Oh Jesus . . . Oh Jesus . . . I'm so unhappy . . . I don't want to be like this . . . I don't want to be like this . . . I'm having one of my panic attacks . . . I can't breathe . . .'

Tatum took the Saab and drove through the night to Ipswich. Due to the late hour when he arrived he could park outside the main entrance of the hospital which had one of those big revolving doors with plants behind glass growing in it. 'At least all this with my dad has stopped me thinking about Clive Hole,' he thought. Then he realised that in thinking that he had indeed been thinking about Clive Hole. So then he wondered if the plants got dizzy going round and round like that, which got him to the reception desk. He was directed to his father's room in intensive care. A woman was pacing outside, his sister Audrey. They hugged.

147

'How is he?'

'Not too bad. The next twenty-four hours are critical apparently, they've got him connected up to all kinds of machines which are supposed to help. Come in and see him.'

She opened the door slowly and carefully as if it had been booby trapped with a hand grenade and a bit of string by a disgruntled former occupant and they slipped inside.

Inside the room Tatum's dad was one of four figures lying each on their own bed, each wired into clusters of machines as if the machines were growing old men like spider plant shoots. A sister hovered over the comatose figure. Tatum had in mind some valedictory speech but he only got as far as 'Dad, I . . .' when a frantic whooping and clanging came from all the machines connected to all the old men. Several invisible Steven Hawkingses suddenly seemed to have entered the room to shout, 'Alert! Alert! Emergency! Emergency! Overload! Overload!'

Using intemperate language you wouldn't expect to come from a nurse the sister yelled, 'Fucking shite what's happening? There's suddenly a massive surge of microwave energy in the room!'

Seeing Tatum she rushed over to him and pulled his jacket open to reveal the two mobile phones on his belt and the three pagers clipped to his shirt.

'Turn those fucking things off,' she shouted.

'Do I have to? Clive Hole might phone.'

'I don't care whose hole might phone! Turn them off!'
Carrying dead people around can make a young woman
very strong; the sister got Tatum by the arm and hauled
him lopsided and yelping out of the door. She said, 'Unless
you want to kill your dad, switch them off! Didn't you see
the signs about switching phones off?'

'I didn't think it applied to me . . .'

'Why not?'

'I'm in television.'

A little later they let Tatum back into the room. His
father was now awake and talking to him in a feeble
voice.

'Son, there's something I have to tell you, something
your mother told me as she lay dying, don't be shocked.
It's about who your real father is. You know how fond
your mother was of Ken Dodd, thought the world of him
she did. Well, when he played the Ipswich Gaumont back
in the Sixties she went backstage then he invited her to his
theatrical digs . . . and well . . .'

Tatum hadn't been listening to any of this. He said in
a rush, 'Yeah right, Dad. Excuse me, I've just got to go
outside and check something . . .'

He got up and left the room. The old man slumped back
onto his pillow. Exhausted by the effort of rallying he had
another series of strokes which left him unable to speak.

Tatum stepped outside the hospital and stood in the
early morning Anglian mist frantically switching on all

his phones and pagers. He checked them all for messages, of which there were none.

'Shit!' he howled.

On one of his phones he dialled a number. When it answered he said, 'Hello ... yes, I'm a subscriber to your message service and I'm expecting ... well, a message obviously ... and I just wondered if sometimes they didn't get lost, messages, because of sunspot activity or something? ... No? I see, well, thank you.'

He stood looking thoughtful. A man with enormous muscles came up to Tatum.

'Hi.'

'Hi.'

'I'm in town for the "World Wrestling Association Bonecrusher II Roadshow" and it's my night off, I wonder if you know an all-night sauna?'

'Sorry, mate, I'm not really from around here.'

He turned and went back into the hospital, leaving the wrestler staring after him.

9

Clive Hole sat at his desk trying to read Tatum and Cherry's script for episode one of *Bold As Bacon*, but the words danced in front of his eyes like those black shapes you get if you punch yourself in the eye. He didn't know what to do. Placing the script carefully down he despairingly put his head in his hands. After a few seconds he was drawn back to the external world by the sound of work outside. Through his window, in the distance he could see some workmen repairing the fallen down bit of fence that he had been escaping over. The men doing the job were supervised by Cherry. She looked in his direction and gave him a contemptuous stare.

Then he had an idea; it swam away from him but he managed to grab onto it and follow it like a runaway kite out of his office and into the small and neglected part of TV Centre where programmes were sometimes made.

Clive entered a basement corridor dimly remembered from his days as a producer, and came to a door marked 'Make-up Room B'. Inside, a couple of make-up girls were sitting in their big barbers' chairs comparing photographs of their cats. They looked up when Clive entered, one of them had worked with him a few years ago on a sitcom called *Dim Lights, Small City*, otherwise they wouldn't have known who he was.

'Hello, Clive,' she said.

'Hello, Clarice,' he said, then rushed on before the decision he'd made was buried under all the counter arguments that were tumbling up from his brain. 'Yes, I'm erm . . . I'm doing a sketch in erm, for erm Comic Relief . . . as erm a ginger-haired erm . . . man and I erm . . . need fixing up with . . . well, a ginger wig and beard . . . yes, a ginger wig and beard to be a erm . . . ginger-haired man in a sketch.'

'Are they shooting that now? I didn't think they were doing Comic Relief this year.'

'No, yes, no in a few days they are and I'd just like to get used to the idea sort of thing . . . of erm . . .'

'Being a ginger-haired man?'

'Exactly.'

'Eugenie,' she said to her assistant, 'can you go to the wig store for a ginger wig and beard.'

A little while later the happy figure of Clive Hole, disguised as a ginger-haired man, walked through the foyer, past the large Henry Moore sculpture of a reclining figure that people said Moore had sculpted while waiting for a meeting with Clive Hole and out of the main gate. Tatum, who was watching all the people leaving using an infra-red sniper's scope from his office window, didn't see him go.

He stood in Wood Lane for a bit then lurched towards the White City tube station; he seemed to remember it contained a form of transport he had used before the BBC had started driving him about. He searched through his pockets for change. In his hand he noticed a coin that looked almost the same as a one-pound coin but wasn't. Examining it closer he saw it was a Spanish one hundred pesetas piece, how had it come to be in his pocket? Had he been going to Spain without knowing it? He was pretty sure he hadn't, but it struck him that he didn't know for certain, he only had the information in his mind to go on and he knew by now that his mind was an unreliable witness.

'A ticket, please,' he said to the man in the ticket office.

'To where?' asked the man.

This was an unexpected problem for Clive who'd had enough trouble getting into the tube station, walking backwards and forwards past the entrance several times like a timid man planning to visit a sex shop. 'Oogh erg dunno, tube ticket.'

'Well,' said the man behind the plexiglass whose therapist had suggested that it might help his anger-management problems if he tried to be nice to the customers, 'why don't you buy a One Day Off Peak Travel Pass, which entitles you to unlimited use of buses and tubes so that you can decide where you want to go and if you don't like it you can go somewhere else for free.'

This seemed like a gift from heaven to the vacillating Clive. Almost in tears he said, 'What a wonderful thing, how much is it?'

'Four pounds ninety pence,' replied the man.

Clive who ate in restaurants where a side order of a little dish of tiny peas cost £3.50 gasped, 'What excellent value!'

The ticket booth man's natural sarcasm couldn't be restrained. 'You're 'avin' a larf ain't ya?' he said.

But Clive wasn't having a laugh at all. He went down

to the platform and got on the first train that came in. This took him to Ealing Broadway where an African woman in a uniform told him to get off because it was going no further. Clive went outside and jumped on a little bus that pulled up on the station forecourt. Showing his pass to the driver made him feel like a detective whose badge got him in everywhere. The bus went to a place called Rayners Lane, where he got another tube train back into town. Clive managed to get off at Baker Street without being told to and from there he took another bus to the edge of Soho. Walking along Old Compton Street he passed a doorway with a hand-written sign on it which read: 'Tania 18 year old Aussie Girl. 2nd Floor.' Again he had an idea. Clive waited wearily for the argumentative voices to chip in but they all seemed to be in agreement on this one, so he went up the rattly stairs.

He entered a very shabby room where a woman who was neither eighteen years old nor Australian sat at a dressing table filing her nails and smoking. Clive said, 'Erm . . . where's Tania?'

Without looking up the woman said, 'She went back to Queensland, dear. Terrible floods they've been having in Queensland, she went back to help dry everything off.'

She finally looked at Clive. 'So what can I do for you, dear?'

'Well, I want something a bit unusual . . .'

'There's nothing I haven't done, love, though it might cost you extra. What is it you want?'

He took the script for *Bold As Bacon* from his coat pocket and proffered it to her.

'I wondered if you'd read this script and tell me what you think . . .'

'Well, that is a new one,' said the prostitute. Taking a pair of reading glasses from out of a drawer in the dressing table, she licked her thumb in a very old-fashioned way and began to read. Clive perched on a hard chair, fidgetily watching her. After half an hour she finished the last page and put the script down.

'So what do you think?' he asked.

'*Bold As Bacon*? Well, I think it's too plotty in the first episode and the characters need a lot more development, they're a bit one dimensional at the moment. Shooting on film?'

'Digi Beta.'

'I prefer film, more texture, know what I mean? But, yeah, should do well in a mid Sunday evening slot.'

'So if it was up to you you'd make it?'

'I don't see why not.' There didn't seem anything more to say after that. After a pause the woman said, 'Do you want that blow job now?'

Clive froze but was saved from making a decision by the woman undoing his trousers.

'You're not a ginger-haired man everywhere then?' she said.

10

In a Thorntons chocolate shop Cherry listened to an obvious actress sitting on the floor and talking on her mobile phone as customers stepped over her.

'. . . course I'm not in as bad a situation as Jenny Tracter, the poor cow. She was about to start on this detective series, starring role. It was about Jane Austen going around solving all these crimes in Georgian England. *Jane Austen, Discreet And Commodious Enquiries*, it was called. You know, one week she'd be a spy at the Battle of Borodino, having an affair with the young Count Tolstoy, the next she'd be trying to assassinate Napoleon. Anyhoo, the day before shooting starts, Clive Hole says there aren't enough Afro-Caribbeans in it and he wants the scripts totally rewritten and a part found for Lenny Henry, so now she's out of work for nine months and if you think I'm mental . . .'

11

On the Northern Line Clive's mobile phone rang, it was Helen his assistant. In a burst of enthusiasm and decisiveness he gave the go-ahead to a huge number of projects including

Bold As Bacon. He rang off and sat back in his seat, happy that his terrible inability to make a decision seemed to have gone away, thank God for that, he felt so much better now. This warm sense did not last very long. While at the front of his brain he was smugly content, in the back room where the bad things were brewed up his thoughts were worriting away at some anomaly. Suddenly a cold, miserable shock ran through him. Mobile phones didn't work deep down here on the Northern Line! He couldn't have had a call from Helen, had he imagined the whole thing? Had he sat there mute and daymaring or had he taken out his phone and shouted mad stuff into it? The looks the other passengers were giving him suggested the latter.

Clive knew then that he was going mad and it wasn't at all how he imagined it. He'd always thought somehow that if he went mad, he wouldn't be there, that it would be like a dream, or something that he could stand outside of, calmly observing at a distance. Or that in the experience of madness he would be so changed that it wasn't Clive at all who was insane but some other person that he didn't have to worry about. Instead he felt himself monstrously, unbearably, still to be Clive, but a Clive whose thoughts had run away from him to operate on their own, screaming and rattling away to a logic of their own devising.

He had once owned at his cottage in Gloucestershire a two-stroke American lawn mower called a 'Lawn Boy'. He'd bought it for the name partly. This machine, either through design or through some fault, just before it ran out of fuel would suddenly speed up to an insane degree, its blades whirling with the force of a fighter engine, giving it enough power to chop garden furniture and bird tables into fragments if he didn't switch it off quickly enough. That's how his thoughts felt now, spinning and razor-edged, chopping and scything and sending clods of earth flying.

A tube, a train, a bus, another bus and he was in a place called Croydon. It was a busy place, there was a market with two different Caribbean stalls run by white people, a place called Brannigans that said it provided 'Drink, Dancing and Cavorting'. Clive did a mad little skip and jump when he read the word 'cavorting'. There were big ugly 1960s buildings and there were trams. Red and grey trams that slithered almost silently along the pavement. A Number 2, destination Beckenham Jnc, appeared over the brow of a hill, travelling at twenty miles an hour. Clive found himself walking rapidly towards it on his short little legs. He wasn't entirely sure that this was a good idea so he consulted the voices in his head. They weren't much use. Some said it wasn't a good notion, that he could be killed, but others drowned them out saying that walking in front of a tram might be a lark, while others said that there was really no way he could be sure that he was in Croydon walking towards a tram at all, so it didn't matter what he did. Closing with the tram he saw it advertised on its side a Malaysian Buffet restaurant in Wimbledon, that offered forty dishes for £5.50. He had a little laugh to himself thinking of him trying to decide what to choose from forty dishes; he wouldn't even be able to pick up a plate. He was very close to the tram now: he could see the driver and he could hear a bell beginning to clang. 'So,' he said to himself, 'are we really certain we want to do this?' And he replied, 'Well, it's hard to say; on the one ha—'

12

Tatum stood at his father's graveside and wondered why he couldn't cry. He had driven up that morning from London. Waking early he had got into a panic because he couldn't find his only white shirt. He'd shouted at a still drowsy Cherry, 'I can't find me shirt, where's me shirt? Do you know? Where's me shirt?' She didn't know but he'd finally found it hanging in the wardrobe where it had been in plain sight all the while.

A light rain began to fall on the small clot of mourners making the graveyard a perfect picture of Victorian melancholy, yet Tatum still could find no tears. He felt a buzzing in his pocket as if a big bee was trapped in his trousers. It was one of his pagers saying it had a message for him. Turning away from the grave, the other members of his family thinking him grief-struck, he surreptitiously took out the device and read its message. It was from Cherry, it read: 'Have been appointed Acting Head Of Media Facilitation. Am cancelling *Bold As Bacon* forthwith. Seems dated, and anyway can't be seen to be helping a relative. XXX Cherry.'

13

Then he cried.

THE ONLY MAN STALIN
WAS AFRAID OF

1

The red flags and banners were cracking in the wind,
Making the NKVD bodyguard edgy and tense, on the
day in the early part of 1937 that Comrade Joseph Stalin,
General Secretary of the Communist Party of the Soviet
Union, paid a rare and frightening visit to meet some of
his subject peoples. The streets were cleared of traffic
for miles around while his armoured American Packard,
surrounded by a legion of NKVD bodyguard in trucks
and on motorbikes, took him to a bakery co-operative
near the Leningrad Station. The reason he was visiting
this bakery was that it had exceeded by over one hundred
per cent its loaf production targets, as set out in the second
great Five Year Plan. That this great loaf leap forward had
been achieved by diluting the flour with various poisonous

metals was of no concern to anybody, apart from those few who were killed by their lunch. He was there to present a medal of Heroes of Soviet Labour (second grade) to each member of the workforce.

The General Secretary went along the line of men and women, uttering the odd gruff word, pinning medals on the rough tunics (made of the same crude fabric as his own) of the bakers and the administrative staff.

Stalin was a small man and most of the faces of the workers were well above his but towards the end of the line he came face to face with the quivering visage of I.M. Vosterov, comrade baker third grade, a short round man with a thick black moustache, round bright brown eyes and a rather delicate, fine, thin nose. When Stalin accidentally looked into the eyes of this sweating little man he was astonished to feel a sudden and violent lunge of fear, a fear composed of nothing but pure fear itself, free floating and anchored to nothing, a horror so deep that a man less dexterous at hiding his feelings, would have run yelping into the street. Yet nigh on nothing showed on Comrade Stalin's face, a slight twitching of his moustache perhaps as he moved down the line, and the further he got from I.M. Vosterov the more the dread subsided. However, if he looked back down the ranks and caught the slightest sight of the little man then the fear returned to him as strong as ever. Stalin didn't know how he kept moving; the fear he felt was intolerable. He thought to himself that he would not be able to endure the next few seconds and minutes. That he could survive through the following days or weeks with this fear seemed an absolute impossibility.

Of course he had felt fear before but it had been of an entirely different order: lesser, altogether understandable. He had feared other men – more or less all other men – for what he thought they might be able to do to him. For example he had feared all the old Bolsheviks, those who knew the secret, the ones who had read Lenin's last letter to the Central Committee condemning him as unfit, a scoundrel and a repressor. They were all now shot or being worked to death in the camps and he feared them no longer. He had feared Trotsky, the only one who could have replaced him in the early days. Trotsky, of course, was banished, waiting on the shelf in Mexico to be dealt with one day. He had feared Bukharin because they said Bukharin had a better mind. For the crime of having a better mind Stalin had exiled him twice and allowed him to come back twice, forcing him the last time to admit his mistakes before the entire Party Congress, playing with a man as if he were a clockwork toy (his confessions wouldn't save him, he would be executed one day, and the thing was that Bukharin, with his fine mind, knew it). Stalin got pleasure from the way Bukharin looked at him, he liked to see the knowledge in his eyes. Stalin had even allowed him to go abroad, knowing he would come back.

And he had. It was terribly hard for Russians not to return to the sacred soil of the Motherland, even if it killed them; it was part of the soulfulness the Russians saw in themselves, a poetic attachment to soil.

The kind of terror that Stalin felt when he thought of the little baker was entirely different. As far as he could tell he did not fear what Vosterov could do to him: what could a baker do to him – Joseph Stalin, General Secretary of the Communist Party of the Soviet Union? Cook him a bad cake? No, it seemed that there was just something about the little man which brought out terror, pure and simple. This dread was clear and burning to the skin, like the finest peasant-grain vodka, distorting and oily in its bottle. Perhaps, Stalin thought, the little baker was some kind of mirror that reflected back all the screaming fear that rose like swamp fog from the entire terror-ity of his empire . . . he didn't know. He didn't know. He, who through his web of secret agents and spies, knew all that was going on in distant frozen Archangel, in sunny Yalta, amongst the minarets and towers of Oriental Tashkent, suddenly he didn't know what was going on inside his own head. He felt furious and very, very frightened.

Sitting back in the leather seat of the car Stalin reflected again on the nature of the anxiety he felt. There were many around him who he suspected of treachery, there were many who he thought might try to kill him, there were many that he hated (the entire Kulak class, for example), but this terror was certainly different. The fear that he generally felt was an enabling thing: a motivation to have this individual or that village or that class liquidated. But with the little baker it was the reverse – it paralysed him.

As soon as he got back to his apartment in the Kremlin and his bodyguard had gone, Stalin ran from room to room in a high-stepping dance, flapping his arms like a bird and saying over and over to himself, 'OhmiGod! OhmiGod! OhmiGod! OhmiGod! OhmiGod!' Then he settled in a corner and beat himself on the temple with the heel of his hand, shouting, 'Stop it! Please stop it! Please stop it!' Then he sat at his desk and issued an order to Yagoda, the head of the NKVD, to arrest and deport to the labour camps the entire workforce of the Bakery Collective near the Leningrad Station. Yet, as he went to put the order in the internal mail, the General Secretary thought to himself, 'Well off you go to the camps, you comrade little shit, I.M. Vosterov' and having that thought caused a picture of I.M. Vosterov to rise up inside his head.

If anything, the fear was worse than before: Stalin fell off his chair to the floor and lay watching the ceiling spin for several minutes. It did, at least, give him the chance to inspect the bottom of his desk for microphones. Eventually Stalin was able to climb back to his desk where he wrote on the executive order in a shaky hand: 'Excluding from deportation Comrade I.M. Vosterov, baker third grade.'

Over the next few weeks, though, Stalin was frequently

struck with thoughts of I.M. Vosterov, each thought carrying its own spear of terrible anxiety. He consoled himself with the notion that at least he would never have to see the man again; after all, there was no chance that a humble bakery worker would ever come into contact with the great Joseph Stalin, General Secretary of the Communist Party of the Soviet Union.

Gradually he became more involved in preparations for the 16th Party Congress and his terror began to fade.

So it was that Stalin strode out onto the podium in the great hall to give the opening speech for the 16th Congress, and in the second row – amongst the Uzbeks and the Tajiks and the Kazaks in their colourful native costumes – standing to applaud the General Secretary's entrance with as much fervour as the thousand other delegates from all over the vast lands of the Soviet Empire, his clapping hands like the blur of a hummingbird's wings, smiling and grinning and sweating, was I.M. Vosterov.

Stalin saw him right away, as those who are afraid of snakes will see a serpent or a coiled hose that might be a serpent, or a coiled hose behind which serpents might be hiding, or a barrel in which serpents might be slithering and twining over each other, where others would only see a hose and a barrel with no serpent-related qualities at all.

Stalin's eyes zoomed in on the features of I.M. Vosterov. Fear had given him the gift of seeing I.M. Vosterovs across phenomenal distances: he would have seen the little baker if there had been ten thousand or ten million delegates, he would have picked that face out if it had been at the back of the hall a mile away, even if it had been wearing a cossack hat, a scarf and a pair of welder's goggles. Stalin staggered sideways as the terror gripped him, and was only able to stay upright by grabbing on to the hammer-and-sickle-draped lectern at the centre of the stage. What was the little bastard doing there?

What had happened was this. When I.M. Vosterov turned up for work the day after the General Secretary's momentous visit, he was a little surprised to be the only person in the entire huge echoing building. Of course he did not mention it to anyone and he did not go looking for everybody. It was as basic as breathing in the Soviet Union that you did not remark on the disappearance of your fellow citizens. You certainly did not report the disappearances to the authorities since it was the authorities who were certainly the ones who had caused the disappearances. You assumed that if they had gone there was a good reason for it: the authorities, under the guidance of the great helmsman, Comrade Joseph Stalin, absolutely knew what they were doing; though, admittedly, it was sometimes hard to divine exactly what their motives were, what lessons you were supposed to take from their actions. So I.M. Vosterov unsuccessfully set about baking a thousand loaves all by himself and somehow the sullen ox of the Russian populace got by with a little less bread. The only one Ivan Vosterov could confide in was his wife. When he got home from the bakery, after filling out his own time slip and docking himself fifty kopeks for late arrival, he told his wife of the disappearance of the entire workforce.

Once he was in the relative safety of his apartment he allowed his emotions some relief. 'Oh how we suffer, us Russians,' wailed I.M. Vosterov. 'Poor Slavs, sons of the soil of Mother Russia, we endure so much,' then he rocketed to the other extreme: '. . . ah but then give us a few friends, a bottle of vodka, some pickled cucumber and how we laugh! Ha, ha, ha!'

'Actually I don't remember much laughing,' said his wife.

In a more concrete way, what the Party meant by its actions was the problem that confronted I.M. Vosterov's branch of the Communist Party: that his entire collective had been liquidated while this seemingly innocuous little man had been spared had to be a powerful message of some kind — but what was it? Supine submission was not an option for Party officials; their lives depended on deciphering the signs and signals that were handed down from the Party, no matter how cryptic. That was how a cow had become director of the Chelyabinsk Tractor Works.

So, after much debate, the secretary and the chairman of the branch decided that the higher reaches of the Party were sending a hint that they, the secretary and the chairman, had been undervaluing I.M. Vosterov. By solely excluding him from the slaughter of his entire collective the Party were saying that he was a man who should be valued more highly. They could, of course, just have sent a letter to this effect, but that was not the way of the Party. So in this manner I.M. Vosterov was elected as the delegate from Central Moscow Branch to the 16th Party Congress of the Communist Party of the Soviet Union.

Once he had stumbled through his speech Comrade Stalin spent the rest of the morning sitting with his hands over his eyes, causing those speakers who followed him to contemplate suicide or a swift run round to the French Embassy and a pole-vault over the gates. The General Secretary also did not attend the buffet lunch – 'a hundred tastes of Kazakhstan' – with the delegates, as he had been scheduled to do.

Stalin had risen to his position of god through the manipulation of the committees and sub-committees of heaven and so he spent the lunchtime arranging for I.M. Vosterov to be transferred to a plenary sub-committee on the struggle against the Kirovite faction, sitting in a side room while the Congress went on in the great hall. As long as he timed his entrances and exits he ran no risk of colliding with the little man.

After the 16th Congress Stalin considered having the secretary and chairman of I.M. Vosterov's Party branch shot for bringing the fearful apparition to his favourite event of the year, but waves of uncertainty seemed to spread out from the delegate for Central Moscow so instead the General Secretary contented himself with half-heartedly deporting some Ukrainians to Siberia. He knew he should at least do the same for I.M. Vosterov, but something in him now wanted to keep the baker close by in Moscow: he told himself that when he had got rid of his fear he wanted to be able to know where the little man was so that he could look on him without feeling the panic, the panic that rose in him that very moment as he contemplated the little baker in his mind. This time he got to check the skirting board for spyholes.

As Stalin spent more and more time thinking about I.M. Vosterov he had less time to stoke his usual resentment and furies, and therefore less people were condemned to death or deportation. This should have been a golden time but many could not enjoy it, expecting the terror to begin again, worse than ever. 'Oh how our poetic Russian souls do suffer,' they thought to themselves and wept suddenly in self-service canteens. Others in the ranks of the Party saw the decline in the deaths of innocents as a sign that Stalin was losing his hold, and began to plot against him.

Meanwhile the General Secretary attempted many things to try and free himself from the fear. He tried, for example, to make the little baker ridiculous in his mind. He imagined I.M. Vosterov sitting on the toilet, his trousers round his ankles; but that only succeeded in making Stalin afraid every time he went to the toilet, since his thoughts would now go 'I'm going to the toilet, I thought of I.M. Vosterov on the toilet. Oh God . . . this floor is cold.'

One day, in desperation, Stalin called in Kuibyshev, the Minister for Health. 'Tell me, Kostya,' he said. 'I was arguing with that shit-talking fool Molotov the other day about who is the best psychiatrist in the Soviet Union. Now you're a clever bastard: who would you say it was?'

Kuibyshev didn't know what to say to this – it could be a fatal trap in so many different ways. A seemingly innocent chat about puppies or mandolins with Stalin could somersault into yelled accusations of high treason within six or seven words; the General Secretary was like a serpent hiding within a coiled hose. So, having no other option available, he decided to tell the truth.

'Nobody, General Secretary,' said Kuibyshev. 'As I'm sure you remember, Comrade General Secretary, it was decided at the Congress of the Academy of Science in '32, which you so ably chaired, that as mental problems were created by the workers' alienation from society, and as the Soviet Union is a perfect society run according to the principles of Marxist Leninism with the workers owning the means of production, there can be no alienation and therefore no mental problems in the Soviet Union. Mental problems cannot possibly exist because that would mean our society is not perfect; which of course it is. The workers live in perfect harmony in the glorious Soviet Union which you, Comrade Stalin, have brought into being following the glorious teachings of Comrade Lenin, and thus there are no mental problems of any kind, whatsoever, at all, anywhere.

Anybody who does show any mental problems therefore must be a shirker or a saboteur and is imprisoned or shot.' Kuibyshev paused to see how all this was going down. Stalin seemed sunk in thought, so he decided to continue, 'Actually it occurs to me, Comrade General Secretary, that the only possibility of mental problems would be if a person were alienated from the workers' paradise because they were not a worker but a blood-sucking Kulak or a bourgeois intellectual Kerenskyite saboteur perhaps . . .'

Kuibyshev was pleased with this elaboration which had just come into his head. It did not do to come up with stuff if there was a witness present because you could make yourself seem cleverer than Stalin, which was a subway token to the Gulag, but on the other hand if there was no one else around then it was essential to come up with things, because then he could later claim these thoughts as his own.

The Minister for Health continued, 'Also, of course, Psychiatry is a Jewish invention and we know that that lot are not to be trusted. So in 1933 we sent all the psychiatrists to chop down trees in the forests of Siberia where, incidentally, lumber production was reduced by thirty-five per cent on their arrival.'

'Well who is the best of them then?' asked Stalin. '. . . Still living.'

Kuibyshev considered for a while. 'None of them, Comrade Secretary General; they are all dead if they have been in the camps since '33.' Then he had a thought. 'Ooh ah, no, wait a minute – there is Novgerod Mandelstim, he came back from the United States with his entire family in '36 after the proclamation of the new Constitution. We didn't arrest them all for sabotage until early this year so I suppose they might still live.'

Kuibyshev waited. Finally the General Secretary spoke. 'If he lives, bring him to me,' ordered Stalin.

2

A few mornings later, far to the east, Novgerod Mandelstim was trying, inexpertly, to cut down a tree in the Siberian forest. The deep snow he was standing in came up to his knees, soaking through the thin sacking of his trousers. He thought this might be the day when he lost his toes. Then the NKVD guards came for him and he thought he might lose more than that.

To his surprise, however, the guards were relatively polite, not beating him much at all. Down the track a car was waiting with its engine running and the heater turned up high. They threw him in the back of it; it was the first time he had been warm in six months. The car set off with a squeal of frozen brakes and bumped along forest roads for over an hour till they came to a narrow black road.

To his right Novgerod Mandelstim saw prisoners filling

some of the holes in the road with rocks, their faces and hands were raw and bleeding. A few took a quick look to see which powerful figure was in the back of this car they were perplexed to see one of their own reflections staring confusedly back at them.

The car drove for another two hours down the black road till they came to some sort of compound with the emblems of the NKVD above its gates. The motor swung through the barrier, not slowing down and only just clearing it as frantic soldiers pushed the gates open. They were now into a large clearing, long and narrow, trailing into the icy acid mist. And here was the most extraordinary thing: a three-engined aeroplane stood on the frozen grass, red stars emblazoned on its shining silver corrugated sides, its propellers slowly spinning in the corrosive air in order to stop them freezing.

Novgerod Mandelstim considered now that he wasn't going to be killed that day after all.

They put him in a seat on the empty plane, then two implacable guards came aboard and sat facing him. Novgerod noted that they were both captains in the NKVD. This got stranger by the minute: he wondered whether he had gone mad and this was some sort of long-drawn-out delusion. It felt real enough, but then he supposed delusions did, while you were having them.

The engine note of the plane changed to a roar, they bumped forward then began racing across the tundra, trees whipping along beside them, until finally they hiccuped into the air. As the aeroplane tore higher into the thin atmosphere, out of the window Mandelstim could see the many, many camps, each a white clearing in the forest, like patches of nervous alopecia in a dark green beard.

For most of the rest of that day they flew west. It was dark by the time the engine note changed again and the Illuyshin began its descent. The psychiatrist woke and looked once more out of the window. Tilted on its side was Moscow! He could see the Kremlin and Red Square clearly, the floodlights illuminating Lenin's tomb casting long black shadows over the rest of the city.

They came into land at Sheremetyevo Airport and another car was waiting on the tarmac, its engine ticking like a bomb and white smoke curling from its tailpipe. By this time Novgerod Mandelstim had gained an idea as to where he was bound, or at least who he was bound to see: there was only one person who could magic these things. In this country it was beyond the power of the average Soviet citizen to get their hands on a potato! Never mind an aeroplane! So NKVD captains, cars, planes, and most of all the sense of purpose, the engines running, the guards waiting and ready to roll, in a land where everything was done at a lethargic half-speed if it was done at all. It had to be him.

The thing was that Novgerod Mandelstim had known him, had been in some ways his friend. Back in the days before the revolution, the sullen pockmarked little Georgian, then called Iosif Dzhugashvili, had seemed vulnerable and shy and conscious of his lower class amongst the flashing, garrulous, intellectuals who controlled the Communist Party branch in Baku. Novgerod Mandelstim had tried (Had he been patronising? He didn't know.) to make him feel less self-conscious, had tried to include him in the debates, had given him preference in appointing him to committees (after all he was a genuine worker, one of those in whose name all this was being done), had invited him to dinner, since he always seemed half-starved; others had done the same. He had killed them all.

After 1917 Novgerod Mandelstim had watched in astonishment and at first with a little pride as Dzhugashvili, now called Stalin, had risen in the Party. In 1928 Leon Trotsky, the last of Stalin's opponents, was sent into exile in Alma Ata and the first real terror had begun. Real in that this was the first terror which had reached into the ranks of the Party. Before this, purges, random murder and imprisonment had been a privilege of the ordinary citizen. In that same year the OGPU, forerunners of the NKVD, had come looking for Novgerod Mandelstim. Fortunately he had been warned by a ex-patient high up in the Party, who he had cured of a morbid fear of frogs, that this was about to happen and thus managed to smuggle himself and his son to the United States in the last days, before the gates slammed shut.

Thanks to the many other Jewish emigres, Novgerod Mandelstim was able to move to the west coast of America and there he set up a psychiatric practice with another of those who had once been in the Party: G.V. Lubetkin.

Yet he was not happy. The corporeal decadence of the United States disgusted him, the seventeen different kinds of motor car that they had, in restaurants the little crackers they gave you that nobody ate, the gaudy suits the negroes wore at the dance halls of Compton; all of it repelled his puritan soul. Most of all he was repulsed by his patients: whining, spoilt, greedy, grown-up man/woman/child without any real problems, who constantly clamoured for his attention and thought he was their friend.

This displacement caused him to fill his son's head with stories of the Motherland. He pointed out at every opportunity the bovine materialism of the Americans, he contrasted this with the nobility of the Russian citizen; he compared the cheap jangling music with the poetry that lived within the soul of every Russian: Pushkin, Chekov, Dostoyevsky – Tolstoy versus Roy Rogers. There was no contest. Maybe this was why the lad had not prospered; despite his obvious intelligence somehow little Misha had not done well at college and had left early. In the years of the Depression he could only get work as a clerk in the accounts department of the Goodyear Rubber Company, and he had married a little girl from Yekaterinburg rather than one of the ten-foot-tall Californian women who ranged the sunburnt streets. So when in 1936 Novgerod Mandelstim heard about the new Constitution, he resolved to return to the Soviet Union. The provisions in this Constitution when it was adopted by the Party Congress included universal suffrage, direct election by secret ballot and the guarantees of civil rights for all citizens, including freedom of speech, freedom of the press, freedom of assembly, the right of return for refugees without persecution, freedom of street demonstrations and the right to personal property protected by law. Later on Mandelstim reflected that it might as well have promised a new type of gravity and perpetual freedom from farting for all the difference it made, but by then it was too late; they were all in the net.

The '36 Constitution had caused a very favourable impression abroad; liberal people said, 'Now the terror is over, maybe it was necessary, who knows? Now it is over, though, the Soviet Union will rejoin the world.' They said this because they wanted it to be so, they couldn't believe that free little crackers was the best that mankind could be.

So Novgerod Mandelstim told his son he was returning to the Motherland but that he didn't expect him to come too. However, as he had secretly hoped, Misha said that he longed too to touch again the dark earth of Mother Russia. Therefore Novgerod Mandelstim, his son, his daughter-in-law and his three grandchildren all returned to the Soviet Union. They were sure that if things went wrong their US citizenship would protect them.

'Hello, Koba,' he said to Stalin, deliberately using the name of the Georgian folk hero that the General Secretary had adopted before he became Stalin, the man of steel.

'Hello, Mandelstim,' replied the emperor of two hundred million souls. 'It's damned good to see you, old friend.'

'It's good to see you too, Koba, especially since I thought I was going to lose my toes this morning.'

'Well now you are here and your toes are safe.'

'For the moment, yes, yes they are,' said the psychiatrist. 'What do you want of me, Koba?'

'Straight to the point as always. So be it. Well, Comrade Psychiatrist Novgerod Mandelstim, I have a small problem.' And the most powerful man in the biggest country on earth told Novgerod Mandelstim about his small problem with the little baker from behind the Leningrad Station.

3

When he had finally admitted to himself that he needed help in sorting out his problem Stalin had felt better immediately. While they were locating Novgerod Mandelstim the psychiatrist, Stalin day-dreamed on what it would be like to confide in another person. All his life Stalin had hidden his thinking behind a thick curtain, his power rested in the fact that his enemies (which meant every living individual in the land and some dead ones) never knew what was going on in his brain, what he was going to do next. To tell all that was in his head to Novgerod Mandelstim, what would that be like? He had no idea. But maybe it was what he needed. To relieve the pressure like a valve, the terrible pressure of trying to make a better world for everybody. 'Oh,' he thought, 'how we suffer, us Russians. I suppose it is in our nature. But what have I done that life should be so hard?' Cautiously he tried thinking about L.M. Vosterov. There came immediately a terrible spasm of fear that forced him to clutch on to his desk in order to remain standing. 'But perhaps,' he thought afterwards, examining the fear, 'it might have been a little reduced already.'

Then another thought came to him, that maybe he didn't need Novgerod Mandelstim at all. He wondered if in some way the little baker was a kind of personal demon of his who could be placated by gifts, just as the ancients made sacrifices to their gods. Even as it came to him this notion seemed absurd to the General Secretary, but he also realised that by now he would try any stupid thing to ease the fear. Armand Hammer, the American who was the only supplier of reliable pencils in the Soviet Union and who bought all their oil, had recently given Stalin as a gift a half-sized metal negro that, via a patented Edison wax cylinder arrangement in its stomach, sang slave songs and negro spirituals at the switch of a lever. Stalin promptly ordered the NKVD to have this object delivered to the apartment of I.M. Vosterov.

The neighbours watched from behind their curtains and felt a little cheered. It made a change to see the NKVD carrying somebody into a house, even if it was a metal negro. Nonetheless, in a society so conditioned to abrupt and brutal change, no happy sense endures and within the hour a rumour started to go around the neighbourhood that all workers were going to be sent to the camps and liquidated: henceforth their jobs would be performed by metal negro robots. ('What was wrong with Russian robots,' many complained, 'instead of these black metal monkeys?')

Stalin waited for the half-sized metal negro to be delivered then thought about I.M. Vosterov. Instantly he fell to the floor and Novgerod Mandelstim's journey from the camps began.

'I see,' said Novgerod Mandelstim after he had heard the story. 'And you wish me to treat this fear that you feel?'

'Indeed, that's what I've dragged you all the way from bloody Siberia for.'

'There will be a price.'

'There always is. You know I always think ahead, Mandelstim, two or three moves, just like you Jews, always thinking, thinking. This is what I propose. Your son, his wife and two of the three children still survive . . .

for now. If you treat me successfully they will be released from prison and allowed to leave the country, along with yourself.'

Novgerod Mandelstim laughed a genuine, hearty deep laugh, the first in a long time. He said, 'You forget, I know you, Koba. I allowed myself to be deluded once but I know you and I know a little of your mind. If I treat this fear of yours successfully you will kill me and my family the instant you feel well, despite any promises that you have made. Patients when they are in the grip of their illness always think they will be grateful, but when you have brought them back into the light they kvetch about the bill. You, especially, will be no different.'

'You're a damned idiot!' shouted Stalin. 'Don't you understand that I could easily have the children brought here and tortured in front of you?'

'Then my heart would be full of hate for you, Koba, and I would not be able to treat you, even if I wanted to.'

Stalin thought for a long time. 'Damn! What are your terms then, bastard?'

'My son, his wife and his children are to be flown immediately to the United States. When I have spoken on the telephone to them and to one of the emigres, Raskalnikov or Lubetkin, then I will begin treating you, not before.'

'Why the hell should I do this?'

'Because you want to be well again. Who knows? It might be part of your treatment.'

'Will it be?'

'I don't know, Joseph; you will have to do it and find out. For once you do not hold all the cards and you are not holding the dealer's family prisoner. You cannot control events this time, no matter how hard and from how many angles you think about them.'

The General Secretary grunted, he pressed a button under the desk and one of his personal guard came in. Mandelstim was taken to a room within Stalin's suite of apartments and locked in it. A cold meal and a bottle of vodka waited for him on a table. There was a clean suit, shirt and tie in his size hanging in the closet.

Three restless days later he was taken by another guard to an office which contained only a desk and a chair. On the desk was an olive-green telephone. After a minute or two the phone pingled in a muted fashion. With his hands trembling, Mandelstim picked up the handpiece. He felt as if it weighed a thousand pounds.

'Misha?' he said.

'Father?'

'Oh my son, I am so sorry for what I've put you through. I was such a fool. This place is . . . is hell.'

'One of my daughters is dead.'

'I know. Where are you now?'

'We are in Lubetkin's house in Beverly Hills.'

'Are you safe?'

'There are Pinkerton men with shotguns all around, guarding the house.'

'Then you are safe for now.'

'Will you be coming too, Father?'

'I don't know, son. Let me speak to Lubetkin.'

The older man came on the phone. 'Hello, Mandelstim,' he said. 'Is he there listening?'

'In another room I expect he is, yes.'

'He will hunt them down if they are not hidden well.'

'I know it.'

'Don't worry. They will be hidden well; we have learnt how to do these things over the years.'

'Say goodbye to Misha, Natalia and the children for me.'

'I will.'

'Goodbye.'

'Goodbye.'

The treatment began the next day.

For an hour each day he would talk to Stalin in the General Secretary's office. Each of them sitting at an angle to the other in a comfortable armchair. Stalin had told his staff that Novgerod Mandelstim was writing a new biography of the great pilot of the Soviet State.

4

Yet, early on in the treatment, Novgerod Mandelstim was presented with an ethical dilemma which he thought no psychiatrist could possibly have encountered before in the short but colourful history of the profession.

The dilemma was this. It soon became clear to Mandelstim, from what his sole patient told him, that for the moment Stalin's fear was considerably curtailing his murderous instincts. He could not fail to learn that deportations were down, that executions were almost as low as they had been under the Tsar, that terror and dread did not stalk the streets with the swagger that they once had. In apartment blocks in the workers' quarters, where citizens had disappeared more frequently than a magician's assistant, the population was stable for the first time in years.

Mandelstim sensed a little, though not all, of the things that were going on beyond the three-foot-thick walls of the Kremlin. Without the perpetual and butcherous attention of the General Secretary, the clamp of the Party on the life of the Republic began to slacken. The secret police and the army did not know what to do and the mesh of spies did not know who to send their lies to any more.

As months went by with no crackdown, so people dared a little to sing the old songs. To worship the old God. In the west, the border guards became lazy on their patrols and each night more and more dark shapes slipped through the wire and into Poland. Via Georgia and Azerbeijan the camel trains again ran trade into Turkey. To the east, in the sea off Sakhalin Island, a thousand tiny boats made for Japan in a single night as the Red Coastguard stayed in port drinking vodka and consorting with whores. In the Ukraine peasants dragged political commisars from their offices and burnt them alive in the market squares and, as was usual in times of upheaval, Jews were murdered simply because it was again possible to do so.

It thus came to Novgerod Mandelstim that if he was somehow to cure Stalin then the murder would immediately begin again. Normally he knew that the patient's wellbeing was supposed to be the only concern of the psychiatric practitioner, but he felt he was beyond hiding behind such spineless evasions. Nothing was normal in the Soviet Union. No, he concluded: every second that Stalin remained ill, others remained well; therefore it was his duty as a human being, though perhaps not as a psychiatrist, to actually strive to make his patient worse! God knows enough of his colleagues had managed to do this without trying.

But how was it to be achieved? Especially without his patient knowing that this was what was being attempted.

In their first formal session Novgerod Mandelstim got Stalin to again go over the details of the fear that he felt for the little baker, I.M. Vosterov. After that they started talking about Stalin's childhood in Gori Georgia. The normal psychiatric practice would be to try and point out the childhood roots of this fear, and through this understanding to alleviate it. Novgerod Mandelstim did not do this but instead constantly professed himself baffled by the General Secretary's illness. He asserted that there could be no possible way that a violent alcoholic father and a cold over-protective mother could possibly have anything to do with their son suffering mental problems.

Often Stalin was forced to move the times of their meetings, and on several occasions desperate phone calls summoned Mandelstim to his bedroom in the middle of the night, when he'd had a particularly frightening dream. Mandelstim allowed him to do this since it was generally considered very bad psychiatric practice to allow the patient rather than the therapist to set the time and place of meetings as this placed too much power in the hands of the patient. These bad dreams that Stalin had were of great use to Novgerod Mandelstim in his project to make the General Secretary more mentally unstable than he already was. The dreams usually featured Stalin either being paralysed or unable to speak and him being menaced by a giant figure – always this person was somebody he had eliminated, such as Bukharin or Zinoviev. Generally the giant figure would be clutching a loaf or a small bread roll. Mandelstim's response to these terrifying reveries was the suggestion that as they were so frightening Stalin should attempt to avoid them by getting a lot less sleep. To this end the psychiatrist prescribed Benzedrine tablets from the

Kremlin pharmacy and within two weeks the General Secretary was a pop-eyed wreck.

Though in the short term this brought benefits to the people in the Soviet Union in that executions were almost down to zero, in the longer run it was a turning point of the wrong kind. Stalin, being no fool, even in his confused state, though he continued to more or less trust Mandelstim, was still suspicious of the fact that he was feeling so much worse after weeks of continuous treatment.

Mandelstim replied with the same responses his colleagues had been using since the birth of analysis: always darkest before the dawn, got to get worse before it gets better, without pain can there be gain? Blah blah blah. Unfortunately Stalin chose to self-medicate and reduced his intake of the amphetamine pills to a level where he was merely distraught. Perhaps taking control of his situation in this small way helped the General Secretary because from this point, despite all the psychiatrist's efforts, inexplicably Stalin began to get better.

One day Novgerod Mandelstim was attempting to probe in the most roundabout way whether what the General Secretary might be feeling for Vosterov was love. After all, he thought to himself, what could be more terrifying for a mass murderer than feelings of affection and desire? It appeared to Mandelstim that all that Stalin did he was able to do because he felt no empathy for other people; his narcissism placed him at the centre of the world and nobody else mattered, nobody else suffered as he did. So for him to be in love, for somebody else to matter, would be profoundly disabling for the dictator. In addition there were the social implications. The love of one man for another was a secret profoundly buried under the black earth of over-protective, smothering Mother Russia. It did not appear, not in literature, not in the ever-present sentimental folk songs, not in the conscious minds of the people; it was profoundly invisible. To raise the possibility of it with an ordinary Soviet worker was to risk a knife in the ribs, so how would Stalin react? However, when he mentioned the name of the little baker Mandelstim noticed that Stalin did not give quite such a large shudder as usual. Mandelstim felt something close to panic at this. Quickly he switched to a line of questioning that in the past had provoked a welcome increase in Stalin's anxiety.

These enquiries involved forcing the General Secretary to talk about the three different people that he had been. In the beginning there had been Iosif Dzhugashvili, the shy pockmarked seminarist in Tblisi; then came Koba the folk hero, the idealist who wished for a better world; and finally came Stalin, the man of steel. One tentative theory Novgerod Mandelstim had was that perhaps it was Dzhugashvili, the child, who was leaking through somehow, who was trying in some way to deflect Stalin from the murderous path that the third man had embarked on. Mandelstim had also in the past wondered if this was why he himself had always been inclined to address the General Secretary as 'Koba', the idealist he had been in the days before the revolution in Baku. Mandelstim imagined himself trying to talk to the man in the middle, the referee in the wrestling match between the child and the monster.

In their earlier sessions Stalin, when questioned about the lives of Dzhugashvili and Koba, had admitted that there were huge gaps in his memory of the early years. Though he retined in his brain the structure of every committee and sub-committee and steering group in the jellyfish tentacles of the Communist Party, he couldn't recall where he went to school, what his boyhood dog's name was or who it was that Koba had first killed: was he a little man with a black moustache? So again Mandelstim began asking Stalin to try and bring back memories of his childhood in Gori. At first there was the usual gratifying unease but suddenly he said, 'Anton! His name was Anton!'

'Whose name was Anton?' queried Mandelstim.

'My dog in Gori, his name was Anton,' said Stalin and smiled a terrible smile.

The only consolation that Mandelstim could take from the hour they spent together was that Stalin did not yet know he was getting better, but if he did not succeed in making his patient regress then that realisation would not be long in dawning.

Through the month of May the daily meetings continued and though Novgerod Mandelstim tried every trick he knew, Stalin continued to improve, to become calmer, and in becoming calmer he again began to sign the deportation orders. The trains began to run again, the spies began to get their orders, the execution squads cleaned their rifles and strode out again into the dawn.

One day Mandelstim was summoned as usual but when he got to Stalin's office it was empty.

Mandelstim knew what this meant; he sat there for the hour then returned to his room. Later the psychiatrist asked his NKVD guard for some sort of small bag which was delivered to him an hour later. Mandelstim packed into this bag the few possessions he had acquired in the past months, some books on psychiatric treatment, a small souvenir samovar from the 16th Congress, a couple of surprisingly high-quality pencils with 'Property of the Kremlin' printed on them, then lay in his underwear on the bed for the rest of the day and into the long night.

The next day Novgerod Mandelstim was again taken by his guard to Stalin's office. This time the General Secretary was in place, sitting behind his desk, though he remained there rather than taking his spot in the armchair from which their therapeutic encounters had generally been conducted. Nevertheless, in a hopeless gesture, Mandelstim took his usual place in the other armchair and waited for Stalin to speak. Finally he said, 'Yesterday, instead of our usual session I went down to the bakery behind the Leningrad Station. When the workers came out for their lunch I saw a certain person. I did not faint, I regarded him as I would regard any Soviet worker.'

'So I have cured you?'

'It would appear so.'

'Are you grateful?'

Stalin smiled. Strangely Mandelstim found himself smiling too, because you had to admit Stalin did have a nice smile. Mandelstim wondered whether people constantly underestimated this terrible creature because of the simple fact that he looked like a nice man. In Stalin's case nature's warning system had failed to work; it was as if the rattle of the snake had started playing sweet music, as if the bright, danger-signal red of the poisonous berries had faded to the fuzzy yellow of a delicious peach.

Stalin said, 'Each worker performs his allotted task within the great Soviet society because he is part of the inevitable process of proletarian advancement. There is no call for gratitude, gratitude is a bourgeois sentiment that has no place in the glorious workers' state.'

During one of their sessions two months before, when the dictator's anxiety had been at its highest, Novgerod Mandelstim had asked of Stalin, 'Koba, why have you killed everyone?'

Stalin thought for a while, considering it a reasonable question. Then he said, 'They threatened my position.'

The psychiatrist asked, 'And why is that bad?'

'I am the only one who can ensure that the revolution continues.'

'But what is the point of it all? The people live in terror, Joseph, millions still starve in the Ukraine, the camps are full to overflowing and the guards indulge in the worst behaviour that humans are capable of.'

'But one day everything will be better.'

'When will that be?'

'When everything is better.'

Now in their final meeting Novgerod Mandelstim stated, 'You said you would let me go back to America if I treated you successfully.'

Again that infectious, charming smile. 'You have looked deep into my mind, Novgerod Mandelstim. Do you really think that is likely?'

'No it is not likely. So what is it for me now? Back to the camps?'

'No, not the camps.'

'No I thought not.'

5

In a blood-splattered yard in the Lubyanka they tied him to the wall. As the firing squad of eight NKVD soldiers, with long Mosin Nagant rifles on their shoulders, marched in, commanded by an ineffectual little NKVD sergeant,

Novgerod Mandelstim began to speak. The execution party all tried to close their minds to what he said; the deranged speeches of those tied to the wall made them uncomfortable, they said all kinds of crazy things.

Novgerod Mandelstim said to them, 'I am a psychiatrist, the only one in this deranged country. Over many months I have been examining Comrade Joseph Stalin, General Secretary of the Communist Party of the Soviet Union –'

The sergeant shouted to block Mandelstim out, 'Come on, you men, line up here at the double . . .'

'– and I have come to the conclusion that he is insane.'

'Zorophets, are you listening to me? I'll have you on a charge if you don't jump to it smartly!'

The psychiatrist had to raise his voice to speak over the sergeant. 'I have a question for you.'

'Now men, rifles to the ready position. Kruschev, do you know what the ready position is? Good.'

Novgerod Mandelstim shouted, 'The name of his insanity is paranoid psychopathy. That is the name of what he is: a paranoid psychopath, a mad man.'

'Aim.'

'But what, I wonder, is the name for a person who unthinkingly carries out the orders of a paranoid psychopath?'

'Fire!'

6

And what became of I.M. Vosterov? Remarkably, the fate of the little baker from behind the Leningrad Station was the only element of Mandelstim's plan that could be judged an absolute and total success, though of course he would never know it. Throughout Stalin's reverse treatment Mandelstim had striven to keep the object of Stalin's terror, the little baker, alive. After all it was not inconceivable that Stalin might suppress his dread for the few seconds that it took to have somebody ordered dead in the Soviet Union. To this end the psychiatrist took every opportunity to plant the idea in the dictator's brain that terrible things would happen to him if any harm came to I.M. Vosterov. For some reason this, of all things, stuck.

As long as he lived – and he lived a long time – the little baker was watched over, day and night, by a special KGB squad of elite officers whose sole duty was to keep him from any kind of danger. A Chechen who tried to rob I.M. Vosterov late one night in the Arbat district was amazed to find himself clubbed to the ground by three silent men who rose from the dirty snow, crippled him with professional dispatch and vanished back into the night. To the quaking, confused I.M. Vosterov what happened on that night to him and the robber seemed like one of the old legends that were told about Koba, the Georgian Robin Hood.

The Vosterov squad became a much sought-after posting

within the KGB until the collapse of the Soviet Union. Just as a soldier had been posted for fifty years to watch over an empty patch of ground in a forest where once Catherine the Great had wished to protect a pretty flower, so the children and grandchildren, the nieces and nephews of I.M. Vosterov were all guarded over by legions of ruthless silent men whose sole mission in life was to protect Vosterovs. Constantly swapping fleets of long black cars followed them wherever they went, beautiful women (all of them fourth Dan or above in long form Karate) offered themselves up to the male Vosterovs as wives and mistresses; the females were also exceedingly lucky in the snaring of handsome husbands with ill-defined day jobs that left them a lot of time on their hands to organise picnics, trips to the circus and excursions to first-aid demonstrations.

Nothing bad ever happened to a Vosterov and they all grew up to believe that the world was a benign and happy place where good things happened to good people and bad people had swift and certain justice meted out to them by kindly strangers.

THE MAU MAU HAT

It was spring when he came, the yellow hammers were darting over the fields of winter wheat and Sam the farmer was out for the first time that year, poisoning wild flowers in the lane.

When he was poisoning wild flowers Sam always wore what looked like a rubber diving suit, on the back of which were twin canisters, with a spray hose attached that he worked with a lever up and down. Like aqualungs of death they were, those canisters, if you were a Bee Orchid or a Bluebell.

The two things Sam the farmer liked were killing things that he didn't get a grant for keeping alive and grabbing land, especially on a nice spring day.

The narrow muddy lane that bordered my house, the lane where Sam stood in his space suit, was solely an access road that ran to the dilapidated asbestos sheds and concrete hard standing that lay behind my home. The sheds were where Sam housed whatever poor creatures he was being subsidised to torture that year: pigs that he sold as pork to the American airbases, hens, sheep, elephants, unicorns. Thus the lane belonged to him, but right up against the lane ran my fence, the side fence of my long front garden, so Sam's road had only a narrow verge. A few months after I moved to the village Sam offered to mend my fence for me, it was falling to pieces in places.

He did a fine job of fixing it but without me noticing he also moved it a foot into my garden, so that Sam now had a fine wide verge. The rest of the village despised me for being so easily duped, for not even noticing that I'd been robbed of a precious twelve-inch-wide strip of grass, for continuing to wave and smile hello to Sam and Mrs Sam as they sat in lawn chairs on their slate smooth grass, in front of their three-car garage. It confirmed their opinion of me as an effete fop.

Nevertheless since that event Sam had felt a strange, uneasy sensation concerning the theft that he had never identified to himself as guilt, farmers knowing only four emotions: self-pity, greed, jealousy and inclinations towards suicide. Certainly since then, in a forgetful sort of way, he had looked out for my interests, if they didn't conflict with his own. He never gave me the land back though.

My name is Hillary Wheat, I am seventy-two years old, I came to the Northamptonshire village of Lyttleton Strachey thirty years ago and I am still nowhere near fitting in. I don't want you to think this is the cliché of rural suspicion towards outsiders. It is just me.

The couple who live in the other semi-detached house joined to mine, a pop-eyed pair of social workers called Mike and Michaela Talmedge, have a sixteen-year-old daughter called Suki. Suki has a boyfriend called Bateman who is a six foot three inches tall, cross-dressing black man with dyed blue hair and a ring through his nose. With her parents' enthusiasm Bateman has come to live with Suki in the parents' house, in her childhood bedroom, still hung with Take That posters. On summer afternoons with the windows open I can hear them having mildly perverted sex, the crack of leather on black man. Bateman fitted right in.

No matter how hard I have tried to shake it off there is some quality that hangs over me of diffidence, taste, restraint, politeness, that really, really, annoyed the inhabitants of Lyttleton Strachey. In the village pub, which our mad quacking landlady had re-named The People's Princess after the famous traffic casualty, I would enter to mumbled 'How do's . . .' then sit quiet and annoying in the corner with a flat pint of Hook Norton Bitter. 'Bitter?' the duck landlady would ask when I entered.

'A little . . .' I would always reply (apart from a 'no,

more rueful I would say . . .' phase in the early Eighties).
It just made people angry. Even couples who had motored
over from Banbury and had never been in the pub before
felt a frisson of irritation at my entrance.

By contrast Bateman would blast in, dressed in a ball
gown worn over lycra cycling shorts, usually shouting
the catchphrase from some television commercial, and all
the lads, Marty Spen, Paul Crouch, Miles Godmanchester,
Ronny Raul, would be pleased as punch to see him. There
would be shouts and banter and lots of admiring questions
for the black man about what it was like to be a black
man or a black woman.

If I had been some sort of spy my diffident qualities
would have stood me in good stead in Lyttleton Strachey.
But I'm not a spy, I'm just a lonely old man.

A lonely old man in exile. At least when the Tsars
sent their troublesome citizens to Siberia they had others
there to greet them, to argue with, to go hunting with,
to make love to and the possibility of escape. It always
sounded like a rather nice winter break to me, excellent
après ski, dancing lessons from Leon Trotsky, a talk on
penguins by Vladimir Ilyich Lenin, a sort of Sandals of
the Steppes.

But I am my own gaoler so there is no escape.

My name is Hillary Wheat, I am seventy-two years old
and once, a long time ago, I was what the newspapers
called a 'well known poet'. I was never avant garde,

preferring clear simple words about love and buttons and buses, that rhymed. God forgive me but I also used my popularity to distend myself into a celebrity. The television made an hour-long film about me that was shown at prime time on the BBC, this being in the time when they used to force feed self-improving stuff down the public's gullet, hoping to swell their brains like Sam crammed bits of their relatives and diseased swill down the gullets of his poor animals. I also had my own weekly radio programme and once made an advert for breakfast cereal in which there was an amusing play on my surname. Wheat.

My descent into Northamptonshire began some time during 1968 and a lunch with my publisher, the late Blink Caspari, of Caspari and Millipede. For some time I had been having difficulty in contacting him. His secretary kept saying he was 'in a meeting'.

Lying in this way was a business practice recently imported from the United States, like time and motion studies, so that when she said he was in a meeting I thought he was actually in a meeting. 'He's in more meetings than the general secretary of the TUC,' I joked. You may not remember it but the TUC was a powerful organisation back then, for trade unionists, run by a man with strange hair. (It occurs to me I should perhaps explain what trade unionists used to be. But then where would I stop? Threepenny bits? Moral rearmament? Emotional inhibition? Ministerial responsibility? Sexual restraint?)

After a lot of phone calls I had managed to get my publisher to invite me to lunch at a restaurant in Camden Town that Blink described over the phone as 'sort of France at the time of the First World Warrey'. It was down some stairs.

I said to Blink as we went down the stairs, 'I thought when you said it was France at the time of the First World War you meant a Belle Epoque sort of thing, a return to the classicism of Escoffier . . .'

'No, what I meant,' said Blink, 'is that it's France during the First World War.'

By this time we were in what I supposed was the restaurant. I stared about me. We had passed through a door into another time. The underground room we had entered was a re-creation of a brasserie in the centre of a town in Northern France sometime in the middle of the year 1917, right in the middle of the First World War. The café had seemingly a few hours before taken a number of direct hits from a salvo of high explosive shells. Jagged holes had been blasted through the walls in several spots, giving views of distant, badly painted underground fields, the shell holes had been, apparently, hastily half-filled with sandbags. Two old-fashioned Vickers machine guns were mounted on top of the sandbags, belts of ammunition coiling from their cocked breeches. There had been a recent firefight between the shop window dummies of the

Allied powers and the shop window dummies of the Central powers: casualties lay blood-splattered in the uniforms of the German, French and British armies, sprawled in stiff attitudes of death across the bags of sand.

All the waiters were got up to look like members of the French general staff and the tables and chairs were rough hewn, shrapnel-blasted mismatches such as would be found in any bunker. On each table there was an old-style field telephone that you could wind up and speak to anybody who took your fancy at another table, these field telephones were taking seriously the current injunction to 'Make Love Not War'. Playing on a continuous tape loop via speakers buried in the walls was the crump and whine of artillery. Every half an hour there was a small explosion of smoke and sparks from beyond the sandbags.

It occurs to me now, thirty-odd years later, that each period interprets the past in its own particular way. So though to myself and Blink (and I expect to the many survivors of the Great War who were still bumbling around in that year of 1968) the brasserie looked utterly authentic, viewed from our own age, from now, the place would appear irredeemably 1960s. And if anybody at this moment would wish to make a brand-new, bombed-out, early twentieth century brasserie, it would look very different.

'You were in the last war weren't you, Hillary?' said Blink as we sat down.

'No, too young.'

'You fought somewhere though, didn't you? I'm sure you did. Had a life-changing experience somewhere, there was a poem about it I'm certain.'

'Yes, Kenya, '52, '53.'

'No heebie jeebies though?'

'Not so as you'd notice.'

'Ah good. I suddenly got a bit worried this place might bring it back . . . if you'd been in France and if there was anything to bring back. Lot of the teachers at my prep school were the most barking mad fellows from the first war, gibbering and crying at all hours and trying to grab your cock in the showers.'

'I don't think war is very much like this,' I said.

'No, I don't suppose it is,' said Blink.

'You in the war, Blink?'

'In the war? Not really. Old enough but medically unfit. Asthma. Eventually after a lot of badgering friends of the family they gave me command of an anti-aircraft gun in Regents Park, in the evenings after work. Do you remember at the start of the war, before things got organised, they let groups of chums form up Home Guard anti-aircraft batteries together? I was in charge of a bofors gun manned by the most ferocious pack of modernist architecture students from the Architects Institute in Portland Place. Spent most of my time stopping them from taking potshots at old buildings that they violently disapproved of! Still not entirely sure they didn't blow up the old Abelard and Helois department store in Oxford Street, one minute it was there then the next . . .' He paused while a shell in stereo seemed to whistle overhead, then went on. '. . . Well, it was still there but it had a lot of really big holes in it and it was on fire and I can't say I remember the sound of any planes overhead or the sirens going off or anything. Still it was a frightful old Victorian pile, better off without it. I think it's an Arts Lab now.' Then, studying the menu which was printed on maps showing the movements of great armies across the plains of Picardy, 'What'll you have, old man?'

I remember I felt myself to be another anachronism. I had dressed that morning in my second-best town clothes: a navy chalk-stripe single-breasted suit made by my tailors in Savile Row, club tie, cream Gieves and Hawkes shirt, silver cufflinks from Aspreys, Church's black Oxford lace ups, silk socks, cashmere navy-blue overcoat, on my wrist my father's old Smiths watch. All a mistake, silly vain old peacock. Dapper I might have looked standing by the Cenotaph or somewhere similarly old fellowish but not in that place. I looked like I was lunching my son, perhaps as a well done for getting his first top-ten disc or to celebrate him choreographing his first nude musical, despite the fact that Blink was ten years older than me.

Once we had ordered and General Petain or possibly

Marshall Foch had thrown our first course down in front of us, I said, 'So, Blink, I wanted to talk to you about where the firm sees me going in the next few years.'

Blink stared unblinkingly into my eyes.

'And I want you to look around, Hillary, the times they are a' changin'.'

Obediently I looked around as I had been told to. It seemed to me more than changin', the times were a' gettin' all a' jumbled up. As was the new fashion, several of the young men and even the young women at the other tables were wearing bright red Edwardian Royal Guardsmen's tunics. They looked as if they had somehow slipped through time into the wrong war and although there were newspapers on sticks to be read they were all from February 1917.

'Yes, if you say so, Blink.'

'Caspari and Millipede has to change with them. Pan global corporatisation is coming whether we like it or not and as of next month Caspari and Millipede will be folded into the publishing arm of the Deutsche Submarine Corporation.'

'Oh dear,' I said.

'Now our top money people have looked at the figures for this merger from top to bottom and they say they can't see any way at all that it won't be total and absolute financial suicide but all the leading futurologist watchers say that pan global corporatisation is the coming thing, so we can't afford to be left behind. Hillary, Hillary, I assure you, you will not notice the difference. There will be absolutely no changes ... except that the publishing department will be moving to Hounslow, authors' editors will be drawn from a pool rather than assigned individually and our poetry list will be slimmed down considerably. On the upside you do get reduced-price travel on West German and Danish ferries.'

'Oh dear,' I said again. 'You know that I've been with Caspari and Millipede since the mid Fifties, your father signed me to the firm. I'm bewildered that he's gone along with all this.'

'I know, remarkable isn't it? But be assured that Dad-dad agrees with me one hundred and fifty-seven per cent.'

Indeed remarkable, since, apart from any other considerations, Paul Caspari had been torpedoed in the North Atlantic during the convoy war and when he amongst the survivors had bobbed to the freezing surface they had been machine-gunned by the lurking German submarine. What I couldn't be aware of at the time was that Paul Caspari was, with good reason, extremely frightened of his son. Not expecting any opposition, Blink had simply told his father that the firm, which he had founded, would be taken over by the DSC. Blink was shocked when the father had for once objected and said that maybe they should think about it. The son had had to roll on the floor spitting and screaming and tearing great chunks of foam out of the furniture with his teeth to try and get his own way, and when even that hadn't worked he'd run at his father and punched him hard on the nose, blood and bone flying everywhere. Apparently everybody else at the board meeting had been terribly embarrassed.

When you know all this, it makes it a lot less surprising that Blink was murdered by his own adopted son a few years later, clubbed to death with a hammer.

You can't stroll down to the shops here in the country like you can in a town. Everybody in Lyttleton Strachey, apart that is from me, likes to do their shopping once a month in one of the out of town superstores that encircle nearby Banbury like Visigoth encampments. On coming home with the carrier bags in the boot of the hatchback they cram their elephant-coffin-sized freezers with ready meals to be defused later in the microwave. The extra time they save by doing all their shopping in one place at one time is used, as far as I can tell, to argue about money with their wives, download child porn from the internet or simply to drool spittle onto the dining-room table.

Briefly a deluded couple with a dangerous dream came down from London and opened a shop in the village offering for sale fresh local produce and poultry from nearby farms, daily deliveries of fish and organic stone-ground bread, all of it beautifully presented

212

with elegant hand-written little notes. The inhabitants of Lyttleton Strachey could hardly contain their horror at the abomination that was come into their midst and all, again apart from myself, boycotted the place with a rare unanimity and determination of purpose. The shop soon went broke and closed down. The husband hanged himself from the oak tree on the village green, which many reckoned was no more than he deserved for trying to make them eat notfrozen peas.

Sam the farmer went one better than the other villagers and did all his shopping in Northern France at a huge discount warehouse called Mutantsave somewhere outside of Arras. This was not an easy option for him to take: Sam did not speak any French and refused to learn, so in the French discount warehouse he often had no idea what he was buying. Sam only knew there was a lot of it and it was cheap. He had once had a violent fist fight with an Algerian over the one remaining gigantic drum of something called 'Akkaspekki' priced at a dazzling FF 28. Sam still had no idea what the stuff was for, nevertheless he knew the answer would come to him one day, he just hoped it would be before September 2009 when the akkaspekki had to be 'à consommer' by. Even when he was fairly certain that what he had bought was food, Sam and Mrs Sam had only the vaguest notion what the 'Conseils de Preparation' were. Dinners at the Sams had often consisted of raw Paella Royale avec Volaille et fruits de mer or boiled pheasant pâté, until they had begun inviting me to dinner so that I could translate cooking instructions. It was a measure of my loneliness that I went.

Sam the farmer had another reason for shopping in France apart from parsimony: it gave him an excuse to go somewhere in his car. In the thirty years that I had lived opposite him he had become rich. Since the hard working hairdressers and photographers' assistants of the European Community had started giving a slice of their income to Sam he had more money than the Sultan of Brunei's brother Prince Jefrey would know what to do with, but coupled with a farmerly dislike of ostentation. Luckily the motor industry had developed a type of car for the likes of him. 'Q' cars the motor magazines called them after the disguised German merchant ships that would sashay around neutral waters in a trollopy way enticing allied warships to get too close then flipping back their sides to reveal dangerous guns. 'Q' cars were ordinary family saloons but fitted with powerful turbo-charged engines, sports suspensions and four-wheel drive; in shades of pale colours they looked the same as plain motors yet screamed past Porsches on the motorway. Sam's first was a 4x4 Cosworth Sierra, then a Lotus Carlton 3.6 litre twin turbo, now he had a Subaru Impreza Turbo P1, 280 bhp, 4 wheel drive, 0 to 60 in 4.6 seconds. He would strap himself into his blue racing harness and hurtle to France at four in the morning, blazing down the M1, M25, M20 onto the cheap-offer ferry. Off the other end, racing spoilers scraping the ramp. Rumbling into the car park of Mutantsave as they opened, turbos crackling and cooling, to fill up his boot with boxes and cartons and pallets of cheap things.

When he came, he came in a green Landrover van.

A few days before, I had dinner with the Sams. As I sat down in their 'clean as a place where they make microchips' living room Sam entered waving a bottle. 'I thought we might have this with dinner, Hillary, what do you say?'

I studied the label.

'Um . . . I don't think so, Sam, you see it's a bottle of shampoo.'

'But it mentions berries,' argued Sam, unable to face the fact that he'd wasted five francs.

'To add lustre to our hair if it is dry or medium to dry.'

Eventually he turned up a box of mixed Australian wines bought at a place called Booze Bonkers, which was just outside Caen apparently.

'Sam, would you by any chance be going to France before Wednesday?' I asked.

His eyebrows went up, wrinkling his forehead and shiny bald pate at the prospect of an adventure. Sam's big yellow farming machines that went about doing his work in the fields were connected to the house by global positioning satellite which he could access from anywhere in the world on his laptop, so he would always be able keep in touch with the damage he was doing, even on the RN1.

'Well, I wasn't planning to . . . but I don't see why I couldn't.' Sam was always ready for a drive.

'Please don't if you weren't . . .'

'No, no a midnight drive is always agreeable and they say penicillin is much cheaper over there so I was plannin' to get some. Is there summink you wanted me to get you then?'

'Well, erm . . . um . . . just some cakes, patisserie if you could . . . I seem to be having a young man to tea on Thursday and it's so hard to get any decent cakes round here.'

'A young man?' rumbled Mrs Sam who had entirely the wrong idea about me and young men since I had had no female companionship in the thirty years they had known me.

Sam's wife, known only as Mrs Sam, was a tall thin woman who kept their house very clean and rarely spoke, but when she did it was in a surprisingly deep voice, rather reminiscent of a Negro from the deep south of the United States. When she addressed you at the dinner table it was as if you were being asked if you would like another serving of mousseline de tête de grenouille by the famous singer Mr Paul Robeson.

'Yes, he's something called a Million Pound Poet. Whatever that is. He telephoned me a little while back and said he admired my work and could he meet me for a chat? So I invited him for tea. It's such a long time since anybody's got in touch with me and well, you know, I did that a lot when I was young, it was quite the done thing. Write to a poet or author you admired and they were often frightfully good about inviting you round for tea, to talk about their work, sort of help out the next generation. Powell, Forster, though I think he was a little too interested in young men coming round; Ted Hughes of the more modern persuasion of poet served a particularly fine sort of scone with currants in it that you could only get at a little bakers in . . .'

Names that meant nothing to the Sams.

'Are you still writing your poems?' said Sam. 'I didn't think you wuzz writin' your poems. I didn't think you'd written any poems since you had come 'ere.'

Sam would always be the one to say to a leper 'Wo's wrong with your nose then, mate?' In fact, he would be pleased with himself, he would think he was doing the leper a favour by being so blunt and outspoken, and by not trying to ignore the deformity but coming right out and mentioning it plain and simple.

'Well, as a matter of fact, as you've been kind enough

to point out, I haven't, hadn't written for thirty years but now suddenly I've, well I hardly dare say it . . .'

I was making the Sams uneasy with my giddy tone.

'But I've started again, only mapping it out at this point. It's a long poem and erm . . .' I was losing them now.

'. . . but anyway I can feel it's back, the power very different but also the same. Would you like to know what it's about?'

Sam said, 'No we wouldn't, no. We're very happy you're writing again but that's about the limit of our interest really.'

'Yes, fair enough. I must say I'm rather sorry that he's coming to see me, the Million Pound Poet, because I can only write during the day for a few brief hours, and even the prospect of somebody coming to see me stops me for days. Still one has to be polite . . .'

Polite. Politeness, my own affliction more disabling than arthritis. I do look on it as an affliction, an inability to make clear my own feelings, to state my own desires. I have always been that way. I imagine I was influenced by all the poets and writers who infested our house in Old Church Street like termites when I was a child, weeping and borrowing money that they never repaid, molesting the staff and stealing the sugar bowls. It would have been good for them to restrain their desires, even if only once a year. Would have kept them out of the courts or the River Thames or the private clinic that everybody knew about in Wimpole Street. But it never occurred to them even for a second.

Surprising then that from when I was a child my only ambition had been to be a poet. At my prep school there were several boys in my class who wanted to be poets, it was that kind of school, others wanted to be fighter pilots, engine drivers and one boy wanted to be a cow, but there was a fair crowd of us nine-year-old aesthetes.

My father, Vyvyan Wheat, had returned from the First World War to become an editor at Fabers. As a baby I had been sick over the first draft of T.S. Eliot's 'The Waste Land'. With my father I had got the Number 14 bus from Chelsea to Red Lion Square then walked past the British Museum to take tea with Leonard and Virginia Woolf, a remote creepy woman whom I was afraid of. As a final pilgrimage I had gone with my ailing father down to Southampton Docks to throw lumps of coal at Auden and Isherwood as the two cowards had set sail for America, just ahead of the Second World War.

I said to Blink, 'I'm sorry but I don't feel I can stay with Caspari and Millipede under this new ownership. I'm sure many other publishers would be glad to have me.'

'Of course they would be, Hillary.'

But of course they wouldn't be, Hillary.

They did a similar thing to Barbara Pym round about

the same time. You can now buy her books again all over the place but in the 1970s and 1980s it would have been impossible. Back in the unswinging Fifties she was enormous, top-five successful novelist, then more or less on one day something in the air changed: the executives at her own publishing company and the critics on all the big newspapers and magazines decided she wasn't any good any more. Though she had been good the day before, somehow now she wasn't. I suppose these people have to believe they have some special power, that they know ahead of time when an artist is played out. So if they bring it about, they make it a self-fulfilling prophecy. They are scientists who can affect the outcome of their experiments. Poor Barbara kept writing books and her editor would be unenthusiastic and they wouldn't get published. And she thought it was her fault, but it wasn't: it was fashion's fault, it was their fault, all the others. Nobody put her books out till they decided to dig her up at the end of her life. Too late, too late.

After my lunch with Blink I went home feeling terribly agitated, perhaps suspecting some of what was to come. My wife was in the hall arranging some flowers on the hall table. At that time we lived in an apartment block on the edge of Hampstead Heath which was called Isopod One and had been designed in the international style, along socialist principles, by a famous architecture collective called the Isopod. There had once, before the war, been a communal canteen on the ground floor that had served nourishing vegetarian meals for sixpence and a bar where there had been folk concerts. It's derelict now.

'How was your lunch with Blink?' she asked.

'Catastrophic.'

'I said you should have gone to Claridges.'

'No, not in that way. Well, in that way too, but the most extraordinary thing. Caspari and Millipede are being taken over by the German Poison Gas Corporation or some such, so I've told them I'm leaving.'

I had married for the second time to a much younger woman. My new wife, Annabelle, was taller than myself, blonde, sweet-faced, with wonderful straight posture that emphasised her perfect breasts, and she had always had terrible trouble getting men to have sex with her. Fellows at the university she went to were always finding her in their beds after parties, looking all tousled and saying things like 'Oh I'm just so tired, can't I stay the night here? We don't have to do anything, honestly, we can just hold each other.' Or she was constantly taking up the bizarre pursuits of men she fancied, such as real tennis or robotics, in order to get closer to them; it didn't work, though she could probably have designed a tennis-playing robot long before Pete Sampras came along.

On the other hand my first wife, Frances, had been a small bandy woman with a substantial moustache and a fine collection of moles who had, sometimes literally, had to beat men, especially Arthur Koestler, off with a stick (which he had liked very much indeed).

My first wife Frances had abandoned me soon after I became famous with my first collection of poems, saying that she found celebrity 'tacky'. She went to live on a kibbutz in Israel which collapsed in violence because of the sexual tension she generated. After that Frances had wandered the Middle East and the ructions she caused were a powerful factor in the rise of Muslim fundamentalism.

My young wife Annabelle had married me because I had felt her up at a bottle party in Mayfair without her begging me to. It was a surprise to me and all in our circle when she gassed herself, after I had left Caspari and Millipede and no other publisher would take me. Nobody knew that my fame had been so essential to her, most assumed instead that she'd been having an affair with Ted Hughes.

In truth we would have been able to stand me losing my publisher but it was the court case that really did for us. Now we live in more crack-up conscious times and it is well known and understood that those under stress, often without knowing they are doing it, find that they have been stealing little things, shoplifting in other words. Even back then, if I had been caught walking out of Fortnums with a jar of pickled walnuts under my coat they might not have pressed charges but the Zoo felt they could not be so understanding. Also I had my accursed ubiquity to blame, for one of the many tasks outside poetry that I had taken on was my own regular radio programme broadcast on the Home Service, called *The Moral Low Ground*, on which each week I would deliver an extemporised lecture, entirely without notes, on some aspect of the decline of manners and morality in society: unmarried mothers, hire purchase, lack of civility in daily life, association footballers earning more than ten pounds a week – plus shoplifting, of course. And although the penguin had suffered no injuries, indeed it was me who had been badly pecked underneath my coat, at Wandsworth Crown Court the beak sent me down for three months and I was pilloried in the press for hypocrisy and animal cruelty. This last charge particularly hurt since I had always been a keen supporter of animal rights and I think in my stress-addled mind I was only taking the penguin home because it looked cold.

With no wife, I sold the flat in the Isopod and with all of my savings bought this little house in Lyttleton Strachey. To exile myself, to punish myself, to not have to come face to face with an old friend in the Strand. I retained the best of the furniture from our Hampstead apartment, at that time the exemplar of restrained urban taste: Hille couch and armchairs in wood and moquette, Heals sideboard in sycamore, an original Ercol dining-room set, Luminator lamps from Arte Luce, Aubusson needlepoint rugs. All as incongruous as myself in what was little more than a rural council house built for the chauffeur of the Manor House, now itself converted to apartments. And I kept my clothes, which also looked out of place in their new bucolic home.

Yet along with my hunting rifle and an ugly PVC hat Larkin had given me that I'd never liked, I seemed to have left the ability to write poetry back in London.

Once my inspiration had been lost and I had come to this place I still stuck to the working routine of a poet. For thirty years, on weekdays, for three hours in the morning and three hours in the afternoon I sat at my G-plan desk in the middle, small bedroom, which looked out over the fields at the rear of the house and wrote ... nothing, basically nothing: the odd line sometimes, a fragment some days; whole poems once or twice convinced me at lunchtime that my gift had returned and as early as the same afternoon they would be revealed as complete rubbish. Once, over four days of fevered creativity, I definitely wrote something that was quite good. Unfortunately it had already been written a hundred years before by the Victorian sentimentalist Coventry Patmore.

Except now was different. In the last two months I hardly dared look at it, hardly dared contemplate it, but something real had come back. After thirty years of being mute a tiny feeble voice had begun to hesitantly speak its lines. I couldn't quite hear what it was saying but I sat each day at the desk in that middle bedroom, grandly named my study, which overlooked the asbestos sheds into which Sam crammed whatever animal it was most profitable for him to abuse that year, and listened closely to what it was trying to say to me.

And what it wanted to talk about was what had been in front of me all along, it was the view out of my study window. When I first arrived, sitting at the same desk and looking out of the same window, the view was of a patchwork of small fields, some edged with trees, one with a large pond in the middle and over to the far left of my vista was a very charming coppice of ancient broadleaf native trees. Now there was nothing except a vast single expanse of bright yellow rape. (Who named it that? Was it someone with a sense of humour?) Such vivid colour, the shade of an RAC man's protective jacket, always seemed out of place to me in the English countryside. Over the years the hedges had started disappearing, the pond was filled in and I could still remember the dreadful day they started the destruction of the coppice. So from diversity had come uniformity, from variety, monotony. It was the same when I went on one of my walks in the neighbourhood: years ago one guaranteed pleasure was hearing and seeing all the different birds — now with the hedges and lots of the trees gone you could walk for hours and hear only the odd wood pigeon. There seemed to be lots more paths back then too, so you could take a turning you'd never spotted before and go on not knowing where it would take you. Now all the local paths seemed to have been tarmaced and they all led to more or less identical housing developments. The realisation crept up on me that my journey from youth to age had been like that – from an abundance of options to none, from countless choices and the promise of an infinity of unknowns to a straight path leading inexorably to the last remaining unknown, the grave.

The poem taking shape in my head was to be an epic or perhaps more accurately a long meditative poem in the style of Wordsworth's 'The Prelude' or 'The Excursion'. I had toyed at first with giving it narrative form, giving my ideas the form of a story, but after some weeks wrestling with an everyman character and his life journey I realised that this was unspeakably banal. Further weeks passed while I re-read some of the greater epics, including Seamus Heaney's translation of 'Beowulf'. I must admit the reviews for this had made me wildly jealous: 'Heaney has chosen the plain prosaic yet subtly cadenced vernacular of his Northern Irish roots as the poetic voice into which he renders the Anglo-Saxon epic. He evokes the highly alliterative texture of Anglo-Saxon verse ... brilliant, genius' etc., etc. And then the bloody thing was a huge best-seller! A lot of those buying it seemed to think he had made the story up himself. I wondered whether I should just translate 'Le Chanson de Roland' into the clipped cadences of a Second World War officer and pass it off as a modern comment on war rather than attempting the great original task ahead of me. I calmed myself down by re-reading 'The Iliad', 'The Odyssey' and of course 'Paradise Lost'. This last seemed, given the subject matter of my poem, an obvious verse form to follow. But since one object of poetry is to arouse emotion, to induce a certain state of being, to enlarge the imagination into unvisited realms, the stanza form and threatening rhythms of Milton's epic did not fit my aim of rousing both melancholy and anger in my reader. The cadence and the emotional emphasis were not what I wanted.

Then, while tending my vegetables, I recalled that for Rimbaud a poem usually first took place in his mind through some folk tune running through his head. He was inspired first by the impelling sense of rhythm, and I wondered for a while if what I had to say could be said in a simple ballad form. I worked with this for a while but realised that it was not subtle enough for the whole poem, though I thought it might work for the middle section. The dawn of false hope. I realised I was being inevitably drawn to the rhymes and rhythms of the 'Divine Comedy'. A vague idea had stirred while I was reading Louis MacNeice's long poem 'Autumn Journal' written in tercets, but it was while reading Part II of T.S. Eliot's 'Little Gidding' that it struck me that, though unrhymed, the poem was also written in tercets, the form favoured by Dante. The pace is subtle but relentless – exactly the mood I wanted to convey in my own epic. Dantesque terzarima has stanzas connected by rhyme (aba bcb cdc . . . and so on), each canto of the 'Divine Comedy' ends with a quatrain linking with the preceding tercet thus: uvu vwvw.

I could use this to emphasise the inevitability of what has preceded and the compelling necessity of what is to come.

When he came he was wearing the most ridiculous clothes. As I said before it really was rather a bother that this Million Pound Poet was calling round at all but I couldn't turn him away.

Excessive politeness appears to be a common disease of the early twentieth century which, like polio and scarlet fever, has largely been eradicated from modern society but I am too old to have been inoculated. I could no more have turned him away than I could be intentionally cruel to a penguin.

Though I was sure that my poem was the real thing at last, progress was still painfully slow. I seemed to need the long hours of solitude that had once been torture to me to bring out the shy voice, it didn't seem to want to come out if there was somebody else in the room, indeed if there was even somebody coming to visit. A note or a scrambled thought was the yield of most days and that left me as drained and wan as if I was having chemotherapy. Now I hadn't even been able to achieve that modest output for fretting about my visitor.

I got back to the house only a few minutes before he came, even though I had spent all morning fussing about the tea spread.

At 7 a.m. Sam had rapped on my door and, looking over his shoulder like some drugs courier, he had wordlessly handed over a big box still warm from the ovens of an all-night Franco–Morrocan patisserie that he knew about, situated on the industrial zone of St Malo. Then at almost the appointed hour I felt it somehow wasn't quite enough, so with only ninety minutes to go I got on my moped and rode into the nearest place that still had shops, which was Towcester. There I planned to buy four of a special kind of small cheesecake that was made only at this one cake shop called Mr Pickwick's Olde Tea Shoppe at the northern end of town next to The Saracens Head Hotel, which was visited by Mr Pickwick in *The Pickwick Papers*. Cheesecakes that only came from one shop in all the world had to mean a pretty impressive tip-top teatime spread, even better than those that Pablo Neruda laid on. I was lucky, I got the last cakes. You had to get to the cake shop quite early and then be quite ruthless in the queue because they ran out of Towcester cheesecakes quite rapidly, always, I have to say, to the total bemusement and bewilderment of the cake-shop staff who were as shocked as anyone to find that there were suddenly no more of the special cheesecakes left. I had once suggested that they might like to consider the option of baking some more cheesecakes. The head woman just shouted, 'No, we're out! We're out of cheesecakes! Have a big Lardy cake or a Belgian Bun, why don't you!' Then all the staff had run into a back room where they hid till I had gone away.

There was still a frisson of fear amongst the serving girls whenever I went in there; they bunched together, static sparking off their nylon coats, and snickered like gazelles at a watering hole snuffing the air, knowing that a lion crouched nearby in the long grass. I also bought some crumpets and an unsliced cottage loaf.

My moped. You had to have some sort of vehicle in the country because there were no buses or trains or trams and everything was a very long walk from everything else, usually along roads down which caroomed giant grain lorries, their drivers steering with, at the most, one hand, their other being used to pin the mobile phone to their ear as they talked to God knows who about God knows what.

Everybody else in Lyttleton Strachey pretty much had a

car except one man at the council house end of the village who had four tanks, an armoured half track and a bren gun carrier crammed into his garden, though I don't suppose they were strictly to get about in. I occasionally got the feeling that even some of the farmyard animals had their own cars. I could have sworn I'd seen one of Sam's pigs at the wheel of an Alfa Romeo 156 on the back road into Banbury one day while I was out for a walk. However, on my modest income, my pension and the small cheques for some of my travel books on the canal architecture of Scotland which still sold well in Turkey, I couldn't afford a car so instead I had a small moped, made in the 1970s and called a Honda Melody. It was purple with flowers stencilled on the side and it had a basket on the front to put things in; it was aimed at the woman rider. I had bought the machine for a hundred pounds from a farmer over near Sulgrave. It had been his daughter's but she'd been mangled in a baling accident and didn't need it any more because she had no hands.

The Honda Melody was powered – though that wasn't really the right word giving, as it does, some image of puissance – by a 49cc two-stroke engine, so weak that going up the hill out of the next village, Woodford Halse, I had to stick my legs out and help it along with a strange man-on-the-moon walking motion. Sometimes I thought that one day if I ever again came into any money I would like to purchase a 125cc Peugeot Speedfight which all the motorbike magazines said was the best of the new style of fashionable scooters.

I buzzed back through the country lanes with half an hour to spare. I took off the brown leather American fighter pilot's jacket that I had won in a poker game in Kampala in '54, clambered out of the boiler suit which I wore over an old pair of corduroys from the Army and Navy Stores and a copy of a Daks shirt made for me by a Malay tailor in Singapore's Orchard Road. I had a wash in cold water and changed into the clothes I had chosen to wear for tea, a brown herringbone wool and mohair suit from Simpsons of Piccadilly, Turnbull and Asser Tattershall shirt, knitted green wool tie and Grendon brogues that I had polished the night before.

Then I stood looking out of the living-room window.

A green Landrover van coming from the north shot past the end of the drive, disappeared out of sight round the bend, then a few seconds later came back in reverse with that characteristic whine of a Landrover gearbox under strain. It went past the house again, then came forward, turned up the drive and rocked to a halt on the concrete hard standing, the rattle of its diesel engine subsiding in diminishing coughs.

The door opened and a long leg stretched out, on its foot was a Cuban heeled boot, the leg itself was wearing a tight black bell-bottomed trouser. The leg hovered for a second then was joined by its twin, together they slid the few inches to the concrete. That was it for a while, perhaps a minute, then the legs were joined by the rest of the man. He was tall, over six foot, long gingery hair parted in the middle fell to his shoulders, sharp features behind a long beard. He wore a frilly white shirt and a knee-length patent leather coat, in his hand a black malacca cane with a silver top; the only note that didn't fit in with the Aleister Crowley look was a hat of some grey material with writing on it, as might be worn by a young surfer or rapper.

My thinking had been that if things flagged between us we might be able go for a walk through the fields and along the green lanes to the knot of Scots pine trees that grew above where the railway used to run. But in his high-heeled boots and tight trousers, the Million Pound Poet had difficulty getting out of his own car and certainly would not be able to totter along the muddy paths or climb the several stiles on the way.

Having wriggled himself out from the Landrover, the Million Pound Poet stood and gazed at my house. He seemed disappointed; I imagine he'd expected a proper poet to live in something made of mellow creamy stone, probably with roses round the door. This looked like a council house, on the edge of a village certainly, with a big garden sure, but otherwise pretty much like some of the old ones in Daventry, from which direction he had come.

I stepped away from the window to fiddle with the tea things and waited for the doorbell to ring so that I could let him in. The first poet to visit me in thirty years.

I looked up from my teapot to see that he was standing in front of me, already in the room. My small living room that looked out both towards the village and Sam's house over the road at the front and Sam's fields at the back suddenly seemed too small. A quince bush that needed pruning tapped insistently on the back window as if wanting to be let into the party. I felt extremely awkward with him staring down at me and he didn't seem in any mood to start speaking.

So I said, 'Erm ... hello. I'm Hillary Wheat.'

'Yes, of course you are,' he replied, stretching out a languid ring-drenched hand, '... and I'm Emmanuel Porlock. Sorry to startle you, the door was open so I strolled in.'

I could have sworn that the door had been shut and locked.

'Well, do sit down.'

He folded himself into my best armchair and looked around him, smiling.

I said, 'Ah um ... I had a vague picture of you in my mind as a smaller thinner man with longer dark hair.'

It turned out, like Gypsy Rose Lees, that there were two Million Pound Poets. He waved his hand dismissively, 'You're confusing me with a ponce called Murray Lachlan

Young, a scribbler of doggerel, disappeared now, a nine-minute wonder, not the real deal like me.'

'So,' I asked, 'what does that mean exactly, a million pound poet?'

'Well,' he said. 'It refers to my record deal. It's a million pound record deal.'

I tried to surprise him. 'Ah I see. But I sometimes watch, I think it's called *Behind The Music*, on VH1 where they tell the stories of bands. And they often go on about how so many costs are built into record deals, by the record companies, that in reality what may seem like a million pounds turns out to be twenty pence in the artist's pocket.'

'Hillary, you are absolutely right, my friend. The Million Pound Poet tag is simply newspaper nonsense. We both know you don't get rich through poetry. That's not why we do it though, is it? It's a need, a compulsion, an irresistible drive. Not for the money, no.'

On a pine trunk that had been dragged into the centre of the room I had laid out tarte armandine, cherry clafoutie, beignettes, raghif alsiniyyeh, muhallabia, quince compote, Towcester cheesecakes, toast: wholemeal and white, strawberry jam, apple jam, coffee and tea.

'Do help yourself,' I said.

'Why thank you.' He leant forward, took a plate and piled it with six or seven cakes.

For a while we talked about my poetry. He told me

how much he liked 'Coventry Town Centre' and 'The Hospital for Imaginary Diseases', was more critical of 'Daddy Wouldn't Buy Me a Mau Mau', and didn't like 'Corrugated Irony'.

Then he embarked on the purpose of his visit. He tried to persuade me to re-enter public life. I felt a bit like Arnold Schwarzenegger in the film *Commando*, where the CIA try and lure him back into counter-terrorism from his life inhabiting a log cabin in the forests, chopping wood in his vest for a living. He said, 'We could go on tour together, there's quite a network of arts centres out there that put on poetry readings, the money's good too and we'd make a great package. Two ages of poetry or something I thought we could call it.'

I said, 'Well, this is all a bit sudden . . .'

He went on, perhaps thinking my horror was a negotiating tactic.

'And there's another thing, seventy per cent of poetry is bought by women, right? They like all that emotional truth, beauty, insights into the human condition and what have you. Some of them that come to readings on the circuit are very keen to sip at the fountain of beauty, if you know what I mean . . .'

I made some other polite evasion and as suddenly as the topic had come it went again. Instead he started to talk about the minutiae of his life in a big terraced house in Daventry.

He was one of those who used the names of people
that they are involved with, without explaining who
they are. So he would say, 'Bev says that I should
get a horse,' or 'Martika was making nasi goreng the
other night when . . .' or 'Lulu has her Urdu lessons
on a Tuesday night.' These three, Bev and Martika and
Lulu seemed to come up in a domestic capacity until
the notion began to dawn that Bev and Martika were
women and Lulu was the child of one of them and
Emmanuel, and that Bev and Martika and Emmanuel
lived together. Lived together like in a pamphlet that a
particularly left-wing local council might put out. 'Lulu
lives with Bev and Martika and Emmanuel. Bev sleeps
with Martika, Emmanuel sleeps with Bev, Martika sleeps
with Emmanuel.'

When I had been a famous poet this sort of thing, while
not unknown in Bohemia, always seemed short-lived and
generally ended in alcoholism, rancour and suicide. This
arrangement, however, from what he said seemed to be
a happy one. I said to him, 'I don't wish to probe but
do I take it that you live with these two women?'

'Yes, Hillary, I do indeed live with Bev and Martika.
I also have sex with Bev and Martika.'

'So how does that work out then?' seemed to have
come out of my mouth without me having anything to
do with it. Fortunately he was eager to expound.

'Well, I do it with each of them and they with each

237

other, though generally not the three of us together, with that you tend to spend all the time rearranging each other like St John's Ambulance practice dummies. Our daughter Lulu's cool about it, all our parents are cool about it apart from Martika's father and Bev's Auntie Glym who we suspect of a drive-by shooting at our house.'

'Even these days I must say it still seems a most unusual arrangement.'

'It shouldn't be, Hillary, it shouldn't be. It makes me crazy. There are so many more ways to live than are sanctioned in our society. Take all these couples, for instance, man and wife living in these little houses all around here,' he waved his arm about as if they were in the living room, '. . . wrapped up together all sterile and tight like a pair of pork chops on a supermarket freezer shelf. Say one of them fancies a bit of a change, a different hole, but they can't, can they? Not without lying, scurrying about like a rat or risking bringing their whole world crashing down. Then there's all this blame that goes around when somebody goes off somebody else. You don't get the blame if you go off prawn tikka masala, do you? People don't go around saying "Have you heard about Toby? The bastard's gone off prawn tikka masala! A friend of Pauline's saw him in town eating aloo gobi and pilau rice with a side order of brindal bhaji! The faithless bastard!" But you would go off prawn tikka masala if you were eating it every night, wouldn't you?'

He leant forward and helped himself to some tarte armandine and a Towcester cheesecake.

'Or take all these single women that there are, lovely girls all about, going without love from one year to the next because, well we know don't we, you and me Hillary, that the single available men out there are, to put it kindly, sub-human, knuckle-dragging mutants with radioactive hair growing out of their arseholes. You wouldn't even want Mrs Thatcher to have sex with one of them would you? So to take on two or three of them, and for them to take on each other, it makes perfect sense. Hillary, what I say and do, is if we live in looser ... tribes if you will, these problems of modern society simply fade away, we spread out the load ... companionship, sex, protection, become available to everyone, not just a lucky few. I do not believe we are meant to live alone, my friend. God created us to live in a tribe then man told us to live in Milton Keynes. It is all wrong, Hillary.'

All that followed in subsequent months sprang from this conversation. I had always lived my life according to Flaubert's dictum: 'Be regular and orderly in your life like a bourgeois, so that you may be violent and original in your work.' It was all that sustained me through my thirty years of self-imposed exile for the crime of zoolifting. Good manners, politeness, moderation, the consolations of conventional morality, these were my tranquillisers. Now it occurred to me, ludicrously, for the first time at the age of seventy-two: 'What if I was wrong, what if I was mistaken in the way I have chosen to carry on my life?' That somebody could live out such a fantasy of perfection as Porlock lived, seemed to shake something loose in me that I had always attempted to ignore. I had maintained to myself that there was a price to pay for immorality, there had to be, hadn't there? But was it simply some idea I had developed when I was a schoolboy and had never revised? I had made myself pay it. I had imagined the gods to be some kind of ticket inspector who would always know if you hadn't paid your fare, and if you hadn't would inflict a substantial fine. But when I listened to commuters talking in the pub they said that these days the ticket inspector rarely, if ever, put in an appearance.

In this village there were so many who did terrible things and never seemed to give it a second thought. In London I had never known anybody who had ever done anything that you would call really bad. Poets, painters, actors, critics, the worst you could say was that one of them might have written an occasional overly waspish review or that another opted for the easy syllogism when a few extra minutes' deliberation might have brought out a more profound and winning argument. But how they suffered, my former friends, for even these minor transgressions! The agonies of doubt and self-loathing, the suicide attempts, the grabbing at drink or psychiatrists or other men's wives, in order to ease the terrible mental pain. None of them had ever crushed a cat's spine for a living, nonetheless they twisted and toiled and sweated in their beds at night, raked by remorse and guilt. Yet in this village, and one can only assume in all these villages about, there were Sams and his kindred whose day's work might involve the tearing up of hedgerows or the barbed wiring of ancient footpaths, the spreading of hormones or the jabbing of antibiotics. Then there were those such as Miles Godmanchester who was a senior employee at Daventry Life Sciences which had taken over the stately home on the bend of the road north of Lyttleton Strachey. At this animal Lubyanka all kinds of experiments were carried out on poor trapped beasts, the vast, vast, majority of these experiments pointless and all of them cruel beyond belief. Surplus rabbits are burnt alive in that place. Yet Miles Godmanchester clearly enjoyed his work, was popular and well-liked, nobody ignored him in the pub, nobody said when he came in, 'Hello Miles, had a good day stabbing cats?' At night in bed, I imagined, he woke for a second, smiled and turned over with a happy, contented sigh.

The Million Pound Poet said, 'No, of course you don't want to come on tour with me right this minute, you need all your time to be here because you're writing again, aren't you?'

I don't understand how he could have known that.

241

*　　*　　*

Emmanuel Porlock went after it was dark, leaving me disturbed and unable to work.

On the doorstep as we were saying our goodbyes he took a cheap Nokia, pay as you go, mobile phone from his pocket and held it out to me on the palm of his hand.

'You see this?' he said. 'Do you know what this is? It's a telephone, yes it is. But it's not connected with wires or anything, it's a mobile telephone that I can phone people up with anywhere in the world, walking about or driving in my car or anywhere.'

'Yes,' I replied feeling confused, 'a mobile phone, nearly everybody's got one.'

'Oh I don't think so,' he said, climbed into his green Landrover and drove off at speed without turning on his lights.

I sat at my desk for the next two days unable to write a word. My mind filled with Emmanuel and Bev and Martika. Bev I cast as WPC Lauren Haggeston, a character on a television police show that I watched regularly and which was called *The Job*. Some days, if you wished to, it was possible to watch two hours of *The Job* since UK Gold, a re-runs channel, would transmit two thirty-minute episodes from a couple of years back in the mornings, then ITV would show a brand-new, one-hour episode in the evening. Recently the producers of *The Job* had culled a lot of the crumpled real police-looking actors in favour of much prettier ones, WPC Lauren Haggeston was one of the new intake, being extremely thin but still with large breasts. I was interested to observe that the actress who played WPC Lauren Haggeston had actually appeared three years previously in the same show but on that occasion she was playing a crack dealer with a boyfriend in the Ukrainian mafia. This happened a lot on *The Job*: actors who were cast in the leading roles as police men and police women had almost always turned up earlier as criminals. I sometimes wondered whether the producers were making some subtle point about the moral duality of the police who must always carry a whiff of corruption about them; but I suppose it was just that the casting people simply liked to work with those they had already met and had found to be professional. In my fantasies of a life filled with sex the part of Martika was played by my dead second wife.

There's that old joke: a footballer is told by his manager, 'Play badly and I'll pull you off at half time', 'Oh cheers, boss,' says the footballer, 'at my last club we only got a cup of tea and an orange.' I was pulling myself off and it was nearly full time.

On the third day after Emmanuel Porlock the Million Pound Poet's visit, I was starting to get back into thinking about maybe getting an idea about starting to work on my poem, when the telephone rang. It was him, Porlock, though he was one of those people who never say who they are on the telephone. His first words to me were, 'Have you got my hat?' No greeting, nothing, very impolite really.

'Who is this, please?'

'Have you got my hat?'

'Hello, Emmanuel,' I said.

'Have you got my hat?' he repeated. 'The hat I was wearing when I came to see you, the grey hat, the Mau Mau hat.'

'The Mau Mau hat?'

'Yes,' exasperated. 'It's a make of hat. Mau Mau, the name's on the front. I was wearing it when I came to your house and now I can't find it. I remember I had it on when I was driving to your house but I don't remember if I was wearing it on the way back.'

I tried to recall whether he'd been wearing it on the doorstep when he'd shown me his mobile phone in the dark. 'Well, I can't remember but I'll have a look for it.'

'Yes, you do that now,' and he rang off. We had only been in the living room and the hall so I turned up all the cushions but it wasn't there. I looked behind the couch and the TV but it wasn't there either. It wasn't anywhere in my house. Fifteen minutes later and the phone rang again.

'Did you find it?'

'No I'm afraid not, I—'

'Shit, fuck, I've got to have a Mau Mau hat. I can't function without a Mau Mau hat. You'll have to go up to London to get me another one. There's nothing else for it. There's a retro hat shop in Berwick Street Market that might just have one.'

'I'm not sure I can drop everything and . . . go up to London . . . my poem . . .'

He started shouting, 'I fucking lost it at your house! You're responsible. You've got it somewhere or you've thrown it out, or you've given it to the boy scouts and you can't remember because your fucking mind is going . . .' There was a pause when I thought he was considering that he had gone too far. Then, 'You're not wearing it, are you?'

'Of course I'm not wearing it.'

'Alright then. I'll ring you the day after tomorrow to find out how you got on in London.' And he put the phone down.

When he'd said he knew I was writing poetry again it gave me an electric shock as if I was being worked over with a defibrillator by an untrained shop assistant in a mall.

'How could you know that?' I asked.

'Oh you've a certain look about you, you know, like a lovely single girl who's getting shagged regularly, after

245

not getting it for a long time. So how does it feel after all this time to be doing it again? Quite a relief, I should think. I'm sure, if you're anything like me, your entire sense of yourself must be tied up with your writing. I mean what are you, Hillary Wheat, without it? Another roly-poly old man in an out-of-date suit. It must have been terribly painful to be blocked out for all those years. I wonder if there's a muse of the writers' block, a sort of anti-muse who descends and uninspires the struggling artist. I mean if there are muses why aren't there un-muses? That would be quite a thing, wouldn't it? I bet you thought when you found you couldn't write that there are loads of other things you could do, mountain climb or do voluntary service in Kenya or learn yoga but you don't do anything, do you? It's simply thirty years down the gurgler really, isn't it?'

I said a trifle snippily, which made me feel immediately guilty, 'You seem to know a lot about it . . . being unable to write, that is.'

'Guesswork, empathy only, I'm glad to say. No, I've always been particularly fecund in the writing department. Can't bloody stop that's more my problem.'

'Well, that is nice,' I said. 'For me it's still painfully slow, only the themes are sketched in, the detailed work is still to come . . . and I don't . . . there doesn't feel like there is much time. I don't know . . . how much time I have left to finish it.'

He laughed so much he spat clafoutie across the room. 'Oh fuck off, Hillary. You are one very chipper old man. Don't try and play the "look at me, I'm a sad old man approaching death" card just yet.'

True. You might have thought that I would at least get on with the villagers of my own age, reminiscing about the war and such and such but I seemed to inflame my contemporaries even more than I annoyed the younger set. My major crime with the senior crowd was that there was nothing wrong with me. While they aged and shrank and stiffened up and died around me, while remorseless diseases left them crapping in plastic bags and rolling around on ignominious little electric carts, I stayed more or less the same. Fit and healthy and spry; slightly greyer, that is all. I sometimes wondered if somehow the suspension of my output had frozen me at the age I was when I left London. I wondered if when I started writing again I would truly start to age and become subject to all the terrible infirmities. It was a price I would happily pay.

It occurs to me that you might have the idea that my poem, my opus, was no good. This had been my worry too, was it just a longer drawn out version of the delusions I had had before? There was only one person I still knew whose opinion I could trust: Paul Caspari, my old publisher, father of the late Blink. Though now ninety years old he was still functional. Like me he had been in a kind of suspension and it was the death of his son that had liberated him, giving him again a seat on the board of Caspari and Millipede, now independent once more after being bought and sold a hundred times, back in the building they had occupied thirty years ago, with the same name after a hundred aliases and the same letterhead after fifty corporate re-designs. What had been the point of all that upset if it only brought them back to the same place? What was the point of driving me mad?

After I sent him such fragments as existed of my poem, plus my plans for the rest, he replied in a letter almost by return of post.

Dear Hillary,

How marvellous to hear from you after all this time and to learn that you have begun to write seriously again. My pleasure at this news turned to extreme excitement when I read the opening stanzas and projected plan of your great poem. I do not want to prevaricate in any way: I think you are working on a masterpiece. You will, with this completed poem, claim your place at the forefront of twentieth century poetry. Indeed, you will stake a claim to be regarded as one of the greats of the twenty-first century also. Janus-like your work looks back to our great tradition and also forward with the yet untried face of the future of poetry in English. I do not know if I would immediately have recognised the work as yours as you seem to cloak your individual personality behind a new voice. This voice you are employing strikes me as absolutely right: so far from mediating between the poet and his experience, it serves instead as a way of lifting that experience to a new power. By means of it each item of sensuously registered and remembered experience becomes, whilst keeping its singular integrity, a sign and manifestation of an energy abroad in the waking world.

How we need this energy and vision now!

I have always thought of you as one of the most under-rated poets of recent times: how wonderful to have this opinion vindicated in what will be far and away your most important contribution to literature.

If I can help in any way with comments or discussions I should be honoured to be asked. I do not intend to get in touch with you in the near future as I do not want to distract you for a moment from your great enterprise, but I hope you will have the time to let me have any new verses as you complete them.

We would certainly be happy and honoured to publish your piece, perhaps also a re-issue of your older pieces . . .

*   *   *

That would have to wait though. The day after my phone conversation with the Million Pound Poet I rode my Honda Melody to the railway station at Banbury and parked it in the motorcycle bay, squeezing it between a 900cc Triumph Speed Triple and a 200mph Yamaha Yakabuza. I went up to the ticket booth and said to the man behind the plexiglass, as I would have said a long time ago, on the last occasion when I went up to town, 'I'd like a first class return to London, please.'

Without expression he printed out the ticket in a machine and slid it under the window at me. 'That'll be one hundred and seventy-five pounds, please,' he said.

'How much?' I gasped.

'One hundred and seventy-five pounds, please. Standard first class return, I'm surprised you asked for it. Nobody buys them any more. See, what you should have bought was an Off Peak City Saver or perhaps a Multi Zone Access Pack.'

'I'm terribly sorry but I don't have a hundred and seventy-five pounds with me.'

He didn't seem surprised. 'No, well there aren't any first class seats on the train anyway.'

He tore the ticket up and printed out another. 'Senior Citizen's Standard Class Fast-track Rail Rover? Twenty-two pounds?'

'I'll take it,' I said.

A train came in fifteen minutes later. When I had first

come to the country I would still make the occasional disastrous trip back up to town. Then the trains were a uniform blue and grey, with the gruesome BR logo on the side. Now they weren't a uniform anything, seeming to be composed of the rolling stock of five different companies from a couple of different countries. Nevertheless I boarded with no trouble and found a seat. We gibbered our way south at only about half the pace I remembered from thirty years ago.

Our train snailed into the suburbs of London and the tracks spread out until they ran like silver streams on each side of us. In a meshed compound I saw Eurostar trains racked side by side, like a display of some imagined near future in a science museum. After that, as if in deliberate contrast, we came upon a district of early Victorian terraces, each backyard a bomb atrocity of disinterred, unidentifiable shards of wood, plastic, metal and decaying vegetable matter. Next there was a sky-darkening twist of concrete flyovers serpenting and intertwining above us, London underground tube stations now mixing with the suburban lines. Suddenly our train shook to a halt, waited for a few minutes throbbing quietly to itself, then crept on even more slowly. Out of the window I saw on the farthest track to us a whole train lying on its side, flame and black smoke only just starting to flick and lick out of the rends in its torn lemon-yellow metal. Several bodies hung from the cracked window frames. One carriage was still the right way up and entirely intact: on the inside passengers beat with their fists on the window glass, mouthing desperate pleas at us as we slid by. In the far, far distance there was the wail of fire engines stuck in unyielding traffic.

A man in a suit with his feet up on the seats opposite me glanced at the wreck, took out his mobile phone and dialled. 'Hi, it's me,' he said, 'yeah, if you're thinking of coming into town today I'd take the car, there's a Hyundai Cotswold Turbo gone off at Larkmead Junction ... Ump ... coupla or five dead at least, I'd say. Yeah, alright, see you this evening ... Bye.'

The grand London terminus that I remembered was now a shopping mall with a big roof and trains in one self-effacing corner. Bumped and swerving I walked out into the shriek of traffic.

Unlike the trains, the bus that I caught was exactly the same as it would have been thirty years ago, apart from the price of the fare, that is.

London did not seem so much changed, I suppose if you watch a lot of television you are kept up with the metamorphoses in the capital, and anyway we've got a Starbucks in Banbury now.

I found the retro hat shop in Berwick Street Market easily enough, the pattern of the streets had not changed at all. It was called Girl/Boy/Whatever and apart from hats of the past it seemed to sell fake fur-covered hand cuffs, whips and patent leather bikinis for men and women. I went inside.

Behind the counter was a most lovely girl of perhaps thirty years of age. She wore a transparent muslin shirt and tight black leather shorts. A y-shaped chain was connected to each of her breasts by rings through her nipples, the slender chain joined above the rib cage before disappearing underneath the waist band of her shorts presumably to end between her legs.

Yet despite the way she was dressed and despite the scowl on her face, somehow her decency shone out of her, somehow I was certain here was a big kind girl, clearly a kind girl, an honest girl. In a previous age, I reflected, she might have been a servant in a big house or a stenographer riding the tram to work in a cheap two-piece suit and cloche hat. Now she was serving in a shop in Soho with a chain clipped to her cunt.

I approached the counter. I suppose I must have presented an odd sight in that shop: several of the items I was wearing had been present at the fateful meeting with Blink all those years ago. The silver cufflinks from Aspreys, the cashmere navy-blue overcoat, my father's old Smiths watch. Not present at that lunch in the past were the white Egyptian cotton shirt from Turnbull and Asser, the dark-blue silk tie, the white crepe de Chine monogrammed handkerchief, or the forty-five-year-old

The Dog Catcher

double-breasted pin-stripe suit, teamed with a pair of black brogues that I had bought from Shoe Express in Northampton the year before for nineteen pounds and ninety-nine pence. In deference to the fact that we were now in the twenty-first century I had decided not to wear a hat.

'Excuse me,' I said to the serving girl, 'I was wondering whether you have a grey Mau Mau hat in stock?'

'Mau Mau?' she said. 'Mau Mau. They haven't made those for years. We do get a few in but not at the moment.'

'Oh,' I said, disappointment settling on me, 'I was hoping you'd have one, I've a . . . friend who's desperate. I don't know what to do. Can you perhaps . . . um . . . suggest another retro hat shop?'

She looked a little concerned at my agitation but replied, 'I can't fink of another place, no.'

'I don't know what to do, I live in a little village in Northamptonshire, this is the first time I've come up to town in decades . . .'

'Sorry.'

As she raised her arms in a shrug the sleeves of her muslin top fell back to the elbow. I saw that almost the whole length of both her arms were covered in distinctive small puncture marks and longer red weals. Some of the cuts were old and almost shadows but others, around her wrists especially, were fresh and deep and rimmed with dried blood. I recognised the wounds immediately, they were familiar to me.

'Those marks on your arms,' I said.

'Yeah?' she replied looking sullenly at me with lowered eyes, instinctively tugging on the thin transparent material of her sleeve to cover the scars. I dropped my voice to show that I understood the situation she was in, and looked her directly in the face.

'You've . . .' I paused, 'you've . . . got a cat haven't you?'

She looked embarrassed for a second then spoke in a smaller voice.

'Yeah,' she said again, trying to remain cool but the light of enthusiasm fired up in her brown eyes.

'What's its name?' I asked.

'He's called Adrian,' she said, excited now, speaking quickly, her voice full of remembered love. 'He's got this squeaky toy on a string that he likes to play with, he likes me to dangle it over him but sometimes he gets carried away and claws my arm . . . and, well, sometimes he claws my arm because he's hungry and sometimes he just claws my arm because he wants to. It's their nature, though, isn't it? You got a cat?'

'Not now. In my time, many, yes.' I sighed and was silent for a second before continuing. 'It's one of the terrible sadnesses of ageing, how many of them you outlive; in the end it becomes too hard. They have such

255

short lives, while ours seem so long, it's like having a succession of children with rare diseases that you know are going to polish them off in ten, fifteen years . . .'

'Yeah,' she said, 'but what about the pleasure they give, the companionship, the company, simply having another heartbeat about the house.'

'Oh I know, I know and I miss it terribly. But over the years losing each cat becomes harder and harder. It's a sort of cumulative thing and finally there comes a time when one particular cat dies and you realise that all the pleasure they have given you does not compensate for the terrible pain their death causes. You realise that, bleak and miserable as it may be, you are still going to be marginally better off without another cat – you will have no pleasure but at least you won't suffer.'

Though I meant all that I was saying there was also an element of calculation in it. I knew nobody else in London, or anywhere else for that matter, who might be familiar with the retro hat world and also . . . I don't know what I thought I was doing flirting with a girl forty years younger than me, but I was. I suppose it was something to do with what the Million Pound Poet had told me about him living with two women. If he could do that why couldn't I at least flirt with a young attractive woman? Anything seemed possible. Actually picking her up, of course, that didn't really seem possible. After all what I would do with her once I had picked her up?

'Oh you know, better to have loved and lost and all that . . .' she said, idly flicking at the silver ring that went through her navel and via which the chain ran on its way to the heart of darkness.

'Not after you've lost the fifteenth pet . . .' I said. 'I've measured out my life in Pollies and Princes and Bingos . . .'

'T.S. Eliot, innit?'

'Sort of.'

'He wrote a lot of poems about cats, didn't he?'

'Yes indeed, though that was my feline adaptation of "The Waste Land". Do you like poetry?' I asked her.

'Only if it's about cats.'

'Um . . .'

'No, I'm only joking with you. I like some stuff from like the last hundred years. Owen, Auden, MacNeice, Betjeman, John Hegley. Before that I don't get it.'

I hadn't expected any mention of me but it was still depressing when I didn't get it. I said, 'There's poems about cats before then. Thomas Gray's "Ode on the Death of a Favourite Cat Drowned in a Tub of Goldfishes" springs to mind.'

She thought about it. 'Nawww. Sounds depressing.' Then she said, 'Look do you really, really have to have a Mau Mau hat?'

I said, 'There's a fellow who feels he really, really has to have one, yes.'

'Well, there's a stall at Camden Market on Sundays, guy I know who might have one. I could take you there tomorrow if you want . . . I was going to go up there anyway, so it's no big thing.'

'Yes alright, that would be terrific. Where shall we meet?'

'Outside Camden Town tube at one?'

'Smashing. What's your name?'

'Mercy, Mercy Rush. What's yours?'

'Hillary Wheat.'

'See you at one tomorrow, Hillary.'

'See you at one, Mercy.'

I felt silly with excitement and had walked half-way back to the station before I came around. I really needed to talk myself down from this ledge of giddiness; she was only being kind, she'd show me the stall then leave me, she'd invite me to a tango club where we'd . . . stop it, stop it, you silly old man.

Which left me with a choice. What was I going to do for the rest of the day? I supposed I could get back to Northamptonshire tonight easy enough. A newspaper hoarding saved me the trouble of considering that option: 'Horrendous Rail Crash, Services Disrupted', it shouted with glee. So I was stuck up in town on a Saturday evening.

Saturday evening has always seemed to me to be the

most melancholy time to be alone in a strange town. Everybody else seems to be going home to have a bath before they attend huge dinners with their laughing, adoring families as you stand in the rain outside their houses looking through the windows into their fire-lit happiness.

Fortunately I had kept on paying the fifty pounds a year it took to be a country member of the Kensington Arts Club so I had a bed for the night and somewhere to eat my dinner at the large round table they kept for members who were dining on their own. I was glad to see that the Kensington Arts was still a bastion of disreputable elderly behaviour with no concession made to the modern puritanism. In the bar, hung from floor to ceiling with proper paintings of things and people and animals in gilded frames, everybody smoked and many who were my age or older were dazzlingly drunk. An old man was telling a story about golf which required him to roll about on the floor, a good-looking woman of forty with long dark hair took her top and bra off then danced on the mini grand piano while a man with an eye patch and a Van Dyke beard played jellyroll jazz, another older woman bit me on the arm while I was at the bar getting a drink at pub prices.

Say what you like about crack dealers they are not ageist: I was offered rock three times in the twenty minutes I stood outside Camden Town tube station waiting for Mercy. When I had last seen Camden Town it was a district of glum Irish drinking holes, black canals, economy cash butchers, Shirley Conran and Dr Jonathan Miller. Now it was as if all the various young peoples of the world had decided to come to this place in order to wear each other's clothes and to talk in each other's languages. Thus I saw what I took to be Nepalese boys in the garb of urban American blacks talking to each other in Spanish, four Japanese girls wearing Andean headgear yabbering to each other in Magreb Arabic, Saree-covered Tolchucks conversing in Cantonese, Malay-speaking Rastafarians, Portuguese-giggling Sikhs, English-speaking Hindu Swedes, Urdu-chattering Nigerian Ortho-dox Rabbis.

I thought she wasn't coming, half wanted her not to come; hope is a harder thing to cope with at my age than prostate cancer. At least you're expecting pros-tate cancer.

Then she was in front of me, smiling, better, more beautiful by far than I remembered her. I'd forgotten how tall she was, taller than me by nearly a foot. I felt ridiculous.

'Hiya,' she said. 'Sorry I'm a bit late. Shall we find this stall then?' She linked her arm through mine and steered me through the crowds. 'It's a funny thing,' she said. 'I have to warn you about this hat stall . . . and women . . . there's something about a hat stall that sends women into erotic spasms. I don't know what it is. This bloke who runs the stall, he operates it at a loss simply because of the pussy he gets. Here check it.'

We had come to a Soweto of stalls crammed just before the bridge that spanned the old Grand Union Canal. One of those that abutted the street was the hat stall and as Mercy had warned, several women stood writhing beside it as they tried on each hat and looked at themselves in the mirror. One teenage Finn unconsciously rubbed her groin against a corner of the table. When the man who ran the stall reached out and adjusted their hats, tilting them one way or the other, visible shivers ran through the women and they let out low moans of ecstasy. Mercy led me over to the stall. 'Hiya, Guy,' she said to the man behind it, then leant across the hats and kissed him on the lips. An audible growling rose from the other women.

To regain the focus one stuck a Cornish fisherman's cap, done in patent leather with spikes sticking out of it, on her head and querulously whined, 'Guy, Guy, does this suit me, would it go with a rubber mini-skirt, Guy? And a red leather bustier, would it, Guy, would it?'

But Guy was gazing steadily at Mercy, peripherally conscious of the other woman but deliberately ignoring her. 'Hi, Mercy,' he said. 'How are you?'

'Oh you know,' she replied then she turned to me. 'Guy, this is Hillary, he's desperate to find a grey Mau Mau hat, mid-90s I'd say, you got one?'

I shook hands with Guy who said, looking me up and down, 'It won't go with that Savile Row suit, homeboy.'

'It's for a friend,' I replied.

'Right.'

He bent down under the table and emerged some seconds later with a hat identical, as far as I could tell, to the one the Million Pound Poet had been wearing. 'Here we are, I only bought this a couple of days ago off some bloke in the Midlands. They're quite a big collectors' item, you know, early Nineties Mau Mau hats. It'll cost you sixty quid.'

'Oh come on, Guy!' Mercy said. 'He can't afford that. Sixty squid for a hat.'

For an instant a look of absolute hatred passed across Guy's face. 'I've done you enough . . .' he began to say, then the fight went out of him. 'OK, thirty, that's what I paid for it.'

'You're a doll,' said Mercy and leant across the stall again, crushing several chapeaux as she hugged him and licked his ear. I paid over the thirty pounds, Mercy flattened some more stock saying goodbye to Guy, then she took my arm again and we walked off as the tide of clamouring womanhood closed in around him.

When you have fought bush warfare you develop an instinct for malevolent eyes and I could feel Guy staring after us with baking anger, which in turn made me feel inordinately pleased that I was taking her away from him.

'You didn't say you were a poet,' she said.

'No.'

'So I read one of your poems last night in an anthology.'

'Which one?'

'"The Cat's Pyjamas".'

I said, 'Are you still a poet if you haven't written anything for thirty years?'

'I guess ... if you haven't done anything else. Have you done anything else?'

'Not a thing,' I said and couldn't help a sigh escaping from me, like a lilo being sat on by a fat man.

'How sad,' she sounded genuinely upset. 'So you've written nothing for thirty years? And you're not going to start again or anything? You've not started again?'

I felt a strange reluctance to talk about whether I was writing again or not, on that day it seemed a distant and infinitely tedious thing. Apart from anything else her sympathy had given me a tingle in my groin that I wanted more of.

'If you don't mind I'd rather not talk about it,' I said in a sad voice.

'Sure, no problem, it's off the agenda.' She considered for a moment. 'You want to go and get some lunch?'

'Certainly,' I replied. 'Where?'

'I dunno . . .' We were in a backstreet, uncertainty seemed to grip her. 'If you don't want lunch, maybe if you want to get the train home instead . . .'

It was slipping away, if I didn't find a place for lunch it would end there. Looking desperately around I suddenly saw a familiar doorway. It was the same basement place Blink had taken me to all those years ago. 'Here's a good place,' I blabbed, 'they do good food here.' Before she could speak I steered her through the doorway and down the stairs.

For those in the basement the First World War was over and it had been won by Kenyan Asians.

As soon as I stepped into the dining room the smells of Rahman's Café in Nairobi forty-seven years ago were all around me. We sat down at a plain pine table, stainless steel water jug and cups already present, a young man brought us plastic-covered menus.

'What sort of food is this?' she asked.

'They're Asians from Kenya.'

'Doesn't that make them Africans then?'

'Not as far as the Africans were concerned.'

'Will you order for me? I'm a vegetarian. I don't eat meat or fish.'

'I'm sure it won't be a problem.'

At Rahman's the others in my regiment had ordered hideous beef dinners of roast camel and gravy that had come from a tree, boiled puddings composed of various naturally occurring poisons and 'fried breakfast meats with a egg', which was a crocodile mother-and-child reunion. I on the other hand had ostentatiously ordered in Swahili: mogo, otherwise known as cassava, served with a tamarind chutney, brinjal curry, karahi karela, tarka dhal and rotis to show my cosmopolitanism. I ordered the same now, again in Swahili and I was twenty-five again.

Mercy said, 'Can I tell you what I did last night?'

'Of course.'

Mercy locked the shop up at six and collected her Piaggio Velocoraptor 125cc scooter from the motorbike bay in Great Marlborough Street, then she rode to a house in Hackney, East London, parked over the road and stood watching the doorway of the house, hidden in the entrance of a derelict shop directly opposite. About an hour and a half later a man came out of the house accompanied by a girl of about twenty-five. The man looked a little older than the girl, was good-looking and fit. The couple paused on the step to kiss, the man sliding his hands down the back of the girl's jeans. They broke apart enough to walk twined up in each other to the man's gas engineers' van parked at the pavement. They then drove off.

Mercy waited for fifteen minutes then went across to the house and opened the front door with a key. Once in the hall she let herself into the ground-floor flat, inside

she did not turn on a light but instead felt her way along
to the living room which was lit by the orange frazzle of
a streetlamp in the road outside.

The room was tastefully furnished with chrome and
leather furniture, framed movie posters on the walls
and racks and racks of vinyl records in bleached wood
cabinets. On a table there was a turntable and amplifier,
the British-made sort that only have one on/off switch
and a simple big volume knob yet cost several thousand
pounds to buy. Mercy filled a kettle from a tap in the
kitchen then returned to the living room and poured tepid
water down the back of the amplifier, she opened a tin
of cream of mushroom soup and tipped that over the
turntable. In the bedroom a number of Paul Smith suits
were hanging in a closet; Mercy decanted the contents
of several cans of Thai Style Vegetables into the pockets
of these suits then dribbled Diet Coke down their inner
linings. After that she let herself out, got on her scooter
and rode home.

Round about eleven o'clock she was sitting on her couch
flipping through an anthology of twentieth-century poetry
when the phone rang.

'Hello, Kitten,' said a man's voice.

'Hello, Dad,' she said, 'how's it going?'

'Fucking terrible! Your mad cow of a stepmother's
broken into my place again and vandalised all my
fucking stuff!'

'How do you know it was her?'

'Who else would it fucking be? Whoever did it had a key, so that pretty much narrows it down.'

'Does it? How many hundred women out there have your key?'

'Not that many.'

'Really? What did she do anyway?'

'Poured soup all over my Nazuku.'

'Painful.'

'Don't take the piss, you know you're the only one I can talk to, Kitten, about this stuff.'

'Yeah, sorry ... So how's everything going with the new one, what's her name, Apricot?'

'Oh yeah, she's great. I think she could definitely be your new mum. Dirty little baggage as well, she sucked me off at the traffic lights in my van last night ...'

'Wow ...'

'Yeah, she's brilliant. We're going to a leather fetish all-nighter in a minute, up at The Cross, you wanna come?'

'Naww, I fink I'm staying in tonight.'

'Sure?'

'Yeah.'

'OK, see ya, Kitten.'

'Bye, Dad.'

Then Mercy said to me, 'Can I ask you something?'

'Of course.'

'Can I come and visit you in the country? Next weekend? I'm sick of this town.'

'Of course you can.'

After that we talked about cats and where she went to school and things like that, then it seemed the natural time to part since there was going to be next weekend.

Outside in the street, 'Great, well then I'll see you next weekend.' She kissed me on the lips and hugged me, then stood back and I walked to the tube station.

I tried to get back to working on my poem when I returned to Lyttleton Strachey but my mind would not fix on it, I could think of little else other than Mercy's upcoming visit.

I was also waiting for Porlock to phone about his hat but he didn't and I didn't have a phone number or an address for him which preyed on my mind as well. What I thought about most was how I would entertain Mercy over the coming weekend. One thing I intended to do was to impress her with a cornucopia of vegetables. I had my own extensive vegetable patch at the top of my field, but I had been neglecting it recently. I needed to get it in good order if it was going to produce a cornucopia of vegetables. Never mind, I had an established asparagus bed so I would be able to cut asparagus for our meals, also I could harvest early lettuce, broccoli and radishes, leeks and spring cabbages, winter cauliflower and winter spinach. Plus turnip tops, don't forget turnip tops.

My house had come with a quarter-acre paddock across the lane running between the church graveyard and one of Sam's fields with some of his concentration-camp sheds in it. Sam had made numerous attempts to get his hands on this triangle of land including hiring some bogus army officers who tried to requisition it for a supposed firing range. My vegetable patch was at the far end of this paddock.

On the Wednesday of the week before Mercy came I was in the field planting out late summer cabbages and purple-sprouting broccoli. Next I was planning to remove any rhubarb flowers, which you have to do as soon as they appear, when I saw Bateman coming up the lane. He waved to me and vaulted the gate into the field. This day Bateman was wearing an off-the-shoulder, knee-length Laura Ashley dress, black Lewis Leathers motorbike jacket and army boots with knee-length black socks. 'Hey, Professor!' he shouted to me. I put my trowel down, knowing I had finished gardening for some time. Bateman had come for a talk.

He liked talking to me, more or less always about the same thing. People I had killed. I had pointed out on more than one occasion that the people I had killed had been black people such as himself but he didn't care, he said he was Antiguan not African so it didn't matter.

'Hello, Bateman,' I said. He sprawled down on the

grass next to me, his skirt riding up over his thumping muscled black thighs.

'Professor . . . I just thinkin' I'd come over an' give you a chance to do some of your war reminiscin' . . .'

I said, 'I don't particularly want to do any reminiscing about my war. I never have.'

'Course you do, all you old ones love the war reminiscin'. Goin' on about Churchill an' Hitler an' Elvis an' all that.'

'Tell the truth, you like hearing about it.'

'No way, man, I'm being social servicin' is all . . .' he tried a pause but couldn't hold it, his impatience getting in the way, '. . . so get on with it.'

'Oh alright.' I gave in as I always did. 'What you have to remember about Kenya,' I said, 'was that while the rest of the British Empire was settled by those from all classes, more of those in Kenya came from the upper classes. They were famous before the war for the life they led.'

Eagerly he asked, 'What sort of life?'

'Drink, fast cars, hunting, extra-marital affairs, sexual perversion.'

'Brilliant . . . and nice weather too, innit?'

'Yes and nice weather too. I don't know why but somehow I always had the feeling the way the settlers carried on led to the Mau Mau uprising, after all it didn't happen like that anywhere else in Africa, sort of brought it on themselves, a price to pay for their decadence . . .'

'Why, they was just enjoyin' theirselves.'

'Maybe. The whole thing's almost forgotten about now . . . odd, really, when you think about it. The Mau Mau starts out as a bloody insurrection and ends up as a hat.'

'A hat, what about a hat?'

'Nothing, sorry . . . You should have seen the settlers' houses, ridiculous Cheshire wooden villas they were, set in acres of flame trees. In 1953 the Africans rose up. They called themselves the Mau Mau. I remember in my first week there, we were called to a farm. A family named Barlow . . . the son was in the yard . . . they'd hacked him with pangas . . .'

'That's like a machete, right?'

'Right, yes, like a machete. He glistened, the son . . . like that sauce they put on spare ribs at the Chinese takeaway . . . purple and deep red . . . His parents were in the house . . . all over the house. And the thing was really that they'd got the wrong people, if that was their concern. Mrs Barlow was pregnant, ran a clinic for the Kikkuyu women and children, Mr Barlow was a model employer, had no intention of evicting the small native farmers which had started the whole thing . . . the son spoke Kikkuyu, the family had built lovely cottages for their workers. On the next farm over was a complete

271

bastard called Magruder, he'd taken many a black woman and raped them, drove them all off his land, got very rich. They never touched him. He's still there now. I think he's in the government.'

'Them's the breaks.'

'I don't know. It wasn't like the Mau Mau didn't know what the Barlows were like, because we found out that it was their head boy who had organised the whole thing, he'd been with the Barlows twenty years, they'd paid for his son to go to university in Leeds. But all over, domestic servants were at the front of it all. You know Graham Greene was out there at that time, we used to have a drink together sometimes at Rahman's and he said that it was as if Jeeves had taken to the Jungle. Even worse, Jeeves had taken a blood oath to kill Bertie Wooster.' I could see Bateman was wondering who and what I was talking about.

'I couldn't hold the chaps back. My sergeant shot the head boy and his wife and his son ... A lot of that sort of thing went on, I should really have put them all on a charge but that would have made me terribly unpopular with my men.'

'They would've fragged ya like they did in Vietnam.'

'I'm not sure there's a lot of that in the British army. There was a terrible panic amongst the white settlers but you know during the whole thing only thirty-two whites died; as somebody said, that's fewer than the number of

Europeans killed in traffic accidents in Nairobi during the emergency. We, on the other hand, the settlers and the British army and our loyal native police, killed thousands of Kenyans and they, the Mau Mau, killed thousands of each other.'

Bateman, becoming bored with my historical contextualising, steered me towards hardware: he loved talking about guns and he bought all those rap records where gangstas sang lovingly about their 'nines'. 'Course you still had the old .303 Lee Enfield rifles then, didn't you? And the 9mm sten guns and the .303 Bren guns for squad support. And they had . . . ?'

'Apart from what little they stole off the native police, the Mau Mau made their guns themselves from odd bits of iron piping, door bolts, rubber bands and bits of wire. Often, of course, these guns would blow up in their faces. I only once was in a thing you could call a firefight . . .'

'You were in a firefight? Wow I bet a firefight separates the men from the boys,' said Bateman.

'A firefight certainly separates the men from their heads,' I said.

'Wow, you saw a guy's head shot off?'

'Not literally, I was being poetic. A lot of the fellows thought they'd shot a whole load of the Mau Mau but when we looked they'd all shot themselves: when your gun blows up the injuries are obviously facial.' Then an idea came to me.

'Bateman, I was wondering if you and Suki would like to come to my house for dinner on Saturday night, I'm . . . er, having a young friend to stay from London and erm . . . well, if you'd like to come to dinner—'

'Sure, man, why not? What time?'

'Eight?'

'Great, give me a chance to wear my new dress.'

I didn't want to appear as if I was trying too hard, as if I had thought of nothing else except her visit the whole six days, so I wore an old Donegal tweed sports jacket, with one of the original Pringle pullovers underneath, brown moleskin trousers, a good leather belt, soft rust-coloured cotton shirt, a dark-green knitted tie, Argyle socks, and my second-best dark-brown Lobb brogues.

I waited with my Honda Melody in the car park of Banbury Station. She was one of the first out from the three o'clock London train with her bouncing walk that made her black hair bob up and down. She had on a black leather jacket, turquoise T-shirt with a sparkling abstract design on the chest, and tight blue faded Wrangler jeans. Over her shoulders she had a backpack shaped like a pair of silver angel's wings and on her arm she had brought her own crash helmet from London.

Angel's wings not being the most space-efficient shape for a backpack she had had to put some of her spare clothes in the crash helmet. A lot of the ease we had with each other the weekend before had evaporated for the moment, still she kissed me quickly on the lips and I tried not to look as she transferred lacy red silk bra and pants underwear from her crash helmet into the little plastic box on the back of my scooter. Then we puffed the nine miles to Lyttleton Strachey, her arms wrapped tight around me, the brave little machine wheezing under the weight of two people for the first time since I had owned it.

I had washed all the bed linen in the spare room and re-made the single bed, I had had to leave the windows open for three days to drive out the musty unused smell. When I had first come to this place I had still entertained ideas of friends coming out to stay with me. I had thought Larkin might come. Though I didn't know him that well we corresponded quite regularly and I think we were friends. For example in our letters we would use forbidden words as close friends do, words unusable even forty years ago, like 'coon' and 'sambo': I thought we were doing this in a spirit of flaunting, between friends, the rules of liberal decency but now, in retrospect, I am not so sure about Larkin. I think he might have meant it. Anyway he never came.

At the end of our ride Mercy put her underwear back in the crash helmet and I showed her up to the spare room and told her where the bathroom was.

All the day before I had been cleaning my little house, I

polished the good Fifties furniture with real wax furniture polish, silicon-based sprays like Mr Sheen are no good for fine furniture. What I was proudest of in my house were the paintings. I had known most of the important artists of the post-war period; this had taken no effort on my part, one simply bumped into them, in those days there simply weren't that many places to go. By and by most everybody would come to the Stork Club, the Kensington Arts or The Mirabelle, in the other party would be someone from school or university or the army and an introduction would be made. In the dining room was a small Patrick Caulfield, in the living room I had several Henry Moore drawings and, in pride of place over the mantelpiece, a small Graham Sutherland oil painting. These I ran over with a feather duster and wiped the frames with a fine cloth slightly dampened, careful not to touch the precious surface of the paintings.

And all that morning I had been cooking and baking. Since all but me were vegetarians I had made a dinner of cream of spinach soup with steamed turnip tops, broccoli quiche, asparagus risotto, cauliflower cheese and a mixed salad. To drink I had got Sam to buy me two bottles of Bordeaux and two bottles of Sancerre from D'agneau et Fils in the Place Gambetta, Calais.

Bateman brought round a litre bottle of vodka he had shoplifted from the off licence in Middleton Cheney plus a gift for Mercy: to supplement his dole money Suki and he made small figures from bits of wire, nuts and bolts that they then covered in a black rubbery coating and which they sold, quite successfully, from a stall in the market at Northampton. They gave Mercy the figure of a cat arching its back and spitting, with its fur sticking up on end. 'Wow,' she exclaimed looking at it from every angle, 'this is brilliant, just like my Adrian. I'll put it on the mantelpiece in front of that painting, so I can look at it while we talk.'

'So, Mercy,' said Suki, 'how do you like our village?'

'Well, I haven't seen much of it but it seems lovely. Really pretty and quiet and that.'

Said Bateman, 'You won't see anybody all day in the outside and all the nature and that around on the hills, trees and so on, makes you feel really calm and centred, know what I mean?'

'Cows and such.'

Mercy said, 'London's so cold, I bet everybody's really friendly here.'

'Oh yeah we all look out for each other, everybody knows what's goin' on with everybody else.'

'And safe.'

'You don't need to lock your door.'

'Well you do, but if you didn't you'd probably be OK if it was only for a couple of hours.'

After dinner we walked through the silent village to the noisy pub. The Young Farmers were holding a disco

277

in the village hall next door, the DJ was playing an old Nineties hip-hop tune 'Like A Playa' by L.A. Gangz, the Notorious B.I.G. Remix I thought. On the door were stationed three or four beefy farmers' sons and daughters; they kept baseball bats tucked behind the door jamb but in easy reach just in case any drugged-up gangs came out from the estates of Daventry or Northampton. The beefy boys rather hoped they would come out, cherishing the opportunity to break a few working-class skulls. The same old story of town versus country, aristocrat versus prole, the General Strike of 1926 played out to the soundtrack of DaCompton Ghettoz.

Suddenly one of the farmers' boys on the door gave a violent jerk then fell to the ground, all life gone from his body. His fellows gathered round, three or four trying to dial the emergency services on their mobiles at the same time and jamming the signal. The ambulance would take an hour to get here anyway, it being Saturday night and them all being in play and the nearest available being in the next county but one.

'What's going on?' I said to Bateman.

'Ah somebody's been pushing semi-fatal smack in Northampton, the scientists are baffled, they don't know what's wrong with it, possibly something to do with anthrax they ain't sure . . . be that he took I spect.'

The car park of the pub was full of BMWs and Audis, Range Rovers and Mercedes; we had to slip in single file between them to get to the front door, the mud on their sides smearing our clothes.

Inside it was if all the noise that had been banned from the rest of the village was let loose in here.

The lads were at the bar, Marty Spen, Paul Crouch, Miles Godmanchester, Ronny Raul. I don't know why in my mind I called them 'The Lads', they are all middle-aged men, all involved in some way or other, as everybody seemed to be in the village, in making the world a worse place.

As I've said before Miles Godmanchester was employed at Daventry Life Sciences, mutilating animals for the cosmetics industry, though I had heard him maintain at the bar in the pub that his work had saved the lives of many 'sick little kiddies'. Marty Spen was supposed to keep it quiet but he was an engineer for a French arms firm whose UK base was in a long gold building, cloistered in a boskey, wooded valley to the east of Oxford. Their main product was the 'Bunuel' ground-to-air missile. Marty Spen was always off to visit some dreadful regime, Turkey or Indonesia, to help them more efficiently strafe their own populace. Such peregrination was not unusual; in any village pub round this way half the customers would be just back from the other side of the globe and half had never been anywhere at all and would need hypnotherapy before they even considered visiting nearby Northampton. And you couldn't guess which was which either. Some yokel straight out of Thomas Hardy might be heard to say in the pub, 'Oiv jarst been instarllin an ethernet modarl intranet system in that thar Yokahama, I bought I a DV camera at the airport . . .' Marty Spen and his wife spent their holidays every year in Saudi Arabia, guests of a grateful government. Paul Crouch had something to do with tobacco promoting Formula One cars and Ronny Raul was a food scientist at US Abstract Foods Corporation on the Banbury ring road, whose factory would fill the air for miles around with the smell of whatever they were concocting that day, nutmeg and cinnamon, coffee and cardamon, saffron and chocolate, the smells of the Damascus souk amongst the tilting roadsigns and squashed-flat rabbit corpses of the A316.

The concentric rings of a sexquake ran through the lads as Mercy came through the door into the pub, then a following after-shock of perplexity when it was clear that she was with me. The other three sat down at a table and I went up to the bar to order drinks.

Miles Godmanchester said, 'Hello, Hillary, who's this? Your granddaughter, is it?'

I just smiled a silly smile and ordered drinks.

'A friend from London . . .' I eventually said.

'You're a quiet one, it's gotta be said.'

'Fucking gorgeous,' said Marty Spen.

'Blinder,' from Paul Crouch.

'Spectacular tits,' said Ronny Raul.

On my way back to the table I sensed the men looking at me and felt ridiculous pride.

After the pub Bateman and Suki came back to my house and finished off the bottle of vodka so that Mercy and I didn't go up to bed till 3 a.m. In the doorway of my room she said, 'I think I'm falling in love with you a little bit.'

I could do nothing except emit a foolish little giggle. She put her arms round me and bent down to kiss me, her tongue in my mouth; I could feel the down on her upper lip. Then she pulled her mouth away and put her head on my shoulder. This gave me a good view of a Bridget Riley etching that I had stopped noticing was there years ago and which deserved a better spot than the upstairs landing. Its migraine swirls seemed appropriate to the moment. She went on, 'You'll understand if we don't . . . you know, sleep together right now, though, won't you? I've got to get my head straight about a few things.'

'Of course I understand,' I said.

Then she went to bed.

The next day I felt quite ill: I had had no reason to stay up late in a long while and even when I went to bed I hadn't slept very well. By the time I got down to the kitchen it was nearly eleven o'clock. Mercy had the

Roberts radio atop the window sill switched on, tuned to MidCounty Melody FM, soft rock trickling like treacle out of its speaker.

We went for a walk together along the bridleways. I showed her where the railways used to run, where the old fishponds and rabbit warrens were, named the few kinds of trees and the one wayside flower the chemicals had left behind.

She thought it was all wonderful. She said, 'Hillary?'

'Yes?'

'It's quite a big thing.'

'Go on.'

'Can I come and stay here with you for a bit? I've really got to get out of London, it's doing my head in.'

My heart leapt though I was not sure with what emotion exactly. However I said quickly enough, 'Of course you can.'

When we got back to my house Bateman was standing by my front door. He waved a ziplock bag at us. 'I got dis good scag in Banbury dis mornin, you wanna try some?'

'Sure,' said Mercy hurrying inside with an eager smile on her face. Turning to me she said, 'Fuck, the country really is brilliant, isn't it?'

We went into the living room, Mercy and Bateman sitting side by side on the couch while I took the armchair; we were like two kids and their dad. Bateman took a roll of tinfoil from his pocket, he tore off a piece and sprinkled some of the heroin onto it, then he rolled some more tinfoil into a tight little tube. Heating the drug from beneath with a little plastic lighter, he sucked up the snow-white smoke. 'You want, Hillary?' he asked. I said no, so he put some more heroin onto the foil and passed it, the lighter and the tube to Mercy. She put the tube between her lips and drew hungrily on the narcotic fumes.

I wanted to stay as alert as I could, although I was feeling drowsy myself from the effects of my late night: it was nearly four o'clock and time for this week's omnibus edition of *The Job* on UK Gold, which I was eager to see as I'd missed a lot of episodes during the week. The reason I admired shows like *The Job* or the hospital drama *Casualty* was because although they were hack work, scripts turned out week after week for an audience who didn't want their intelligence stimulated too much after they'd had their chemical-packed, ready meal dinners, they were good hack work providing the cleansing catharsis of Greek drama.

Once, a few years ago, I tried my hand at writing an episode of *Casualty*. We were all writers after all. Sitting at my desk day after day I thought I might become a different sort of writer. My idea was that as usual in that show the chemical tanker would leave the depot, its driver complaining of chest pains, the Sea Scouts would set out in their kayaks despite warnings on the radio of bad weather, the bickering couple would begin working on their house not having seen what we had seen, that the power saw with the whirling silver shark-finned blades was faulty and unsafe. We would keep cutting back to these scenes, the tanker on the motorway, the Scouts on the increasingly choppy sea, the couple arguing and slicing. However at the very end of the episode, after fifty-five minutes, the tanker would arrive safely at its destination with no undue incident, the driver suffering from nothing more serious than wind, the leader of the Sea Scouts would decide it might be prudent to seek shelter from the bad weather so they would paddle to a safe bay where they would sit under a tree eating their sandwiches, and the bickering couple would notice that the saw was faulty and would immediately take it to a registered dealer for repair under its warranty. All this time Charlie and the rest of the cast at Holby A & E would sit around drinking tea and saying what a quiet day it was and how they'd like a bit of action and something would happen any second now. Then they'd all go home for an early night.

I got a very nice letter back from the producer's assistant saying that they didn't accept unsolicited scripts but she had included a signed photo of the cast.

Bateman and Mercy slowly slid sideways on the couch, their arms lying twisted under them on the cushions, drifting steeply into narcotic dreaming. It felt like a traditional English Sunday afternoon. Everybody in a coma and the TV on.

*   *   *

One of the cable TV companies was currently running an advertising campaign: it featured two office workers standing by the water cooler on a Monday morning. One is handsome, tall and confident, the other is shorter, uglier and more nervy. The Nervy one says to the other, 'I had a fantastic weekend. Went to a club . . .' – we then see the club which is crowded and noisy – 'met a great woman . . .' – we see the woman slapping his face – 'didn't get home till 3 a.m.' – we see him walking home alone in the rain. Then he says to the handsome man, 'What did you do?' We cut to all the great cable TV programmes this man has watched over the weekend. 'Oh, just stayed in and watched TV,' he says and smiles smugly. The tag line of the advert is: 'A Life Worth Watching.'

The implication is that the handsome man has had a better time by staying in and watching the television. But really it's the ugly one that you should admire, doggedly ploughing on with going out into the world, despite it relentlessly coughing great gobs of rejection and hawking them into his face. Brave, brave, ugly, nervy little man.

Most weekends before Mercy came I stayed in and watched television.

Bateman went up to London in his van to get her stuff. There was a lot of it. Such as: an exercise bike, a dressmaker's dummy with the face of Cliff Richard, a hundred pairs of shoes, her Piaggio (which I was looking forward to riding), two inflatable armchairs and, in his travelling basket, Adrian, a furious-looking black tom cat whose continual yowling only stopped when he was let out into the living room and went straight about attacking the moquette of my Hille couch with his claws.

It took so long to get her stuff in that it was ten o'clock by the time we'd finished, which meant that I'd missed a special two-hour episode of *The Job* when Kurdish terrorists took the whole station hostage and threatened to blow it up. One of the old cast members was certain to die, my money was on kindly old desk sergeant, Ron Task. I had been interested to see how the new prettier cast would work out in their first big two-hourer. I thought they had been slow to bed in: partly it was that their appearance was now so at variance with what real police looked like. They were all young and thin with full heads of hair. There were no fat old men working out their time for their pension and, strangest of all, none of the WPCs were stumpy-calfed lesbians.

Mercy would stand at the living-room window every morning and say, 'It's so peaceful, I can't get over how peaceful it is, it's so peaceful, I can't get over it,' then she would go next door to smoke dope with Bateman and Suki if she hadn't gone to school, the sound of his electric guitar thumping through the walls as I sat in my office sparring with my poem.

Tuesdays and Thursdays she would go with them into Northampton to help with their stall on the market, but then all her stuff stayed behind to represent her and I could hardly get to my study for training shoes.

When she was home Mercy would often walk around the house naked except for her pants.

I went out for longer and longer walks, issuing from paths round the blind backs of villages that I had only ever seen from the lanes, bursting upon unmarked NATO radar stations and on one occasion emerging through a hawthorn hedge onto the eastbound carriageway of the M40 motorway.

With regard to headgear my strong feeling is that felt hats should solely be worn up until Royal Ascot which is held in the third week of June, after which straw is permissible, so, deep in the fields on the Friday afternoon, I was wearing grey flannel trousers, a cream cotton jacket, white cotton shirt with no tie but instead a silk paisley cravat, stout brown walking shoes from Hogg's of Aberdeen and a fine straw panama hat when I came upon Sam stretching razor-wire fencing across an ancient drovers' road. I hadn't seen much of Sam lately so I was pleased to encounter him, though as a lifelong member of the Ramblers' Association I should really have reproved him for lethally blocking off the footpath; instead I said, 'Hello, Sam, I didn't know this was your land.'

'Oh aye, all around 'ere, my land.'

'I see.'

'Not for much longer though, sellin' it for an 'ousing development. Three hundred warehouse-style loft apartments for sophisticated rural singles.'

'Goodness,' I said, 'but I heard on the radio the other day that the population is shrinking. Who are these places for?'

'The government say, the housebuilders say, they need four million nu 'omes.'

'But who for?'

'Ah it's for all these people who're living by themselves these days, they need a whole apartment to live by themselves in, to wander from room to room, naked, I expect. I 'spect they've lost the knack of gettin' on with other folk, seeing as they spend all their days at computers, talkin' to ghosts across the other side of the world. When I was young we all lived together. Generations all together on top of each other. My old gran in the loft, my mum, my dad, brothers and sisters, cousins, lodgers, aunts fallen on hard times, uncles that took a shock and took to their beds never to get up till they died. It were fuckin' horrible.'

A look crossed his face. 'Must be like your house these days with all the comin' and goin'.'

'I suppose so.'

'No, we don't see you so much now. An' how's that poem of yours that you was tellin' us about comin' on?'

'I can't seem to get on with it . . .'

'No well, I expect you're having too much fun, with your new friends.'

'Is that what it is?'

'I would have thought you'd need to get a move on, though, don't you? I mean how long have you got left?'

'In what sense?'

'In your life sense, might only be a year or two after all, what are you?'

'Seventy-two.'

'What's the average, seventy-six, is it? Then there's all the stuff that happens, strokes, cancer, even if you survive beyond that, your mind goes, a year or two and I imagine your powers will be waning considerable. There's not a minute to be lost when you think about it, is there? Time must be running through your fingers like sand. There's not a minute, not a second to be wasted.'

When I got back to my house, out of breath from trying to run some of the way across ploughed fields, my mud-splattered flannels torn from my having unsuccessfully attempted to vault a stile, there was a van parked on my drive, on its side was written 'Barry Rush, Certified Gas Heating Engineer'.

Mercy was in the kitchen looking tense, trying to grill some toast. She said, 'Hillary, my dad's here.'

'Yes,' I said, 'so I see.'

I went into the living room. Sitting on my couch was a youthful-looking man: it was hard to believe he was Mercy's father. The young image was compounded by his clothes, he wore a coat from Dexter Wong, black leather Prada trousers and the new Nike cross trainers, his hair was shaved to mask his baldness and his arms were muscled and buffed from gym training. Sitting next to him was a girl of perhaps twenty-five, her clothes were more ordinary, torn Gap jeans and a pale blue T-shirt, her small breasts clearly defined, dark blonde hair in dreadlocks and a ring through the centre of her bottom lip.

'Hello,' I said, 'I'm Hillary Wheat.'

They stood and shook my hand.

'Barry Rush.'

'Melon Gabriel.'

'Please do sit down, is Mercy looking after you?'

'Yeah, she's getting us coffee and stuff,' said her father.

'Lovely little house you have here,' said Melon. While Barry spoke in working-class Scottish, her accent had been forged in a barrio bounded by Knightsbridge to the north and Sloane Street to the west, Eaton Square to the south and Grosvenor Place to the east. 'My brother Rollo has a place over towards Daventry. Fawkley Hall – do you know it?'

'I've been round it.'

'The Van Dykes are particularly fine, aren't they?'

'Indeed. So are you here to stay for the weekend?'

'Naww. Me and Melon are attending a weekend pony club that's being held at a stately home over Byfield way. Starts tomorrow morning, so I thought we'd get here early and spend the night with my darling daughter.'

'Well, yes, of course. You can sleep in the erm . . .'

'The spare room,' said Mercy coming in with a tray piled with coffee and burnt toast.

'Yes, the spare room . . . You know it's shaming but I don't know as much as I should about these country pursuits. Is a pony club some type of point to point?'

Barry and Melon sniggered. Melon took it upon herself to explain in a voice vibrating with a kind of self-regarding excitement. 'No, Hillary, what happens at a pony club is that all the women there dress up in special leather costumes, bustiers, high-heeled boots and so on, plumed headdresses like you see on horses at funerals, we all have nice swishy tails, the other end of which, of course, are butt plugs, big rubber dicks, which are stuck up our arses. Then we're leashed to little pony carts and we pull the men around in them. And the men whip us when we don't go fast enough, somebody might get branded and such and such.'

'I see.'

Barry chipped in, 'It's fantastic and we've made so many friends of like-minded individuals at these weekends. As soon as it's over we can't wait to get home so we can all get on the e-mail, chatting to each other.'

'Toast?' said Mercy, setting the tray down with a crash.

After coffee we showed them up to the spare room. At some point Mercy seemed to have moved all of her substantial amounts of possessions into my bedroom, her underwear and her stuffed toys and her punchbag and her weights. She followed me in there after we'd shown Barry and Melon the bathroom and they'd gone in there together, carrying a coiled length of rubber tubing and locking the door behind them.

Mercy sat on my bed. She said, 'I'm sorry about putting my things in your bedroom, I don't know . . . I didn't want my dad to think I was sleeping in the spare room.'

'Why not? You are sleeping in the spare room.'

'I know but I didn't want him to think I was.'

'Why?'

'I don't know. Don't give me a hard time please, Hillary. Just don't, alright?'

'I'm sorry, Mercy.'

'That's OK.'

*   *   *

That evening we all went for a meal in the village pub, the pub which had been called the Royal Oak for three hundred years, which had been called The People's Princess for three years, and which the landlady had now changed to The Stephen Lawrence. Barry, Melon, Suki, Bateman, Mercy and me. Last orders weren't called until sometime close to 2 a.m. Afterwards we all filed through the pesticide-scented night air back to the house and squeezed into the little front room to carry on drinking with an assortment of portable stuff brought from the pub.

Because I was drunk I tried to tell them the truth about the countryside, how it wasn't what it appeared to be, but somehow the conversation wriggled like an eel and swerved onto appearances in general. Bateman said that despite overwhelming appearances to the contrary he was in reality a really anxious person. He said, 'Oh yeah, I suffer real bad from my nerves. Like I've got this terrible nervous alopecia, except its only on parts of my body where I don't have any hair, like my knees.'

Mercy said, 'Yeah, nature's cruel, isn't it? I mean you're all upset about something and then on top of that all your hair falls out! So then you feel even worse. I mean wouldn't it be nice if, say, you were a baldy bloke and you were feeling really fed up and instead of all the rest of your hair falling out, it grew instead? So like even though you were feeling depressed at least you'd have a nice new head of hair?'

Bateman said, 'Yeah or if you were a woman and you were feeling anxious about your life, about not having a boyfriend or something but instead of getting agoraphobia or becoming an alcoholic, you grew a really nice big pair of tits. I mean that would be more fair, wouldn't it?'

'And you'd probably get a boyfriend because of your tits,' said Melon.

'Maybe there's some sort of reason for alopecia and agoraphobia and that, maybe some sort of balance in nature.'

'But that's what I was trying to say before: nature's a mess up, isn't it? Look outside – that's not nature, it's a factory, a green factory. It's not meant to be like this . . .'

Barry Rush who had been quiet for some time said to me, 'You got kids, Hillary?'

'Noo I'm afraid not, I never . . .'

'You never stop worrying about them, know what I mean?'

'I think I . . .'

'Yes, I was really worried about my daughter, my Mercy. I mean she hadn't had a good seeing to for God knows how long, then a quiet old fellow like Hillary moves in on her. Not the conventional boyfriend I imagined for her but I'm not one to talk.'

I didn't know what to say to this so I simply simpered and uttered a noise something like 'nnggnmam'.

Barry went on, 'So what's she like? You know, as a fuck? I've always wondered. What dad doesn't? Is she passionate, like her dad? Is she good at sucking you off? She's got that big wide mouth, I'd think she would be. Do her tits feel as good as they look?'

I stood up. I said, 'Sir, I count myself as a good host but I will not have anyone, especially her father, talking about Mercy like that. I'll thank you to leave now.'

Barry stared up at me, looking confused.

'If you don't leave I'm sure Bateman would be happy to assist you.'

'Will I fuck, Hillary,' said Bateman.

'Don't be a twat, Hillary,' said Suki.

I looked in appeal from them to Mercy. Surely she would support me. She stared me straight in the eyes and said, 'Take a chill pill, man. What's the matter with you?'

As I left the room I heard Barry say to the others, 'I never fucked her, did I? Even though God knows plenty of fathers do.'

There was a general murmur of approval at his restraint.

I lay on the bed. 'I suppose I'm a stupid old man,' I said to Mercy who was standing in the doorway. Downstairs I could hear the party still going on. She came in and sat down next to me.

'Hillary, don't talk about yourself like that. You're a lovely man. It's my dad, I can't stand up to him, I know I should but I can't. I know you were only trying to be honourable and I love you for it. How come, though it's my dad who's the awful shit, it's me who somehow feels guilty?'

'Well I'm not sure, but I think it's a parent thing, Mercy. I think that he's holding the child that you were hostage, and you'll be paying her ransom for the rest of your life.'

'I ooo. Thank you.'

'Don't mention it. You wanted to know.'

And yes, like her dad said, her wide mouth was good for that thing and her breasts were as he imagined them to be. I know a poet should do better than this but it was like riding a horse again after many years, the movements, the postures unaccustomed, yet familiar, mounting her, sliding into her, the sweating twisting body, except now there was a consciousness, a part of me that wasn't subsumed in the act, a part that worried about falling off. Like riding a horse again after years and the traffic had got faster and more frightening.

The next day Mercy's father and his girlfriend had gone by the time we got up and she went back to sleeping in her own room. She said to me, 'I don't want us to be a couple, not yet. I want us to be friends who sometimes do stuff. Do you know what I mean? That's much more original, isn't it?' It was certainly much more frustrating as far as I was concerned since I never knew when she would choose to activate her franchise and I didn't seem to have much of a voice in the matter. Needless to say, this not knowing did not help my poem to progress. Plus my days seemed to be full of housework and cooking. My evenings were no longer as empty as they had been either, since I'd been recruited into the pub table-skittles team. This strange game, peculiar to Northamptonshire, was exclusively the province of the village proletariat: Cedric Gull the owner of the local garage, Len Babb who worked on one of Sam's farms, that sort of person. Twice a week I would be taken to skittle games in Cedric's 1969 Rover Coupe, enveloped in the smell of cracked leather and lead replacement petrol. Mostly we would talk about Mercy or rather I would answer questions about Mercy for this fifty-year-old father of five as we rocked along the country lanes, Cedric working the big bakelite steering wheel like a ship's tiller.

There were several pub-skittles leagues: Byfield, Gayton and Town which was Northampton itself; there were fourteen teams in the Byfield League including Lyttleton Strachey. Each team has nine players. As to the game itself, there are nine pins arranged in a square on a table in three rows of three. Each player has three cheeses and has three throws of the cheese at the skittles. A cheese is a piece of wood shaped like a small cheese and painted cheese colour. Each player has five legs for his turn to knock down as many pins as possible. There were various strange terms for the success you could achieve: a flora is when all the pins are demolished with one cheese, a stack is when all the pins are demolished with two cheeses and so on and so forth. Though my recruitment onto the team denoted some raising of my status in the village I had not risen too high as there had always been a problem getting new members: a lot of the newer inhabitants of the Northamptonshire villages had difficulty in seeing the point of throwing cheese-shaped bits of wood at skittles in the evening after a hard day spent designing new forms of poison gas or new methods of torturing animals.

It was summer by the time he came again.

One morning I was sitting in my study, the poem inert on my desk. Bateman had just shouted up the stairs that we were out of milk and I needed to ride to the nearest garage to get some, he said; I should also buy Suki some Tampax while I was there. Then the phone rang, and before I spoke a man said, 'Hello, Hillary.'

'Yes?' I replied in a 'who the fuck are you?' tone.

'I was thinking of coming over to pick up my hat.'

'Is that Emmanuel Porlock, the Million Pound Poet?'

'Yes indeedy.'

'I've been hanging on to that hat for three months.'

'Well, I better come and get it then, hadn't I? Saturday morning alright for you, round about brunchtime?'

'I suppose so.'

'Excellent, see you then.'

It was only after I put the phone down that I thought to myself, 'How did he know I'd bought him a new hat?' I had never spoken to him since the day he had phoned me, badgering me into going up to London and causing me to flirt with Mercy.

Brunch to me is a silly meal and difficult to devise; it's really a breakfast that's been lying in bed too long. Nevertheless I have never been able to be inhospitable and, it being later in the year, at least there was more produce available from my garden, so in the end I decided upon courgette fritters with mayonnaise dip, eggs Florentine, Spanish omelette, kedgeree, broad bean dip, nasturtium salad and roast tomatoes with garlic. For cocktails I would do Long Island Iced Teas.

Recently Sam had taken to driving through the low countries and into Germany for his shopping: twice he'd been to Austria and once he'd got as far as the Hungarian border before the lack of a visa caused him to be turned back. There were a couple of bullet holes in the tailgate of his Subaru from where Sam had tried to sneak across the border on a rural back road – he'd heard that things were even cheaper in the ex-east than in the hypermarkets of France. He seemed to be going further and further on each of his trips and to be more distracted and edgy when he was at home. His farms literally ran themselves and he'd pretty much killed all the wildlife for hectares around so one day, I suspected, he simply wouldn't come back, though I'm sure Mrs Sam would be able to monitor his progress, zig-zagging across the world via GPS satellite and her laptop. Maybe she would be able to see him drive head first into the onrushing Autobahn traffic, a popular method of suicide in Germany so I'd heard. Still it's an ill obsessive compulsive disorder that brings no one any good, so Sam was able to fetch me from Austria a cake called a Wiener Apfelstrudel Gugelhupf, a Gottinger bacon cake, a selection of wurst and eight bottles of a decent Gerwurtstraminer.

His Landrover van swerved into my drive just after 12 o'clock. The day was extremely hot and I was wearing a short-sleeved fawn linen shirt made for me by Domediakis in Berwick Street, Soho, pale cream tropical nine-ounce double-pleated gabardine trousers from Adeney and Briggs and blue-and-white canvas yachting shoes. Earlier that morning I had found the Mau Mau hat still in its paper bag at the back of my sock drawer.

On this visit Emmanuel Porlock was not alone: he had brought his tribe along with him. What a shock. Bev and Martika and the kid Lulu were not as I had imagined them and Emmanuel was not the man he was when unaccompanied by these three.

To paraphrase Tolstoy: all thin families are alike but a fat family is fat after its own fashion. It was truly remarkable to my mind how three human beings could be so fat in three such distinct and individual ways. With Bev the surfeit manifested itself mostly in width, she was a very, very wide woman, enormous flat breasts stretching out to the side of her like stubby wings, gigantic hovercraft-bearing hips, a rolling, boiling stomach that hung down almost to her knees. In Martika, by contrast, the fat was confined solely to her bottom and her stumpy little legs that seemed to bend backwards in an entirely new way, like you see on one of those TV programmes where they try and pretend that they know how dinosaurs walked but really they haven't a clue so the computer-animated puppet looks all wrong and impossible. In fact Martika might not have known she was fat at all unless she got a good look at her rear view in the mirror, or somebody unkind videoed her. The kid Lulu was just fat all over: fat scalp, fat elbows, fat eyelids, fat heels.

And they were not jolly fat people these three. Though I suppose I am a bit prejudiced, I have never been what I understand is called these days a 'chubby chaser'; all my women have been trim and capable of looking good in the clothes of the day. I have never been that keen on fat women, so I believe that jolly fat people are only those who try and keep the self-hatred and disgust hidden under cover of jocundity. With this trio the loathing was out in the open and expressed itself mostly in a contempt for Emmanuel Porlock: each thing he said was greeted with a roll of the eyes or a look at the other two or a 'tsking' sound. Sometimes one would say to another, 'What's he saying now?' in a scornful tone. Porlock himself was very subdued; overshadowed by them both physically and verbally, he took little part in the conversation and when he did speak his voice had an apologetic, humble note I had not noticed before. Over brunch the women merely jabbed at their food, nibbling at corners and tearing off small strips so that I was left with a great deal of it, which I took away, wrapped in cling film and left on the work surfaces and in the fridge in the kitchen. After they had gone I found the food had somehow departed with them.

I would not have flirted with Mercy in the hat shop three months before if my mind had not been filled with erotic reveries of the life I thought Porlock led with Bev and Martika, taking turns of each other, truffling away with their heads between each other's slender legs. It was all a great big mistake.

After brunch the three females said that they would like to perform their chi gong meditation in my paddock, so Porlock and I had an hour alone to sit in deck chairs out the front. Porlock had the Mau Mau hat on his head even though the sun was bright in the sky. I said to him, 'There's something I want to say to you.'

'Go ahead.'

'In the year 1797 the poet Samuel Taylor Coleridge was staying at a farmhouse, near a place called Porlock, in the county of Somerset. Of course everybody knows that Coleridge was addicted to opium; he took some one particular day, then fell asleep in a chair. Before he took the opium he'd been reading a book about the palace of Kubla Khan. In his opium sleep he started dreaming and in his dream there came into his mind an entire poem of something like two hundred or three hundred lines. When he woke up, what a gift, a whole poem complete! No need for months or years of work but a masterpiece delivered from the subconscious straight to the page. Of course as any of us poets would have done he began furiously writing: "In Xanadu, did Kubla Khan, A stately pleasure dome decree . . ."

'But after writing for a short time, he says in his diary he was "called out by a person on business from Porlock", who for some reason he didn't tell to bugger off, politeness maybe, I don't know. He says this "person from Porlock detained me above an hour". When he finally got rid of this man he found he had forgotten the rest of the dream. All he had left was fifty-four lines. And that's all there is of "Kubla Khan" – fifty-four lines, unfinished.'

'They're a very good fifty-four lines though,' said Porlock, 'so all wasn't lost.'

'That's one way to look at it. The thing of it is, though, I've looked for your name all over the place and I can't find it. There are no books written by you in the bookshops, no poems written by you in any anthologies and the only reference on the internet I can find to your name, connected with poetry, is this "person from Porlock": not a poet but a man who stopped a great poem being properly written.'

'There's something odd here, what are you saying, Hillary?'

'I don't quite know what I'm saying except that you don't seem to be who you say you are and that you have brought terrible disruption to my life.'

'Me? How have I brought disruption to your life?'

'You made me go up to town to buy you a new bloody hat. When I was up in town I met Mercy, through meeting Mercy I am now living with a girl who is forty years younger than me, my house is full of noise and her friends, I'm in the stupid skittles team throwing cheese-shaped bits of wood about twice a week and I haven't written a line of my poem, my great opus, my final testament to the world that will echo down the centuries, in fucking months!'

'Well, first off, I don't understand why you can't find any reference to me, I'm all over, you must be looking in the wrong places. I mean what are you saying, that I'm some sort of sprite who travels through the ages stopping poets writing?'

'Are you?'

'Why would such a person exist, what would be the point?'

'I don't know, you mentioned something the last time you came: a sort of anti-muse . . . Maybe there are Porlocks all over the place stopping poets writing, stopping painters painting, for all I know it's you who stops the gas board coming on the day they say they're coming and makes the builder abandon his job half completed.'

He was looking discomfited. 'Look, Hillary, you're going off the deep end here,' he paused. 'Now what may have happened, I admit, is that I may have exaggerated a little bit how advanced I was as a poet. There may not be a lot, well any, of my poetry in actual print. I might have wanted to sort of associate myself with you to help my own career, I admit that. It's only because I love poetry so. But I tell you this, Hillary, I would give anything to be at the point you are. To be on the edge of a masterpiece must be the greatest thing on earth and I know I wouldn't let anybody stop me finishing it. You know what? I bet there was no man from Porlock, Coleridge probably only wrote that much and was making up an excuse for not writing any more. You blame me. There is nobody who's stopping you working except you.

If you can't write with all these people around then get rid of them. Get rid of Mercy, she's a nutcase anyway if you ask me, a right mental case. If you get rid of Mercy then the darkie in the dress and the schoolgirl won't come round either. Hillary, I'd give anything to have your gift and at the moment you're squandering it. Be ruthless, be focused, get on with it, man!'

Over the next week as the heat of summer shimmered above the fields I thought about what I should do. Looking back I am aware that the options I considered are not those that another person might have considered. They were: One. Going over to the Sams and saying to them, 'Can I live in one of your sheds?' I was sure they would let me. I would survive on out-of-date pâté and vacuum-packed saucisson sec while I worked on my poem. Two. I would go and live wild in a bender in the woods, eating foxes or something. I had been trained in bush warfare so it would be like in the old days back in Kenya. Again I would work on my poem while daylight lasted. Three. I could murder Mercy. Murdering Mercy seemed like a situation in which I won either way. If I got away with it then I would have my solitude back to write and if I was caught then I'd have a nice cell in prison to work in. I'm sure they'd let me have a pad and a biro.

You may have noticed none of these options consisted of me simply asking Mercy into the living room for a chat and then saying to her outright, 'Look, I'm sorry but, Mercy sweetheart, could you just please go away. You're stopping me working on my poem what with all these people coming round to see you and this thing with us being "friends who touch each other", which is just a recipe for a cerebral embolism as far as I can see.' But there was no way I could be so impolite. You might think that murdering someone was a tad rude in itself but I'm sure many women and maybe some men were murdered out of politeness. I'm certain a lot of husbands who wanted to break away couldn't stand the idea of upsetting their wives, couldn't imagine themselves saying the hurtful words, couldn't endure the tears, the shouting, really couldn't stand the thought of the pain they would cause, so instead they crept up behind them with a ballpen hammer and stove their skulls in.

I thought of a way to do it as well. The bad stuff they were selling in Northampton. If I could get some I could give it to Mercy as a present. Junkie dies, happens all the time.

I rode Mercy's Piaggio to the back of the bus station on market day. I thought to myself that really he wouldn't have any of the bad stuff but at least I would have tried. I said to the dealer, 'I don't suppose you have any of the bad smack that's killing people do you?'

'Oh yeah,' he said, 'I've got lots of it, it's very popular.'

I was a little surprised. 'Why is it popular if it's fatal? I'd have thought people would steer clear of it.'

'Well there, sir, you don't understand the mind of the drug taker. See, they think that if it's near fatal it's got to be an A1 great buzz. It's one of my most successful lines.'

I bought some but when I got it home I knew I couldn't do it. I went out to the paddock and threw the deadly heroin into my compost heap where it would decompose and give my courgettes an extra zing next harvest time.

That evening in my tiny living room as usual Bateman and Suki were there as were a couple of new friends Mercy had made, Jessie and Gunther. They lived on a barge, Jessie was a juggler and Gunther spent his days miming as a silver statue in Northampton market. It was a trifle disconcerting seeing him on the couch as he had not taken his statue make-up off. I had just served them all welsh rarebit and coffee and was about to bring in a walnut cake I'd made earlier. With the TV bellowing in the background Bateman said, 'You know when we was up in London, Merce, bringin' your stuff back?'

'Yeah . . .'

'Well, when we wuz going through the West End in my van, I saw loads of people wearin' them sweatshirts from like Harvard University and Princeton University but I don't think them people went to them universities, or if they did then goin' to one of them Ivy League places don't help you so much, cos a lot of them peoples wearing them sweatshirts was sellin' hot dogs from a stall.'

Suki said, 'Did you go to college, Merce?'

'Yeah, I did media studies at Harrogate University,' said Mercy, 'but you know I can't remember a single thing about it. Not a thing. I think we went to a big place once to . . . no it's gone. What about you, Suki?'

'I'm still at school, remember.'

'Oh yeah I forgot, and you, Bateman?'

'I got a woodwork O level in prison. Which is harder than you think when they won't let you have anything sharp. So, you know, the exam was like, largely theoretical, though I did make a teapot stand using a plastic chisel, paper nails and a rubber hammer.'

And finally, 'Hillary, what about you?'

'Oh ummm . . . well Cambridge, just after the war . . . you know.'

'Oh yeah?' said Bateman. 'What was that like, then?'

'Well, it was a unique and rather odd time to be up at university, because on the one hand you had ordinary schoolboys like myself, and on the other a huge number of fellows straight back from the war. They seemed terribly fierce those men, commandeering cars in the middle of the Great North Road when they wanted to go to the pub and so on. And the thing that struck me most was that they were so determined, knew so clearly what they wanted to do. While most of us schoolboys had no idea what we wanted from life, these men had it all figured out. They felt they had been through such a lot that their generation could do things in an entirely new way: write theatre plays that would bring about socialism in Scotland at their first performance, design monorails that ran under the sea powered by plankton, make typewriters that you could wear as a sombrero. And apart from re-making the world they knew they could also re-make themselves. These boy soldiers would study like never before because they had walked through the gates of Buchenwald; they would no longer be drunk because they had ridden a Superfortress to the canopy of the earth; they would no longer be shy around girls as a memorial to their best friend who they'd seen drowned, gargling in black engine oil, slipping beneath the cold North Sea. But after a year or so had gone by, their true natures, who they really were, suspended for the duration of the war, like Association Football, began to re-emerge. The drunks were brought back to college by the police having parked their MGs in cake-shop windows, the lazy stayed later and later in bed, the shy lost the composure that killing had given them and ran in fear from girls as they had never run from the Japanese. You see what I'm trying to say? You cannot be other than who you are and you cannot act in any other way than your nature permits you to act, do you understand that? It's no use trying to fight it, you're stuck with yourself.'

They were silent for a while then Suki said, 'I heard about this bloke, right, got a terrible shock, right? But instead of his hair turning white, it turned red!'

'What colour was it before?'

'Dunno, brown I expect.'

That morning I had sat in front of my unfinished poem for what I think will be the last time. I had gathered up the bits of paper and put them in a drawer: not even the fifty-four lines of 'Kubla Khan'.

There was high-pitched mewling from outside in the back garden, I looked up. Adrian jumped up onto the window sill and stood there crying to be let in, his pink mouth opening and closing in petulant supplication. The others seemed to be too sunk into the furniture to get up so I went over to the window and opened it, the cat jumped down into the room and began clawing the moquette of the one Hille armchair that had so far escaped his depredation. I sat back down and the cat climbed onto my lap, sinking his claws into my best Gieves and Hawkes moleskin trousers and coiling himself with his nose up his bottom; after a few seconds he began purring.

Mercy said to me, 'You got a cat after all, didn't you, Hillary? You said the first time we met in that shop, you said that you thought you couldn't stand the pain of having another cat. That you get to a point in life where the pain wipes out the pleasure. Where you'd rather settle for no pleasure than pay for it in pain. But really it's better, isn't it, having another heartbeat around the house and all that?'

'Well, I'm not sure . . .' I said, but then I saw she was looking at me with an expression of such savage entreaty on her face that I changed my tone and said in a cheerier voice that sounded in my head like clattering tin trays, 'Yes, it's better having one rather than not having one . . .'

Then I added, '. . . just.'